TEST OF STRENGTH

The first part of her marriage-in-name-only had been easy for Amanda. Her husband, Lord Mainwaring, had been suffering from a broken leg, and the only use he had for his bed was to lie helplessly upon it.

But a man's leg could heal, and Mainwaring was very much a man.

Now Mainwaring was up and about, and it was not only his leg but his male appetites that were as strong if not stronger than ever.

Her husband's renewed strength, however, was but a small part of the independent Amanda's growing concern.

Far more dangerous was her own unsuspected weakness. . . .

D1070279

SIGNET REGENCY ROMANCE
COMING IN MARCH 1994

Marcy Rothman
The Kinder Heart

Emily Hendrickson
Miss Cheney's Charade

Patricia Oliver
Miss Drayton's Downfall

AT YOUR LOCAL BOOKSTORE
OR ORDER DIRECTLY
FROM THE PUBLISHER
WITH VISA OR MASTERCARD
1-800-253-6476

THE
TEMPORARY HUSBAND

BARBARA ALLISTER

A SIGNET BOOK

SIGNET
Published by the Penguin Group
Penguin Books USA Inc., 375 Hudson Street,
New York, New York 10014, U.S.A.
Penguin Books Ltd, 27 Wrights Lane,
London W8 5TZ, England
Penguin Books Australia Ltd, Ringwood,
Victoria, Australia
Penguin Books Canada Ltd, 10 Alcorn Avenue,
Toronto, Ontario, Canada M4V 3B2
Penguin Books (N.Z.) Ltd, 182–190 Wairau Road,
Auckland 10, New Zealand

Penguin Books Ltd, Registered Offices:
Harmondsworth, Middlesex, England

Published by Signet, an imprint of Dutton Signet,
a division of Penguin Books USA Inc.

First Printing, March, 1987
11 10 9 8 7 6 5 4 3

Copyright © 1987 by Barbara Teer
All rights reserved

 REGISTERED TRADEMARK—MARCA REGISTRADA

Printed in the United States of America

BOOKS ARE AVAILABLE AT QUANTITY DISCOUNTS WHEN USED TO PROMOTE PRODUCTS OR
SERVICES. FOR INFORMATION PLEASE WRITE TO PREMIUM MARKETING DIVISION, PENGUIN
BOOKS USA INC., 375 HUDSON STREET, NEW YORK, NEW YORK 10014.

If you purchased this book without a cover you should be aware that this book is stolen
property. It was reported as "unsold and destroyed" to the publisher and neither the
author nor the publisher has received any payment for this "stripped book."

For my mother and dad

1

"Jeremy, you must. You promised." Amanda glared at her cousin, who was standing in front of the fireplace gazing at the small fire burning there. "Why have you changed your mind?" she asked, her brow creased with anger and hurt.

Her cousin straightened his rather bony shoulders and turned toward her, his face unusually serious. "When you forced me to promise I'd help, I had no idea to what lengths you were prepared to go." Amanda opened her mouth to answer him but his frown silenced her. "Taking a caning from Grandfather for following your lead when we were children was one thing. Deliberately breaking the laws of the state and the Church is something else."

"If everything goes right, no one will ever know anything about it."

"No one but the lawyer and the man involved."

Amanda crossed to his side and put her hand on his sleeve.

"Please," she begged. Her hazel eyes filled with tears. Her bottom lip started to quiver and a lone tear trickled down her alabaster cheek.

"Still pulling that old trick, are you?" Jeremy asked. "You're better than you used to be. But you should remember I used to watch you practice that to use on Grandfather." His voice, so coolly amused, did little to calm his cousin's already stormy emotion.

She stamped her foot in a way that ten years earlier would have earned her a lecture from both her mother and her governess. Her eyes snapped with anger. The tension in her body made every wispy dark curl quiver.

Refusing to give way as he usually did, Jeremy returned stare for stare.

Amanda whirled and flounced across the room to her favorite chair, a large red leather piece more suitable to a gentleman's study than a lady's sitting room.

As usual when she was disturbed, Amanda ignored the rules of ladylike behavior, curling her legs under her in her chair. The blue plaid merino she wore as a concession to the day's coolness settled about her, and she tucked her skirt around her legs. The rich red leather of her chair framed her dark hair and made it seem darker than it really was. She picked up a small miniature on the table beside her and caressed it softly, her anger slowly seeping away. She looked up, her eyes faintly shadowed by sadness. "Then tell me what I can do. I could not bear to lose Robert." Amanda traced the soft blond locks and smiling lips of the painting, her touch as delicate as a feather. Her voice, usually soft and quiet, broke.

"You could accept one of those offers I know you have received." Jeremy watched her closely.

Her face, already pale, lost more color. She shivered and wrapped her arms around herself for a moment. Jeremy frowned as he watched her, cursing softly under his breath. Catching sight of his face, Amanda let her arms fall to her lap. With a false smile, she asked, "And how can I arrange that before the major arrives? Jeremy, be realistic. Most of them are in London for the Season."

Her cousin grinned wryly. "Been regretting those refusals, have you?"

"No," she said firmly. Then her voice sank to an almost purr, soft and persuasive. "My way would be so simple. A few days of pretense and then back to my normal life again."

He glanced at her before crossing to the bellpull.

"That's the coward's way out," she accused as he stood waiting for the butler to appear. "I might have known you'd go back on your word just the way you did when . . ."

The door opened. Amanda bit back the rest of her remark.

"Tell the cook I'll be staying for dinner, Thompson. And send word to the stable also," Jeremy said quietly.

Amanda released the breath she had been unconsciously holding and settled into her chair more comfortably. She stared at her cousin, shifting impatiently while he gazed at her thoughtfully.

Marshaling his thoughts, Jeremy looked around the room. It was, he believed, a very appropriate setting for his cousin. Designed by the lady when she inherited the estate, it had set off comment both in the family and in the neighboring countryside. The controversy made little impact on Amanda. She had proceeded to turn her sitting room into a place that glowed red in any light. The walls were covered in ivory silk figured in red, a pattern so unique that everyone was certain she had designed it herself. Her settee and drapes, both red damask, added to the warmth of the room. The other chairs, except her red leather haven, were ivory and red damask. With her hair and clear complexion, Amanda glowed in the reflected richness.

Finally, when Amanda's patience was almost at an end, Jeremy crossed to a chair near Amanda. She had been known to fly in the opposite direction after a definite no. "Tell me once again about this man your lawyer has found," he suggested. A smile of satisfaction lit Amanda's face only to be quenched as he continued, "I'll have a look at him myself, and then we'll talk again."

A few days later Jeremy stood in the door of the common room at the Ship's Anchor at Bristol. He stared across at a man seated at a table alone, half-hidden in the shadows. "How long has that man been here, Jenkins?" he asked the innkeeper, who stood close by.

"About an hour, sir."

Jeremy frowned as he noted the man's weak chin and shifty eyes. His eyes narrowed as he watched the man signal the barmaid for another ale and then run his hand suggestively over her generous curves as she put it before him. His decision made, he entered the private room that he had bespoken earlier.

A few minutes later Jeremy stood in the doorway to the common room once more. "Give this to the young man over there." He handed the innkeeper a packet. "And, Jenkins, it was delivered by a messenger." Noting the cold anger in his patron's eyes, the innkeeper nodded and hurried away.

Jeremy melted back into the passageway, heading toward the inn yard. Watching the hustle and bustle as two horsemen dismounted, he leaned casually against the doorjamb, a true smile crossing his face for the first time since he had agreed to Amanda's plan.

"Tell the innkeeper I'll need a room for the night and a private parlor as well as a room for my groom," the taller man commanded.

"Afraid I have the only one, old man. Care to share?" Jeremy asked.

Startled, the man turned slightly, his eyes widening as he saw the tall, thin figure standing there. "Jeremy Desmond. What are you doing in Bristol during the Season?" asked Andrew Fairleigh, Lord Mainwaring, his usually stern face breaking into a smile.

"I might ask the same of you, Drew. I thought you were heading back to Wellington's staff."

"I sold out after my father died." He glanced around at the listening ostlers. "Where's that private parlor?"

Jeremy led the way down the passageway, relieved to have an excuse to postpone the confrontation with Amanda that he knew to be inevitable. The next hour or so was filled with pleasant memories, lively conversation, good food, and an excellent wine.

Finally, Drew leaned back in his chair and asked, "Gad, Jeremy, how do you stand it?" Drew watched as his friend stretched his long legs out in front of him and reached for the wine.

"Stand what?"

"All the fawning and chasing. Six years ago mothers of sweet young things were happy for me to ask their daughters to dance. Now they're after something more serious — marriage." Drew's voice was as bitter as his smile.

"Six years ago you were only the heir to a moderate fortune, and rather ordinary. Now . . ." Jeremy paused and looked at his friend appraisingly. They were both the same height — a few inches above six feet — but there the resemblance ended. Jeremy was blond, tall, and thin — wiry, as he liked to refer to himself. Drew, on the other hand, had dark hair and a tan that made his blue eyes seem darker than they were. His shoulders, once as thin as his friend's, were broad. More than one young lady had dreamed of being held in his strong arms. Although neither of the men was handsome, both had regular features and pleasant smiles that made them worth a second glance. "Now, my friend, you are wealthy, a hero, and anything but ordinary. What do you expect them to do?"

"Leave me alone."

"That's unrealistic, Drew. What matchmaking mother wouldn't rejoice to see you at her ball."

"What do you do about them?" Drew asked, his face losing its scowl for a moment.

"Ignore them." Jeremy smiled, his face sardonic rather than amused. "If that doesn't work, I bring in Amanda." He chuckled ironically as he remembered the neat way his cousin had put to rest the hopes of one mother a short time earlier.

"Amanda? Your cousin? Have you decided to marry her at last?"

"Amanda? Never! It would be like marrying my sister." Jeremy laughed. "Besides, Amanda is as reluctant to marry as you or I." He ignored Drew's questioning look. Amanda's reasons were her own. "It's too bad you don't have someone like her in your life." If the man Amanda had sent him to meet had been more like Drew, he would have had few objections. Jeremy's eyes narrowed speculatively as he glanced once more at his friend. "How long do you plan to be in Bristol?" he asked thoughtfully.

"A day or so. I'm to meet one of my father's ship's captains here tomorrow morning." Drew ran a hand over his slightly rumpled dark hair. "It's taken me six months to see them all, but he's the last."

"Rather difficult trying to handle all those details, isn't it?" Jeremy stretched and reached out a hand for another glass of wine. "Fortunately Grandfather took me in hand early on, or I'd have been lost." He hesitated and then asked quietly, "What are your plans when you are finished here?"

"Back to London, I suppose," Drew said ruefully.

"Why not stay with me awhile? I've promised Amanda I'll stay in the country to help her with a problem. Of course, you will be disappointing all those eager mothers."

"Does Amanda still come up with all those schemes?" Jeremy looked at Drew, a smile lighting his face. "That's right. You got caught in one of them that last summer, didn't you? Remember the look on Grandfather's face when he had to explain to the lord lieutenant?"

"And my father's comments? That summer helped persuade him that the military life might be best for me. We should have had better sense. And at our age too." Drew laughed. He looked at the toes of his polished Hessians and then at his friend.

"Take care of your business and then come to Hedge-field. There are no matchmaking mamas there."

"Only Amanda. If I remember her correctly, she can be worse than any mother."

Jeremy smiled and stood up. "Not even Amanda," he promised. "When the estate next to ours, Applecroft Manor, went on the auction block, Grandfather bought it for her. After he died, she moved there to prevent gossip, she said." His voice was rather wry.

"She lives alone?" Drew asked, his voice revealing his shock. "But why didn't she join her mother?"

"Aunt Elizabeth was in Brazil with the Portuguese court."

"She refused to live with you because of the gossip and set up her own household?" Drew tried to remember how old Amanda was but couldn't. But she wasn't as old as they were. "I suppose the county was in arms at first?"

"Have you known a time when Amanda was not gossiped about? But enough of that. I have a lovely stream filled with trout." He raised his eyebrow questioningly.

"With pleasure, my friend," Drew assured him. "Why not stay in town tonight? After my meeting tomorrow, we'll ride back together."

"Let me send Amanda a note. She's expecting me," Jeremy said as he called for paper.

All day Amanda had been restless. The day had begun well enough. After their usual ride, she and Robert had shared an early-morning picnic on the hills overlooking Bath. The briskness of the early-spring day gave them a reason to gallop home. Robert was a fearless rider. Even their chief groom had to admit that. But he was so reckless. Her heart was in her throat as she watched him jump a hedge, his blond curls tossed by the wind.

When they walked back into the manor, her day began to deteriorate. "A letter just arrived by special messenger, Miss Amanda," her butler said.

The laughter on her lips was silenced as she took in his serious face. She bent to hug the small boy beside her and sent him up the stairs with a kiss. "Remember to practice your sums, love. And, Robert . . . ?" The small boy halted on the third step, his blue eyes wistful and his mouth pouting. Amanda smiled at him. "Take that pout off your face, young man," she said sternly. "Then tell Nurse to bring you down for luncheon." His shout of glee made the smallest smile appear on the butler's face. "Now, where's the letter?" Amanda asked. As the butler opened the door to the sitting room, Amanda entered. "Be certain to send word to Nurse that Robert truly is expected for luncheon, please."

Pulling her riding gloves off, she crossed to the table

where the letter lay. Recognizing the handwriting though she had seen it only a few times before, she stood for a moment, trying to control the shaking of her hands. She took a deep breath and reached for it. The words that leapt up at her were no more welcome the third time she read it then the first. "I will be arriving on Thursday next to discuss the disposition of our ward, Robert Shilling." Amanda stared at the flourishes of his signature, "Major Derwood Besley," and shivered.

"Thursday next," the words burned themselves into Amanda's brain. So little time. Catching a glimpse of herself, still dusty and disheveled from her ride, she hurried up the stairs.

Even Robert's cheerful recitation of his latest knowledge brought only an occasional smile to her lips during luncheon. By the end of the meal her cook, a woman who had known her mistress for years, was wringing her hands in despair. "None of the turbot?" she asked, her voice edged with doom.

"Only an omelette and a peach," the footman told her gloomily.

"She's sickening for something," the cook said knowingly.

"Or she's worried about our lad again," the butler said quietly as he entered the kitchen in search of his own meal now that his mistress had left the table. None of the servants gathered there had to ask what he meant. The usual gossip had kept them all informed. Unless their mistress could find a way to stop it, Master Robert would be taken away.

"It's not right," the cook said angrily. "No Christian child should be forced to go to that heathen land."

The butler pulled off his glasses and polished them carefully, running his handkerchief over his face before replacing them. "At least all is not lost yet. Miss Amanda has a plan." He glanced carefully at each serious face around him as if to gauge their willingness to help. Each face gleamed with resolution. Their mistress would find a way.

Upstairs in the schoolroom Amanda was listening to Robert read, her face attentive but her mind wandering. It was still some hours before Jeremy could possibly return.

"You are not listening," a small hurt voice declared firmly.

Amanda pulled her thoughts back to the present. "I'll do better, I promise. Do you want to begin again?" she asked as she hugged the small boy sitting beside her. He nodded. She followed the words carefully until his eyes began to droop.

Sitting beside his bed sometime later, she held his hand lightly in one of hers. With her other, she brushed a lock of hair off his cheek. He had added so much to her life. From the moment of his birth when the doctor had laid him in her arms before hurrying back to her cousin, he had fascinated her. His fingers had twisted themselves around her heart as surely as they had captured her finger that cold December morning. Even the pain of losing her cousin a few hours later was easier with that little bundle in her arms.

Amanda smoothed Robert's hair again, released his hand, and stood up. She smiled at the older woman who sat knitting in the rocker in the corner. "I'll be up to see him later, Nurse," she promised.

The clock struck the hour as she walked downstairs. "Have you heard from my cousin yet, Thompson?" she asked as she saw her butler standing in the hallway.

"No, Miss Amanda. Shall I send a groom with a note?"

"He is supposed to come here first. Perhaps he was detained." She smiled at her retainer, hiding her own nervousness. "Send Mrs. Thompson to see me. With a guest arriving we must make some plans for his entertainment."

Unfortunately for Amanda's plans, Mrs. Thompson was determined to oppose them. "Even with your cousin in attendance, Major Besley cannot expect to stay here, Miss Amanda. It wouldn't be proper. Shall I send word to Master Jeremy to expect a guest?"

Amanda bit down hard on the inside of her mouth, reminding herself that her housekeeper was only echoing what the neighborhood would say. "I have thought of that, Mrs. Thompson. Everything will be all right, I promise." She smiled at the older woman, willing her to accept her statement.

The housekeeper glanced at Amanda and nodded. Like most people in the two households, she was ready to do anything to help her mistress.

Much as Robert had done years later, Amanda had captured the hearts of her retainers. In a time when wages were low and goods were high, she paid her people well—too well, her neighbors complained. Her rents, too, were another source of annoyance in the neighborhood. They were sentimentally low. Her tenants, like her retainers, took pride in the fact they worked for her. Only in the early days after the purchase of the manor had there been any dissension. And as soon as she had proved to the farmers that Coke's methods really worked, they were also her supporters. To those who claimed she was too easy with her tenants, they just smiled, remembering how their mistress had sent one lazy farmer packing. Of course, she had given his wife enough money for passage to the colonies.

Her discussion with the housekeeper concluded, Amanda entered her sitting room, her spirits lifted at least momentarily by the warmth of the room. She had finished her tea and was trying to read a book when she heard the knocker on the front door. Reminding herself that ladies do not run into the entrance hall when they hear a noise, she sat still, her book forgotten, her breath light and shallow, her eyes anxious.

Her anxiety increased a few minutes later when Thompson entered—alone. "A message from Master Desmond."

She took the note with a hand she held steady only by determination. Nodding her dismissal, she missed the worried look the butler gave her. For a moment she sat there staring at her cousin's seal. Then she slipped a finger under the wax and opened the note.

Even with the difficulty of reading Jeremy's handwriting, Amanda read the first few sentences and crumpled the letter, realizing that her fears had indeed come true. She curled her legs under her and rested her head on her hand. She stared at the crumpled ball of paper again. Smoothing the letter out, she read the first few lines again, her fear fast being replaced by despair.

"I could take him away," she whispered, knowing that she had early rejected that way of keeping Robert. "Why did my cousin Alice leave her affairs in such turmoil?" she asked for the thousandth time, conveniently forgetting that it was not her cousin's will that had them in this state. "Or why didn't the major stay in India?" she muttered rebelliously.

About to toss the letter into the fireplace, Amanda read it one last time, this time finishing it. She stared at her cousin's words as though they were Egyptian hieroglyphics. "Ran into Lord Mainwaring (Drew Fairleigh) today. He'll be staying with me for a time. We'll join you for dinner tomorrow. I'm staying Bristol tonight."

Amanda stared at the note for a moment, her face puzzled, her mouth in a bitter smile. She had been so naïve that last summer Drew had spent with them, so sure of herself. "And so sheltered," she whispered, her eyes wistful.

She crossed to the fireplace and tossed the note into the coals, watching the edges of the note darken, then burst into flame.

If only her problems could disappear as easily . . .

2

The simple, ordinary tasks of sitting with Robert as he ate his supper and hearing his prayers before bed helped Amanda push her problems into the background for a few hours. Only once had she felt so frightened, so helpless. Then her grandfather and Jeremy had been her strength.

With Robert asleep, she sat down to the dinner her cook had so carefully prepared. The long table, with its gleaming silver candelabra and the one place set at the foot, seemed to mock her, to cry out for guests. This was the one room where she could not hide from her loneliness.

The footman ladled a clear broth sprinkled with fresh herbs into her soup plate, but she didn't really see it. Eight years earlier, the last time she had seen Drew, everything had seemed so simple. She would return to London for her second Season, fall in love (at that time she was certain that the man of her dreams was certain to appear momentarily), marry, and have a wonderfully large, happy family.

As an only child, she had longed for several brothers and sisters to share her dreams and adventures. Even when her father died and she had joined Grandfather's household, where Jeremy was in residence, her cousin had only filled part of that need. He became the older brother she longed for, but he was only at home during the holidays and for summers. The boys nearby had teased him unmercifully when she accompanied him, but he had refused to tell her to stay at home. Eventually her daring and her refusal to tattle on them made her a part of the group.

She was the despair of her mother and governess until she was seventeen. Suddenly the boys who had been good friends had begun to stand in line to fill her card at the assemblies in Bath or London. The next summer only Jeremy and Drew did not seem to notice the difference. With them she could be herself. After having her first heady draft of the exciting world of an adult, she had practiced her flirting, knowing that the two of them, so recently graduated from college, had no interest in being serious. They were ready to forget decisions and be her age once more, daring and reckless.

At first her grandfather had only raised his eyebrows when her mother complained bitterly that Amanda was running wild. But the problem with the lord lieutenant had raised his ire. Even now Amanda smiled ruefully as she remembered that brouhaha. Even Drew's father had been forced to attend that conference. Shortly thereafter Drew bought a commission, Jeremy started studying their holdings with Grandfather, and she had been shipped off to her mother's cousin in Brighton.

As usual when she thought of that summer in Brighton, she jerked herself back to the present. Amanda toyed with the soup, giving permission for it to be removed after only two sips. The fish and the capon received as little attention. And when she refused her favorite apple tart with clotted cream, even the housekeeper agreed that something must be done.

"It's as though she can't be bothered," the footman said in a puzzled voice.

The cook, the housekeeper, and the butler exchanged worried looks. They had been underservants in her grandfather's home when she had returned from Brighton. For months afterwards she had eaten only when someone had reminded her.

"I'll speak to Nurse tomorrow," Mrs. Thompson said quietly. "If Master Robert shares her meals, she will have to eat something if only to encourage him."

Her husband and the cook nodded their agreement.

For a while the next morning their plan seemed certain of success. Their mistress, herself determined to put her worries behind her until she talked to her cousin, had taken a long ride alone. When she returned, she joined her ward in the schoolroom for breakfast. Usually not a picky eater, Robert was in an unusual mood.

"Here, darling, just taste the toast and eggs," Amanda coaxed when he refused to eat them for his nurse. By eating a few bites herself, she was able to get him to eat a little.

Finally leaving him to his nurse, she met with her estate agent. Usually interested in even the smallest details, she found her mind wandering. When a footman appeared at the door, she excused herself and hurried to him. "Has my cousin arrived?"

"No, ma'am." He cleared his throat and then blurted out his message. "Nurse requests that you come to the schoolroom as soon as it is convenient."

"Why? Has something happened to Robert? Did he go for a ride without me?" Startled by the unusual message, she was on her way out of the room, halting only for a moment to make her excuses, her blue kerseymere dress swirling around her in her haste.

A few minutes later Amanda was in the schoolroom, where the harried nurse held the sobbing boy on her lap. They both looked up as she entered the room.

"Manda," Robert said plaintively, and held up his arms to her. Transferring the boy to her mistress's arms, Nurse helped her make him comfortable on her lap.

Amanda ran her hand lightly over his curls and brushed them back from his forehead. Startled by its heat, she looked at Nurse questioningly. The silent message gave her no reassurance.

"Would you like something to drink, Robert?" Amanda asked quietly. "What about some lemonade?"

He nodded and closed his eyes. His arms wound their way around Amanda's neck so tightly she was afraid for a moment that she might choke.

"Here's some lavender water, Miss Amanda. I tried to put some on his forehead earlier, but he wouldn't let me." The nurse put the bottle on a table beside her mistress and handed her a handkerchief damped with the liquid. Squelching her own dislike for the smell, Amanda rubbed the cooling liquid over Robert's face and neck, ignoring his protests.

When the housekeeper entered a short time later, Robert was moving restlessly on Amanda's lap. Mrs. Thompson poured a small glass of the lemonade she carried and held it out to her mistress. Containing a chunk of ice from the cold cellar, the glass seemed invitingly cool.

Robert eagerly took a sip and then pushed it away. "It hurts, Manda. Don't want it." He buried his head against her. Once again Amanda felt his forehead. It was warmer than earlier.

"Have someone bring up a tub and some cool water," Amanda said, remembering her first battle with his fever.

A couple of hours later, she and Nurse slipped into the hall.

"Did you notice those red dots, Miss Amanda?" Nurse said quietly.

"Yes?"

"I heard that three members of the children's choir went down with measles this week."

For a moment Amanda just stared at her. Then she said, "I'll have Thompson send a footman for Dr. Weston." She had turned to go down the stairs when she stopped. "Did I have them?"

"That you did, miss. Something fierce. I only hope Master Robert has a lighter case," Nurse told her.

With the footman on his way, Amanda returned to her ward. Looking down at his sleepy figure, she smiled wryly. No one would be able to take Robert away from her—at least for a little while. As soon as the doctor had confirmed their suspicions, she would send the major a letter.

"I suppose it would be too much to hope that the major

had never had them," she whispered, not realizing she was speaking aloud. Nurse and the nursery maid exchanged worried glances.

"Miss Amanda, you must have something to eat. Mrs. Thompson said that Cook would keep dinner until you rang. If Master Robert does have the measles, you know he will demand you beside him as soon as he wakes up. You must keep up your strength," Nurse said, almost pushing her from the room.

Persuaded finally, Amanda retired to her bed-chamber, also decorated in the ivory and red of the first-floor sitting room. Throwing herself on the chaise, Amanda picked at the contents of the tea tray. As usual, her fertile imagination had her terrified. Only the knowledge that Nurse would send her unceremoniously from the nursery kept her from rejoining Robert.

By the time her maid brought her word that Dr. Weston had arrived, the quietness and solitude of her room had done its work. As much as she longed for a large family, at times Amanda simply had to be alone. The fact had caused much friction between her and her mother. Always happiest in a crowd, Elizabeth had tried to force her daughter into the same pattern. Looking at the calendar on her ebony desk, Amanda realized that it was almost time for another of her mother's monthly letters detailing the joys and eligible husbands to be found in Vienna and bemoaning her lack of grandchildren. Lately even her stepfather had begun to add a note along the same lines.

As usual, thoughts of her mother's manipulating ways helped her pull herself together. Rising, Amanda climbed the stairs. In Robert's rooms, the doctor was just finishing his examination.

"Just as you thought. It is measles," he said quietly, pushing his glasses up on his nose. He smiled and patted Robert softly on the head. "Keep the lad in bed—no easy task, I'm sure. He'll feel better presently." He smiled down at his small patient, and as usual, the smile was returned.

Drawing Amanda and Nurse into the adjoining school-room, Dr. Weston added, "I'll leave an elixir and a sleeping draft. He'll be restless at first, and it's best he be kept quiet. Get as much rest as you can now, especially you, Miss Desmond. As I remember from when he fell out of that tree last fall, Master Robert is not always a good patient."

Nurse and Amanda exchanged rueful glances. They nodded.

Before they could question the doctor about specific treatments, the door of the schoolroom flew open.

"Thompson said you were here, Doctor," Jeremy said abruptly. "You must come at once."

"What happened?"

"Are you ill?"

"What's wrong?" The three listeners seemed to speak at almost the same time, their faces puzzled.

"It's Drew, Lord Mainwaring. Doctor, you must come at once."

Before either of the women could utter another word, both Jeremy and Dr. Weston were out the door.

"Best you follow them, Miss Amanda," Nurse suggested. "Master Robert is asleep and will likely remain so for a time. And Master Jeremy is in a state."

Agreeing, Amanda hurried downstairs, stopping three steps above the hallway on the next floor. Her eyes wide, she watched as four sturdy footmen struggled to move a gate and the tall figure lying upon it up to a bedroom.

"Put him here," Jeremy said, flinging open the door of the first bedroom, the one that was part of the master suite. Jeremy looked up and saw her shocked expression. "It's the closest, Amanda. We'll move him to my estate when he is better, I promise."

Dr. Weston looked at the twisted right leg of the man, who was trying to hold back his moans and held his counsel. "Gently, men. You, Mr. Desmond, and I will need to move him from the gate." The doctor directed the footmen to the bed, frowning at its height. "Get a couple more lads up here. And we need more light."

Jeremy moved to the bellpull to send for the men. Amanda crossed to the windows, moving the small cloth package of lead shot from one side of the window to the other. She turned back to the bed to find the doctor watching in amazement as the gray satin drapes seemed to rise under their own power.

Reminding himself of his duties, the doctor looked back at his patient and then asked, "Are there any razors in the house? That boot will have to be cut off."

Thompson, who had just entered, nodded to his mistress and hurried out. "My butler is bringing his. Is there anything I can do?" Amanda asked, keeping her position close to the windows, her back straight and her face pale.

Drew, who was hanging on to consciousness by sheer strength of will, turned his head toward her voice. Silhouetted by the afternoon sun, she was simply a dark figure. The movement jarred his body. He moaned softly and fainted.

The doctor breathed a sigh of relief. "Miss Desmond, find a nightshirt to fit him and have someone prepare a restorative broth. We'll get him settled in bed while he's still unconscious. It will be less painful for him, poor man."

Amanda nodded and hurried out of the room, her face calm and determined.

A short time later Jeremy, the doctor, Thompson, and the other men were breathing heavily, their faces edged with uneasiness. To their dismay, Drew had regained consciousness just as they lifted him. Even though they were careful, the movement was agony for him. He bit his lip, drawing blood. Not until the doctor, using Thompson's razor, split his once gleaming Hessian from his leg did he faint again.

Almost as one, the men let go the breath they had been holding.

It was at this point Amanda hurried in. "Will this do?" she asked. "Mrs. Thompson thought it might be too small."

Looking at the breadth of the shoulders of the young lord, Dr. Weston had to agree. "He had some clothes in his saddlebags," Jeremy remembered, looking around the room wildly until he spotted Drew's groom. "Fetch those saddlebags, Prescott. Then I'm sure you want to check on his mount."

Nodding, the groom slipped from the room, his face concerned.

The doctor turned from the depressing sight of Drew's twisted leg to Amanda. "We'll need strips of strong cloth. And send someone to my buggy for those pieces of wood in the back." He noticed her pale cheeks and suggested, "Perhaps you could check on Master Robert while we are setting this and getting Lord Mainwaring settled. Then we'll discuss all of the treatments. It looks as though you will have two patients."

"We'll move him to my place soon, Amanda," Jeremy promised, his eyes on the damp, pain-racked face of his friend.

Dr. Weston and Amanda exchanged rueful glances.

Hurrying downstairs, Amanda gave the additional orders. "And send for Master Jeremy's valet," she told her housekeeper. She paused thoughtfully. "Be sure the groom asks if he has had measles." She stretched tiredly. "Ask Cook if she will have something light ready for the doctor. If there are measles in the village, the man has had a hectic day."

Checking on Robert again, she found him still asleep, his curls plastered to his forehead. She smiled tiredly at Nurse. "I'll be with Lord Mainwaring. Send for me if Robert awakes."

As Amanda entered the master suite, she found Jeremy seated on the settee, his head in his hands and his cheeks drained of color. "Did you try to help the doctor?" Amanda asked anxiously, knowing her cousin's reaction to anyone's pain but his own. "You did!" She rang for her maid. Before long the woman was back, a bottle of brandy and a glass on a tray. "You drink this right now,"

Amanda commanded. "And stay right there until I return." Watching for a moment until the color began to return to his face, she nodded in satisfaction.

Entering the bedroom, Amanda paused just inside the doorway. With the aid of two husky footmen who looked as though they were about to faint themselves, the doctor repositioned the bones in Drew's leg. Running his hands down the leg, checking the set, he nodded to a third servant, who slid the wrapped splints under the muscular lower leg. The leg firmly in place, the doctor wrapped the split to the ankle and upper leg and motioned the footmen away. A soft curse broke from him as he felt the bones slip out of place again. He looked up in dismay, but Amanda refused to let him apologize. Once again, they pulled the bones back into place. Once again they slipped out as soon as the footmen released their hold.

Dr. Weston ran his fingers through his already disheveled gray hair. "If only we knew more . . . If the bones don't stay in place, this young man will have one leg shorter than the other. There has to be some way," the doctor ranted softly, almost to himself.

Amanda looked at him, startled, and then back to the man on the bed. He was so changed from the young man she had once known, she would never have recognized him. His skin, now with a sickly green cast under the rich tan, reminded her that Drew was obviously a man who enjoyed being outside, being active. "Isn't there anything you can do?" she asked, her eyes shadowed. Forgetting her own fears, she stepped close to the bed, smoothing Drew's hair back much as she had done Robert's. For the first time in years she forgot her fears, more worried about the man who lay there quietly than about herself.

Drew groaned and opened his eyes, their blueness startling in his pale face. Seeing Amanda and frowning, he asked, a worried tone cutting through even the pain, "Is your grandfather angry again, Amanda?"

Startled, Amanda looked across at the doctor.

"He's confused. He did the same with Mr. Desmond," the doctor reassured her. "Here, your lordship, drink this." The doctor held the cup laced with laudanum to

Drew's lips and held it there until the cup was empty. He watched carefully until his patient drifted off again. "If only there were some way we could keep that pressure constant," he muttered as he felt the bones slip back into place again. "We need a constant pressure."

Wanting additional light, Dr. Weston crossed to the closed drapes of a second window. Remembering Amanda's movements earlier, he looked for the bag of lead shot and moved it to the other side. As the drapes began to move upward, he stopped, stared at them thoughtfully, and turned back to the bed. He picked up the splints and looked at them. "Take these out to the stables and have the groom drill holes here and here in each," he said quickly. As the footman hurried on his way, the doctor turned to Amanda. "Can you find me at least eight bags of shot like those at these windows and some cord?"

Slightly puzzled, she nodded and turned to the bellpull.

"You had better get a board to go under the mattress too," he added as Thompson answered the bell.

When Thompson left, Amanda once again crossed to the bed. Even unconscious, Drew had a white line around his mouth. Groaning slightly, he flung out an arm and tried to turn over. Amanda jumped back. The footmen held him in place while the doctor checked the leg once more.

"He'll have to have someone with him constantly for the first few days. Even if my idea works, he must not be allowed to turn over," the doctor explained.

"What do you plan?"

"I'm going to weight the splints much as you weight the drapes to keep them open or closed."

"How?"

"We'll attach the bags of shot at the end of the splints closest to the end of the bed and drop them over the edge."

"And the pressure may keep the bones in place," Amanda said quietly.

"If we are lucky. He may still have a limp, though. If

only there were some way to tell if everything is in place," he muttered almost to himself.

Jeremy poked his head in the door. "My valet has just arrived, Doctor. What do you want him to do?"

"Send him up immediately. I want to be certain he understands what I am doing." Jeremy turned to leave once more. He stopped as the doctor said, "Mr. Desmond, I do not recommend moving this patient."

"But he can't stay here," Jeremy said, totally surprised.

"And he can't be moved either." The doctor looked at the tall man closely, as if just realizing why he had originally been sent for. "Has your friend had the measles, Mr. Desmond?"

"The measles?"

Amanda's eyes grew round. "Oh, no," she whispered.

"What?" Both men turned toward her.

"Jeremy, you were at school when I had them. Have you had the measles?"

"Measles? Will someone tell me what you're talking about?"

"Master Robert has the measles, Mr. Desmond," the doctor said quietly, "as do several children in the village." He watched Jeremy's face grow alarmed.

"He's resting," Amanda assured him. "And Nurse is with him. Jeremy, go ask her immediately if you had them."

He shook his head. "No need. I haven't."

"Well, sir, I hope your affairs are in order. I think with the situation as it is now you had better stay here," Dr. Weston ordered. "And, Miss Desmond, find out which of your servants have not had the disease. Those are not to leave the house or stable area for the next three weeks."

"Three weeks?" Their voices echoed their shock.

"With any luck that will be the end of it," the doctor tried to reassure them. As the footmen hurried back in with the splints, cord, and bags of shot, he turned back to the bed, oblivious of the rueful glances the cousins exchanged.

Jeremy glanced at his friend, guilt clear in his eyes, if

anyone had been looking. Then he looked back at Amanda thoughtfully.

"Three weeks," Amanda repeated softly, a soft smile lighting her face for the first time all day.

3

The next two days were so busy that Amanda hardly had a chance to think. Keeping Drew quiet was no problem. With Jeremy's valet on hand to be certain he did not turn and reinjure his leg, Amanda could divide her time between Robert and Jeremy.

Amanda's nerves were on edge; therefore, her first discussion with her cousin was less than calm. "How dare you dismiss the man! What do you expect me to do now?" Her arms folded around herself, Amanda tapped her foot impatiently and returned her cousin's stare.

"I told you I would decide what to do when I saw the man," he reminded her, his voice deliberately calm. His eyes flashed his true emotions. "The man was a Greek. He'd have taken your money and created a scandal broth."

"You learned all this and you didn't even talk to him?"

"Some things are evident."

Amanda glared at him for a moment and then took a deep breath. "And what am I supposed to do now?"

"I suggest you write the major about the measles. With any luck, he will postpone his visit," Jeremy said, maintaining his calm only with great effort. He walked slowly about the room until he neared the door. "I will be with Drew. We can talk about this again later." Making his escape, he closed the door to the sitting room. He took a deep breath and hurried up the stairs. If he were not careful, he might give his plan away.

Amanda stared at the door angrily. Forcing herself to

take several calming breaths, she regained her composure. Planning how she would gain her revenge, she smiled. Her smile grew as she thought of the letter already on its way to the major. Of course, her cousin would probably take credit if the man did postpone his visit.

A short time later, her frustrations carefully hidden under a deceptive mask of calm, Amanda entered Robert's bedroom. As he caught sight of her, he stopped turning restlessly and held up his arms. "Manda," he cried plaintively, "hold me." She picked him up and carried him to the low rocker. He snuggled against her at first; then he began to shift restlessly. "Hot," he whimpered.

Amanda held him for a short time, her hand soothing his hair. Then she put him into bed again and sat beside him, her fingers caressing his forehead.

As he grew quieter, he looked up at her and said in a grumpy little voice, "I don't like being sick."

Blinking back tears, Amanda smiled at him and hugged him gently. As soon as she was certain her voice would not quaver, she whispered close to his ear, "No one does. Now close your eyes and I'll tell you a story." As his eyes obediently shut, her voice dropped even lower. "Once upon a time in a land where the sun never sets a wicked. . . ." Before she could finish, he was asleep once again.

The nursery maid slipped to her side. "Mrs. Thompson said to tell you that dinner will be served in a few minutes. She thought the dressing bell might disturb Master Robert and Lord Mainwaring. I'll sit with Master Robert if you wish to freshen up. Nurse is asleep next door if I need her," the girl said in a rush.

Amanda rose and stretched, feeling cramped from sitting on the low bed. She watched as the nursery maid took her seat in a chair beside the bed, picking up the knitting from the basket placed there.

"He'll be fine, Miss Desmond," the girl said quietly, wanting to smooth the line of worry from her mistress's eyes.

Amanda smiled gratefully.

After a short visit to her bedroom to change into a more formal but simple muslin gown, she entered the ivory-and-red sitting room. In her visit to Robert, she had been able to put her problems out of her mind. But when she saw her cousin, she halted, her despair and anger as fresh as they had been earlier.

Used to their easy relationship, Jeremy greeted her casually. He held up his glass of wine as if to ask her if she wished her own. Their grandfather had always poured them a glass before supper. Noting her frown and refusal, he hurried into speech. "Drew is rather restless. Huttle has had quite a time keeping him quiet." He glanced at her again. Then he stared. "Are you still angry at me?" he asked, rather surprised because Amanda's temper storms were usually forgotten as soon as they happened.

"Yes." The clipped word told him that her anger was serious. She stalked to the door. "Some things are not easily forgiven."

The door opened, almost hitting her. Jeremy stifled a bark of laughter as he watched her jump back. "Supper is served," the butler stated primly. Although his face never lost its impassive stare, Thompson correctly read the uneasy atmosphere. Later he told his wife, "It's not her way. Master Jeremy must have distressed her greatly."

"Most likely it's the strain of two sickrooms to oversee. You know how she worries about Master Robert," his wife said quietly, resolving that she would ferret out the truth in her meeting with her mistress the next morning.

By the next morning a possible rift between the cousins was the least thing on the housekeeper's mind. The youngest groom and a kitchen maid were the latest victims of measles.

Realizing the importance of keeping the situation manageable, Amanda came up with a plan to care for them. "Empty two of the bedrooms near the schoolroom and set up extra beds. We'll put the females in one and the men in the other." The housekeeper nodded. "Put someone who has had the disease on duty with them at all times."

"But that's not possible," the housekeeper protested, mentally running down the number of servants already doing double duty. Amanda raised one eyebrow. Mrs. Thompson explained, "Several of our younger servants haven't had the disease. Those that have are already working helping with Master Robert and Lord Mainwaring."

Amanda thought for a moment. Then the slight frown on her face disappeared. "Send to Hedgefield. With Jeremy our guest for some time, they'll be willing to share. How many people will we need?" Sitting at her small desk, Amanda picked up her pen and sharpened it. As she pulled the paper toward her, she asked, "Is there anything else we need?"

"Master Desmond asked me if there were any strawberries for breakfast this morning?"

"I'll ask for them and for anything else that might tempt an invalid's appetite," Amanda assured her. "Hmm. I wonder if the forcing houses have any lemons?" Nodding her dismissal, Amanda turned to her letter.

With the aid of the older servants from Hedgefield, Amanda and Mrs. Thompson set up the sickrooms, each gradually gaining population. Although Mrs. Thompson tried to discourage her visits, Amanda checked the rooms at least once a day, totally ignoring Mrs. Thompson's ideas about propriety by personally overseeing the men too.

"They're only a few steps from the schoolroom," Amanda explained when Jeremy commented on her visits. "If I visit Robert, I feel guilty when I think of the people, children really, in there without anyone but servants to care for them. I never stay long. But I want them to know I care."

Wisely, Jeremy held back his comments and simply nodded.

There was one sickroom that Amanda rarely visited: Drew's. Only in the presence of Dr. Weston, who stopped in at least once a day, did she venture inside. Then her eyes darted around the room, looking anywhere but at the man in the bed. Even with him, she was able to avoid entering some days, sending Jeremy instead. Jeremy spent much of his free time there.

Feeling guilty because his suggestion had resulted in such an accident, he spent hours each day at his friend's bedside, talking about their school days and that summer and the fun they had had with Amanda. As soon as Drew began to regain consciousness for longer periods, Jeremy helped him feel part of the world again. "Your groom told me your horse suffered a slight sprain only," Jeremy reassured his friend.

"And my saddle?" Drew asked, his voice low and husky.

Jeremy frowned. "Not like you at all to have such a worn girth, Drew. Better fire that groom of yours. He should have caught it." His back was to the bed as he raised the drapes. So he missed the thoughtful look that crossed his friend's face. "Now, I suppose I must write your mother."

"Never!"

"What?"

"There's not a single thing she can do that is not already being done. When I've recovered somewhat, I'll let her know." Drew pulled himself up higher on his pillows, digging his elbows in the soft mattress. He winced as he jarred his leg.

"Stop that! Amanda and Dr. Weston will have my head—and rightly so—if you hurt that leg again. Keep still before you knock it out of place." Calling for Huttle, Jeremy crossed to stand by the bed. As soon as the man arrived, he directed him. "You move his body; I'll keep the leg still." Lifting carefully, they rearranged Drew, if not to his total satisfaction at least more comfortably.

As careful as they were, by the time they had finished, Drew's face was a sickly green. He leaned back on his pillows gratefully and closed his eyes. As if sensing his friend's withdrawal, he opened them again. "Promise me you will not tell my family, Jeremy," he said, his breath still shallow from pain. Bowing to the agony in his friend's eyes, Jeremy agreed.

As Drew improved, Jeremy spent even more of each

day with him. Developing their own version of the White's betting book, they listed trifling wagers on the health of the servants. One afternoon Drew glanced at his friend. Then he reached for the betting book he kept close beside him. "A monkey that you're in bed in a week," he said quietly.

Jeremy raised an eyebrow slowly and nodded solemnly, against his better judgment. "Determined to lay me low, are you?" He adjusted the sleeves of his dark-blue jacket and inspected the polish of his gold buttons. His friend merely smiled. Jeremy dealt another hand of piquet, using the edge of the bed as a table.

Two days later Drew won his bet. Complaining of a headache and feeling hot, Jeremy had gone to bed the night before at an hour early even for life in the country. Early the next morning Drew woke suddenly, startled. Something was wrong. Someone was pounding on the door. As he tried to raise himself, he groaned as he jarred his leg. Huttle, Jeremy's valet, who had been sleeping in the dressing room on a trundle bed, stumbled to the door. "You're to come at once, Mr. Huttle," a tall footman said. "It's Mr. Desmond."

"What's going on?" Amanda, asked, rubbing sleep from her eyes. She had entered only minutes after the footman.

"A chambermaid lighting the morning fire found Mr. Desmond ill and called Mr. Thompson. Mr. Huttle is needed."

"Has Thompson sent for the doctor?" Amanda asked sharply, the last edges of tiredness dropping from her like scales. She gathered the deep-blue velvet robe she wore more closely around her, tightening the ties under her full breasts. Her short curls tumbled in disarray around her forehead. Totally unaware of the appealing picture she made to the man who watched her from the bed and unaware of the proprieties she had violated, Amanda stared at the man in her livery.

"I'm not certain," the man mumbled, startled by her appearance.

Drew, used to the staid, quiet picture she usually made, stared in amazement at the vibrant figure that stood on the threshold. She ran a hand through her disheveled curls, and he caught his breath.

"Huttle, get dressed," Amanda said firmly. She turned toward the footmen. "You tell Thompson I will see him in my sitting room as soon as possible." The two men disappeared. Her audience gone, Amanda sighed and covered her face with her hands.

"He'll be all right," Drew said, wanting to wipe the despair from her face.

Startled, Amanda dropped her hands and turned toward the bed. Her face burned under her blush. "Oh," she whispered as she realized just where she was. Her heart raced and she looked at the floor in embarrassment.

"Will you send me word about Jeremy?" Drew asked, trying to ease her discomfort.

She nodded and slipped from the room.

Although she had not forgotten Drew—his dark hair against those white pillows was a striking sight—it was hours later before Amanda could bring herself to face him again. After settling Jeremy, soothing Robert, and checking on the sickrooms, she finally slipped into Drew's chambers, her maid her shadow.

"Is he all right?" a gruff voice asked.

"Not at the moment. He has a particularly nasty case of the measles."

"Then he owes me a monkey," Drew said, his laugh covering his own worry.

"What?"

"I told him he would be sick in a few days."

Drew's calm statement raised Amanda's ire. Her morning had been less than calm. "How dare you! I suppose you also bet on whether he'd die?"

Had Amanda been one of Drew's subalterns, she would have recognized the too-quiet voice that said, "No, but he bet me that I'd always walk with a limp."

Amanda looked at her unwilling guest in horror. Then, overwhelmed, she totally gave way. She started shaking, her face turning white. Her maid shot the man in the bed a sharp look and put her arms around her mistress. "That's all right, miss."

Drew raised himself slightly on his elbows, feeling panic. "Jeremy will be fine, won't he?" he asked, a slight uncertainty evident in his voice.

That uncertainty reached Amanda as nothing else could. She sat in the red velvet chair Jeremy usually occupied and tried to control herself. As soon as she had stopped shaking enough to speak, she whispered, "Forgive me for being so missish. Jeremy would tell me how silly I've been."

Drew, resting awkwardly on one elbow, murmured a polite response. Then in a voice rough with worry, he asked again, "He will be all right?"

Amanda began to shake again.

Drew's anxiety increased. He tried to pull himself higher in bed, gritting his teeth as he dragged his leg up higher on the bed. "Amanda, tell me what the doctor said," he demanded through clenched teeth.

"He's, he's sicker than . . ." Amanda took a deep breath and held it, determined to regain her composure. Since she was normally able to handle any crisis, her trembling had surprised her. She took several deep breaths. Watching her face carefully, Drew held his tongue. Calmer, Amanda began again. "Measles are more dangerous for adults than children," she said as calmly as she could. No matter how hard she tried, her voice still had a definite quaver.

"What does that mean? Will he be in bed longer?"

"Probably." Amanda refused the restorative her mind held out to her. She rose and crossed to the window, fingering the heavy pale-gray satin drapes figured with birds and flowers in reds and blues. Finally she straightened her back and turned to face the bed. "The doctor has said that there is a possibility his lungs will be affected. That and the fever are the worst problems." Amanda took a deep breath. She walked closer to the bed. "The next few days should tell us something."

Drew lost what little color he had. He turned his face

away from her, muttering something under his breath.

Amanda crossed to the opposite side of the bed and stared at him, trying to determine what the problem was. Her eyes stared into his for a moment. Drew dropped his eyes in front of her questioning look. Then she realized what he was saying in a voice so low she had to strain to hear. "My fault."

In spite of her own fears Amanda recognized his folly. "For falling off your horse? Come, now, Lord Mainwaring, even you cannot blame your worn saddle girth for my cousin's bout with measles." Her attention focused more on her own worries than on him, she missed the angry look that swept over his face before he could guard his expression. "If that were true, I would then have to trace the problem to Robert, and I refuse to do so. Anyone can catch measles." She stepped up on the steps beside the bed and stared him straight in the face. "You behave yourself, your lordship. I'll keep you posted on my cousin." Her maid clucking behind her, Amanda swept from the room as the footman came in. "Take care of him," she said quietly. "I'll be with Master Robert if you should need me."

Cursing his inability to do anything to help, Drew worried. With Jeremy ill, he was left with servants most of the time. They answered his questions, brought him the books he requested, and took care of him physically. Too restless to be able to read, Drew shifted nervously, waving away the footman who came to stand beside the bed. He closed his eyes briefly, remembering for the first time in years an old governess.

He had made her so angry. He had stolen out of the schoolroom to the stables, his favorite spot on the estate. Slipping past the grooms, he had taken his pony and headed for the practice jumps that he had been forbidden to use. He had made the first one. At the second he came a cropper, hitting his head. When his pony wandered back into the stables, they came looking for him.

The next week he had spent in isolation in bed with a

concussion, a suitable punishment for one who had broken the rules according to the governess. His little sister had slipped in to see him as often as she could dart away from her nurse. Standing on tiptoes by the edge of the bed, she had lisped her support and kissed his cheek when he had tried to hide his hurt. Now Drew wished she were there with him. Then he had second thoughts. Calling for paper, he did send an express to his household, telling them not to worry about his absence. That finished, he drifted off again.

The door to the suite opened. Drew snapped out of his dreams and sat up as much as he could. At the sight of a maid with the teatray, he dropped back down on his pillows. The only thing he was hungry for was news. Drinking his tea and waving the rest away as he had done with his other meals that day, Drew wondered once again about his friend.

In spite of years of separation, Jeremy was one of the few people he still trusted. But he regretted the impulse that made him accept his friend's invitation. "No matter what Amanda said, if I had not returned with Jeremy, he would not be ill at Applecroft Manor," he muttered almost under his breath.

"No, he would be at Hedgefield, and I should have to travel back and forth to keep an eye on both Robert and him," Amanda said snappishly. Her eyes took in the almost untouched teatray. She gestured toward it and then asked, "Well, are you trying to push yourself into a decline? Or is the meal not to your liking?" She tapped her foot impatiently, already worn to the bone with her efforts to keep Robert in bed and to oversee Jeremy's care as well. Only the crackle of the letter in her pocket kept her spirits up. The major had decided to postpone his visit until "The contagion has been eradicated."

Drew shrugged, feeling guilty at adding another problem on her slender shoulders. "I don't seem to have an appetite," he said apologetically. Then his voice grew more gruff. "Is Jeremy any better?"

Taking a good look at Drew, Amanda sat down in the

chair beside the bed and then sent the footman for fresh
tea. By the time the teatray arrived, she had forgotten her
own hesitation and fear as Drew asked one question after
another. He seemed more like the young man who had
urged her to one prank after another. "What will you do
if Nurse continues to insist on nursing Jeremy?" he finally
asked, noting with satisfaction that the tired look in
Amanda's eyes was disappearing. She was so different
from the girl he remembered yet still brave and beautiful.

"As long as she and Huttle agree, it is probably the best
solution. Jeremy is the one who needs the most care right
now," Amanda said, the question that had been worrying
her all day now clearly resolved.

"And you are certain the doctor said Jeremy was
improving?"

Amanda looked with satisfaction at the almost empty
sandwich plate on the edge of the bed. "I promise. And if
you don't believe me, you can ask the doctor yourself
when he comes to check on you tomorrow morning."
Promising herself that she would find some time to
entertain Drew, preferably at teatime, she made her
excuses and hurried back upstairs to the nursery.

Alerted by the noise within that Robert was awake, she
slipped in quietly. "You may go downstairs now," she told
the nursery maid quietly, smiling at her to show that she
understood what Robert had been trying to do. As soon
as Faith had disappeared, she turned to face her ward.
Her voice grew stern. "Now, young man, please explain
exactly what you were doing before I came in."

Robert took one look at her stern face and hung his
head. But the feeling of contrition did not last long. He
raised his head and pouted. Then he tried his wistful
look. Amanda had to suppress a laugh as she
remembered doing much the same herself. Finally, his
patience at an end, Robert demanded, "Manda, I'm
well. I can get up now." His chin, usually so boyish, was
set in a firm, square line.

"The doctor has been here, has he?"

Blue eyes stared into her hazel ones defiantly for a few
moments. Then Robert lowered his. "It's hard being sick.

I'm tired of it," he said in what tried to be a gruff manly voice.

Thinking about the man she had just left, Amanda agreed. She sat on the bed beside Robert and pulled him close to her. "Have patience, little one."

"I'm not little. Nurse told me I'm as tall as Cousin Jeremy was when he was a boy." Robert frowned but did not protest when Amanda laughed and hugged him. Then he asked, "Doesn't Cousin Jeremy love me anymore?"

Amanda drew back and stared at him thoughtfully. "Why do you think that?"

"He hasn't come to see me." Robert's chin quivered.

"Oh, darling, he loves you. But he has the measles, too."

"The same as me?"

"Yes."

"Then I'll go see him." The little boy pulled away from her and tried to slip from the bed. Amanda pulled him slowly back into bed. "Do I have to ask the doctor first?" the child asked wistfully.

"You can visit him. But you need to wait a few days. Remember when you were first ill, you didn't want anyone but Nurse or me around," Amanda reminded him.

He settled back on his pillows and looked at her solemnly. "But I'm almost well now."

"Cousin Jeremy just got sick."

Robert considered the situation. "I can go see him when he gets better?" Amanda nodded, her face as solemn as his. "Then I'll wait."

For the rest of the evening, Robert was his charming, happy self, only pouting a little when he discovered that "his" nurse would not be there to tuck him in.

"Remember she was Cousin Jeremy's nurse first," Amanda said quietly, watching as Faith handed him a cloth to wipe his face.

"He's too old for a nurse," the little boy muttered under his breath.

Amanda and the maid exchanged rueful glances.

A short time later Amanda listened to his prayers and tucked him in bed carefully. "You go to bed now," Amanda said quietly to the maid. "Mrs. Thompson has promised to send someone up as soon as the kitchen is clean. You need to be fresh for tomorrow."

A short time later Amanda checked on the nearby sick-rooms one last time, waving the maid who was dozing by the fireplace back to her place. Then she looked in again on Jeremy, pleased to see he was less feverish than before. As she headed back to her own rooms, she paused outside Drew's door and then hurried on.

4

The next day was no easier than the previous one had been. When Amanda accompanied Dr. Weston on his rounds, she was treated to rare displays of temper. Jeremy refused to take his medicine; Robert demanded he be allowed to go outside to see his "friends." Drew, who had his own grievances, wisely held his tongue until the doctor, reading his patient correctly, suggested that Amanda prepare the servants in the sickrooms for his visit.

As the door closed behind her, he turned to Drew and asked, "Now, Lord Mainwaring, what may I do for you?"

"Let me go home."

"And reinjure your leg? Do you know what could happen?" The two men stared at each other for a moment. The dark-blue satin robe Drew wore made his eyes burn like sapphires. Then the doctor asked, "Why?"

"To relieve her of the burden of my care. Miss Desmond has enough problems to worry about without my presence adding more." Drew pulled himself up slowly, allowing the doctor to help him only briefly. He had watched Amanda carefully the last few days, worried that she was doing too much, yet helpless to prevent it.

"And who would see that you got there? I understand that even the grooms have been pressed into service in the house for part of each day." Dr. Weston paused and ran his hands over Drew's leg, noting with satisfaction that the bone seemed to be knitting nicely. Drew winced as the doctor adjusted the fit of the splints. "If it is this tender while you are lying still, your lordship, think what a coach ride would do," the doctor reminded him. The leg rebandaged to his satisfaction, he stood back. "And think of the worry it would cause Miss Desmond."

"What?"

"How would she feel when she knew you had refused to stay in her home? Especially since she knew moving might cause you further injury?"

"But, she doesn't . . ."

"Have to know? My dear Lord Mainwaring, Amanda Desmond would know in a heartbeat what you were doing. Besides, the worst is over. If you could persuade her of that and get her to sit with you and get some rest herself, you would be doing all of us a favor." The doctor let his glasses slip down his nose and stared over them at the man in the bed. "But if you insist . . ."

Drew, never one to maintain a faulty battle plan, gave in. But trying to follow the doctor's advice was very difficult. Amanda flitted into Drew's room with her maid at her heels at least once a day. His heart always raced when he saw her. But she rarely stayed for long. In fact, to Drew's dismay, her visits grew shorter as Robert was released from his bed for short periods. Amanda had to supervise these times carefully, for he and the nursery maid did not agree on what a short time out of bed should be.

When Dr. Weston returned the following day, he frowned as he noticed new lines of exhaustion around Amanda's eyes.

They had just left Jeremy, who was beginning to show a marked improvement, when Thompson materialized, his face shadowed. He said breathlessly, "Master Robert is not in his room."

"What?"

"How did it happen?"

"The maid was looking for Master Robert's favorite book when he slipped out," the butler explained. "As soon as she realized what had happened, she reported it to my wife."

"We must find him at once," Amanda said, her hands clasped to keep them from shaking.

"I'm certain Thompson has everyone looking," the doctor reassured her, looking at the butler questioningly. Thompson nodded. "There is nothing to worry about. He'll be found shortly. And he is almost completely recovered, as this excursion proves." He smiled reassuringly at her, his eyes twinkling above his glasses.

Before they could reach the entrance hall, Robert, his face mutinous and his arms folded across his chest, was carried in by the head groom. "He was heading for his pony's stall, Miss Desmond, when young Will caught sight of him. Gave us quite a start." He placed the boy on the floor and stood quietly.

"Thank you, Hilton. I appreciate your quick work." Amanda smiled and nodded her dismissal. She waited until the servants were gone and turned to her ward. "Well, young man?" she asked sternly.

"My pony was lonely," Robert began. Realizing from the look on Amanda's face that that tack would not work, he shut his lips tightly and stood glaring at her.

"And Dr. Weston gave you permission to go outside?"

"He said I could get up. Didn't you, Doctor?"

The older man looked at him sternly for a moment, as if reminding him silently of their conversation. The boy looked at the floor in embarrassment. "Up, yes. Outside, no," the doctor said quietly. Robert blushed. "And I want you to rest for several hours each day." He smiled at Amanda, who sighed and nodded.

"No, I won't." Robert stamped his foot.

"Young man," Amanda began.

"There's nothing to do," Robert said, his usual cheerful face twisted into a pout.

"Bored, are you?" the doctor asked, dropping down on one knee in front of Robert. "Well, I know someone who fits that description better than you." He stood up and took the boy by the hand. "Let's go up and see him."

As they started up the stairs, leaving an astonished Amanda behind, Robert began chattering. "Who is it?

Manda says my Cousin Jeremy is too sick for me to visit. Is it Huttle? I like Huttle. He lets me practice tying neckcloths just like Cousin Jeremy. 'Course they're still too big for me."

As they turned the corner and headed up the next flight of stairs, Amanda broke from her brown study and hurried after them. She arrived, breathless, to hear Robert ask, "Who is here? Manda's rooms are next door. Nobody is supposed to be here. I'm not even supposed to play hide-and-seek here."

"Doctor, I don't think this is the right thing to do," Amanda said quickly.

"Nonsense. It will do them both good." Dr. Weston threw open the door and ushered Robert inside. "Good morning, Lord Mainwaring, I have brought you some company."

Drew looked up from his book without much enthusiasm. Then he dropped it. "Good morning. Who is this?"

The little boy walked to the end of the bed, fascinated by the bags of lead weights. "I am Robert Shilling, and I live here. Who are you?" He reached, curious, for one of the bags.

"No," Amanda said sharply, and Robert jumped back, startled.

"I, sir, am Andrew Fairleigh, Lord Mainwaring." Drew bowed his head.

Robert made a very credible leg and then hopped up the stairs beside the bed. "What happened?" he asked, looking at Drew's leg as it lay encased in splints and propped up on pillows. "You didn't have the measles, did you?" He looked at Amanda and then back to Drew. Dr. Weston smothered a laugh.

Drew chuckled. "No. I took a fall from my horse." The doctor drew Amanda into the suite's sitting room. They smiled as they heard Robert's questions continue. "When?"

As soon as he was alone with Amanda, Dr. Weston explained. "This is just the thing. I have been worried about Lord Mainwaring. He has seemed so unhappy, so alone."

"But what if Robert jars his leg. You know what he's like when he's well." Amanda smoothed the rather plain gray morning dress she was wearing, wishing for the first time in some time that she had taken more care when she had dressed that morning.

The doctor hid his frown at her pulled appearance and said firmly, "I'm certain Lord Mainwaring will not permit the boy to do anything foolish. The bone seems to be healing, and slight movements will not hurt it. Besides, Master Robert will grow tired very easily. After his adventure, I'm certain his eyelids are drooping right now."

"But, but . . ."

"You can put him to bed in your dressing room. I'm certain that nursery maid would keep an eye on him. And I'll have a word with the footman who has been sitting with his lordship about what Master Robert should not do." He nodded and then asked, "How has he been eating?"

"Robert?"

"No, Lord Mainwaring. You said he had been eating poorly. Has his appetite improved?"

"No. He usually has a good tea, when I pour for him, but at other meals . . ." Amanda cleared her throat, remembering her promise to herself to check on him. "Is there something we can do?"

"I think that young man in there now will do most of it. Let them share their meals. And your cook can do the rest. By the way, compliment her on the contents of the basket that I found in my carriage yesterday. The meat pie was delicious. Thank you."

"It's the least we can do, since we are taking up so much of your time." Although she said the right words, Amanda's attention was focused on the bedroom behind her, listening to the deep rumble and the shrill questions.

When the doctor left to check on his other patients, Amanda entered the room quietly. There was Robert curled up in the red chair beside Drew's bed, fast asleep.

"Shh." Drew whispered as she opened her mouth. "Let him sleep here for a while. He's comfortable."

"You're certain? He won't be too much trouble?"

"You can stay in your room next door," Drew suggested, noting the same lines of exhaustion the doctor had seen earlier. "When he wakes up, we'll call you." He sighed in relief as she nodded and left. Maybe she would rest awhile.

Drew looked at the sleeping boy, comparing him to his nephew. Two years older than Daniel, Robert seemed so much more masculine, so determined. He laughed at his comparisons and picked up his book again. "At least I'll have something more to do than count the stripes on the wall," he reminded himself.

To a man unaccustomed to being still for longer than a few hours each night, Drew was finding the prospect of more time in bed boring. Robert, with his inquiring mind, was a welcome diversion. The next morning as soon as he was dressed, Robert appeared in the gray bedroom, noting carefully the order of Drew's abbreviated toilet. With Jeremy on the mend, Huttle was once more free to shave the injured man, a blessing for which Drew gave thanks fervently, having already suffered several nicks from lesser individuals.

Robert watched the whole procedure, fascinated. He peppered Huttle with questions. "Why do you do that? What's that for?"

Patiently, the man replied. The only time the valet refused any of Robert's requests was when he asked to try the razor. "No, Master Robert, your hand is not steady enough yet. In a few years ask me again." For a moment, Drew had wondered if the wish would be granted, and he breathed a sigh of relief. "I'll see you again tomorrow, your lordship," the valet promised as he gathered up his equipment.

When the maid and footman entered a few minutes later, they were followed by Amanda. Her short curls were carefully tousled around her face and threaded with a pink ribbon that matched the cambric of her morning gown. "Well, here you are, pixie. Did you ask permission from Lord Mainwaring before you disturbed him?" she asked as she bent to kiss Robert's cheek.

"He is not disturbing me." Drew paused, wishing that he too could command her kiss. "We promised to continue our discussion over breakfast," Drew said quickly, exchanging a men-only look with Robert. A smile flashed across the boy's face as he nodded firmly. "Would you join us, my lady?"

Amanda looked from one to the other and then took her seat, her feet carefully lined up side by side, her back straight. Accepting her tea, she smiled at Robert.

Drew noted that she looked more rested. He tried to sit up alone to accept the egg and toast from the maid, but Amanda forestalled him. "Help his lordship," she directed the footman quietly, holding his leg carefully in place herself, trying not to blush. Breathing rapidly, she sat back down, her eyes carefully avoiding his. Once sitting up, Drew accepted his breakfast and took a swallow of ale.

He almost choked when Robert asked, "Are you going to be my cousin, Lord Mainwaring?"

"What?" Two heads snapped to look at him quickly. "Nurse told Thompson Manda could be in Cousin Jeremy's bedroom alone because he was a relative. But she should have her maid when she visited you. Are you going to be Amanda's relative too?"

The maid and footman exchanged speaking glances. The other two blushed fiercely. Dew took one look at Amanda and knew that now was no time for a teasing remark.

"We're not alone," Amanda stammered. "You're here and so are the others." She waved her hand toward the servants, who were busily clearing the table, their backs carefully turned away from the scene.

Robert frowned and opened his mouth as if to continue, but Drew spoke up. "I'm a friend of your cousins'. I suppose I could be called an honorary cousin," he suggested, wishing he could be more. He could certainly hear the conversation in the servants' hall as soon as those two finished clearing the table.

Robert considered the situation for a moment and then agreed. Tilting his head to one side, he asked wistfully, "Did you know my mama or papa?"

Amanda drew a deep breath as she realized once again how much Robert had missed by losing his parents. As much as she and Jeremy loved him, they were not a family in the ordinary sense. Her own yearnings as a child seemed to be repeated in Robert. Saddened by her thoughts, she leaned back in her chair. She patted the space beside her, and Robert hurriedly climbed beside her.

Wanting to fill the silence, Drew took a deep breath and said quietly, "Your mother and father were younger than I. By the time they met I was on the Peninsula."

Robert sat up straight. "Were you in any battles?"

"More than I care to remember." As Robert began bombarding him with questions, Amanda made her escape.

A short time later her already sagging spirits dropped even lower. "When?" she asked quietly.

"A short time ago. The silly girl thought she could keep it secret, and her with red spots all over. Embarrassed, I suppose," her housekeeper said briskly. "I've had her put to bed."

"But she said she had already had them," Amanda protested.

"Now, now, Miss Amanda. She's little more than a child herself. But it does create a problem in the nursery. I simply have no one else to replace her." She stopped, giving her mistress time to collect her thoughts.

"Another nursery maid? No. Let me speak to Huttle and the footman assigned to Lord Mainwaring. Between all of us we should be able to care for one small boy." Amanda nodded her head briskly, each detail falling into its precise place in her plan.

Unfortunately, Robert had never seen her plan. To

him living with the adults all day in the adult rooms was one big adventure. He played hide-and-seek in Amanda's wardrobes, much to the dismay of her maid, Jennings. Growing bored with that, he slipped away from the footman who was attending Drew and slid down the banister to the first floor, saved from a headlong plunge to the marble below only by Thompson's quick thinking. Fortunately for her sanity, Amanda was nowhere in sight when the butler returned him to Drew.

"Put him up here with me, Thompson," the gentleman demanded. "No, no. He will behave. I'm certain he does not want to cause me pain."

The butler, who had been about to complain, swallowed his protests. For a few minutes the boy was as still as a rabbit hiding from a fox.

During those few minutes, Drew suggested, "Perhaps Thompson could arrange for some of your favorite things to be brought down from the schoolroom. What do you suggest?" He smiled ruefully as Robert began his list. By the time the servants had discovered everything the child wanted, Drew hoped to be walking again.

This time the plot was more successful. When Amanda returned to check on them later in the afternoon, she found Robert curled up beside Drew on the bed, reading him a story from his book on horses. Spread out at the foot of the bed was Robert's newest dissected puzzle, and his regiment of soldiers had pride of place on the newly emptied table beside the bed. She caught her breath at the sight. Drew's dark head bent over Robert's bright one. They looked like father and son. Suppressing a dream she had just acknowledged, Amanda cleared her throat nervously.

Catching sight of her, Robert sat up hastily, dislodging Drew's leg slightly.

"Manda!"

"No." She hurried to the bedside, anxious to stop the child before he hit Drew again.

"He didn't mean anything," Drew assured her through clenched teeth.

Robert's eyes filled with tears, and he threw himself on Drew's chest, sending pain rippling through the man's body again. "I'm sorry. I won't do it again," the child sobbed.

Drew waved Amanda away and hugged the boy tightly. "It's all right." He waited until Robert's tears ceased. Then he added, "You just have to remember to move carefully around me. Now, I believe your Cousin Amanda wants you to freshen up." Robert looked from him to Amanda, who nodded. Then he slid to the edge of the bed, moving carefully.

"Run next door, pixie. Jennings is waiting with a fresh shirt," Amanda told him as she smoothed back his curls from his forehead.

Stopping just short of the door, Robert turned. "You won't go away, will you?" he asked Drew, his blue eyes shadowed.

"No, halfling. I'll be here when you return." The joking tone of his voice was in sharp contrast with the white line around Drew's mouth. The door closed behind the boy. Before Amanda could utter the protest that was on her lips, Drew said quietly, "It was an accident."

"But he should not have been on the bed with you. Robert may be a child, but you should have had more sense." Amanda glared at Drew and then at the footman. "I will keep him with me for a time. You, Lord Mainwaring, are to go to sleep." Her eyes flashed. Her cheeks burned. She tapped her foot impatiently, waiting for a response. Both men nodded. Turning to leave the room, she stopped suddenly, glaring at the footman. "If he doesn't drop off to sleep soon, give him that sleeping draft the doctor left." In a swirl of pink she was gone.

Over the new few days Amanda spent much of her time visiting Drew and Robert or with Jeremy, who was almost as bad a patient as Robert. To her amazement, her ward had learned his lesson that first day. Though he still played on Drew's bed, never again did he make the mistake of jarring his leg.

His trips to see Jeremy were not as successful. Excited

and anxious to tell his cousin all about his newest friend, he chattered incessantly. "He didn't know my papa. But he was a soldier. Just in a different place. Cousin Jeremy, did you know that India is around the world? Drew read me about it."

"Drew?" Amanda looked at the little boy sternly. Jeremy rubbed his head and wished for quiet.

"My friend said I could call him that," the boy said almost pompously, daring her to disagree. Realizing that she was not, he returned to his questions. "Drew said you were his friend, Cousin Jeremy. He said you met at school." Jeremy groaned. Robert stopped and stared at him. "I'm not jarring his leg. What's wrong?"

"He is still not himself," Nurse said quickly, for once ready to see the back of her small charge. She wrung a cool compress out and placed it on Jeremy's head.

"But I don't understand? Who is he?" Robert asked.

Amanda put her hand on the boy's shoulder and guided him to the door. "Who?"

"Cousin Jeremy? If he isn't himself, who is he?"

Jeremy groaned as Amanda laughed and left, sending Robert to Drew once more.

Watching Drew spend his time entertaining Robert over the next few days, Amanda began to lose the last remnants of fear of the man. His broad shoulders clothed in white lawn nightshirts seemed less threatening than they had earlier, and who could be afraid of a man who had laughing blue eyes and who loved children?

After two evenings when she returned from her solitary dinner to tuck Robert into bed and listen to tales of what had happened at their shared dinner, Amanda joined them, but not without incident.

"I won't," her housekeeper declared emphatically. Her usually pleasant face was set in stern lines.

"Jennings will be with me."

"It is not proper, Miss Desmond."

Amanda raised her eyebrows. "Lord Mainwaring cannot even get out of bed!"

"That is part of the problem," the housekeeper said

huffily. "It's one thing to visit Master Robert in the daytime. Sharing an evening meal is different. Eating dinner in a man's bedroom! Humph!"

"But I've often shared Robert's," Amanda began. Then she thought a moment, her face impassive, and tried another approach. "With so many invalids, I thought it might save you some work. Surely it would be easier to serve the three of us at the same time?" Her voice was very soft and concerned.

"Well?" the housekeeper softened for a moment. Then she grew stern again. "It simply isn't done."

"Nonsense. Who will know? Think of the time you'll save. As soon as the other servants are ready to resume their duties, I'll return to the dining room."

Shelving her reservations for the moment, the housekeeper finally agreed. "Only until the servants are well again."

Had the housekeeper been present in the red sitting room the next afternoon, those reservations would have returned in full force. The vicar's wife, a pleasant woman who was known for her wagging tongue, came to call. Hardly had Amanda poured her first cup of tea than she began. "So wonderful of you. How courageous. So many single ladies would have refused house room."

"To an injured man?"

The vicar's wife continued as though Amanda had not spoken. "Of course, most ladies your age do not live alone, do they?" The woman smiled benignly. Amanda gritted her teeth and returned the smile. "I have never understood how you could be so daring."

"Daring? When my grandfather helped me establish my home?" Amanda said as calmly as she could.

"Men. They never think of the consequences. How could he have known that a situation like this would happen? My dear, you should have sent for me immediately."

"And have you leave your own family? Oh, no, I would not be so cruel," Amanda said firmly. "Is everyone in the village recovering now?"

"Yes. And not a minute too soon. The vicar mentioned that the doctor has missed services the last three weeks. Poor man, he's looking so drawn." She looked at Amanda accusingly. "Of course, some people say that he has been spending more time here than at home. However, I am not one of them," the woman said pompously.

By biting her tongue and smiling inanely, Amanda preserved her dignity. Before her temper could get the best of her, Thompson appeared. "Master Jeremy is asking for you, Miss Desmond."

"I shan't keep you from your sickroom duties then," the vicar's wife said graciously, drawing on her gloves. "We will expect to see you in church again soon. Do tell your cousin that our thoughts are with him."

"If they are, Jeremy really will be restless," Amanda muttered to herself as she headed up the stairs. Opening the door to Jeremy's bedroom, she saw him, as she expected, asleep. Farther down the hall she discovered a full-scale battle under way on the table beside the bed, the bed stairs, and the edge of the bed itself. Smiling to herself, she slipped into her own room. The quiet seemed to wrap peaceful arms about her, soothing her. Yielding to Jennings' urging, she took a short nap, putting her anger to one side for a time.

That evening, though, as she sat beside Drew's bed watching the chessboard carefully, the scene replayed itself in front of her eyes. Without thinking she moved a pawn into a direct line with Drew's bishop.

"I knew you would admit I was a superior player," he said jokingly, "but are you just giving up?"

"What?" Amanda jumped and looked at the board, a word learned from her cousin bitten back quickly.

"Shall we call it a night?" he asked as he stifled a yawn.

Moving the board to the top of a high cabinet Robert had shown no interest in, Amanda said coaxingly, "If you are so certain that you are the superior player, I'm certain you will allow me an edge."

Sleepy as he was, Drew's eyes snapped open. They sparkled. "Now I know you are ill. After watching you play, you expect me to give you an advantage? Not likely, Miss Desmond." His voice lowered, and he said with a smile, "All I can promise is a continuation of this match tomorrow."

5

The chess game continued nightly. Amanda found herself regaining her comfortable feeling around him, a feeling he deliberately fostered, watching for her reactions carefully. Finally one afternoon after Dr. Weston had given Robert permission to visit the stables, Drew decided to change the game. He waved away the chessboard and produced a deck of cards. "I suppose Jeremy taught you to play piquet, too?" Drew asked.

"No," Amanda said demurely, lowering her lashes coquettishly. Drew sighed theatrically and wiped his brow in relief. "My grandfather did." She laughed delightedly at the look on his face and fanned out the cards. "You may draw first."

When Thompson entered a short time later, Drew was ahead, but not by much. They looked up startled when he cleared his throat.

"It isn't the vicar's wife again, Thompson?" Amanda asked, a frown creasing her brow.

"No, miss. A letter has just arrived." He held it out.

Amanda, recognizing the seal although she had only seen it a few times, blanched. Her hand shook as she reached for it.

Drew, worried but not knowing quite why, looked from Amanda to her butler and back.

For a minute, Amanda simply held the letter, staring at it like it was some poisonous snake that had just appeared. She nodded her dismissal to Thompson. As though she had forgotten where she was, she sat back in the chair, curling her legs under her, the soft folds of her pomona-green muslin skirt falling like curtains in front of her. Drew held his breath. Then hesitantly she broke the seal and opened the letter. She read through it quickly; then she crumpled it angrily.

"Amanda, what is it?" Drew asked, his voice quiet.

Startled, she looked up. Her face flamed. Her feet dropped to the floor. Her back straightened. She smiled hesitantly and smoothed the letter. "A small problem. I need to talk to Jeremy."

Before she could get up, Drew reached out his hand to stop her, stretching sideways as far as he could reach comfortably. "He'll be asleep." His voice dropped lower until it was almost a deep, resonant whisper. "Tell me. Maybe I can help." He longed to hold her, to soothe the worry from her face.

Amanda crossed to the window and looked out at the green lawn that surrounded her home, its expanse broken only by flower gardens just beginning to bloom. For a few minutes Drew respected her silence. Then he asked, "Is there anything I can do?"

By the time Amanda turned to answer him, she had regained her composure. Her face was pale and her hands still trembled slightly, but her voice was calm. "No." She smiled bitterly. "This is something I must deal with myself."

"Are you certain? I've always found talking things out helps."

Amanda's eyes flashed. She opened her mouth and then shut it quickly. She took a deep breath. "This problem involves my household only," she said as calmly as she could.

"Then that includes me: I demand that you allow me to help." Drew sat up in bed and used his command voice.

The only effect it had on Amanda was a negative one. Her eyes flashed. "Demand. You 'gentlemen' do that very well. Why can't you leave us alone?"

Her words struck Drew as though they were cannon-balls. He sank back into his pillows without another word, his face whiter than normal. He pressed his lips closed tightly and closed his eyes.

"No, please." Amanda hurried to his bedside. "Drew, please. I didn't mean you."

"Are you certain? These last few weeks cannot have been pleasant for you," he said quietly, still stunned by her words.

"No. Oh, yes. Oh, please. You don't understand." The tears she usually had kept for her times alone tumbled down her cheeks. "Please. You don't understand." She sat down in the chair beside his bed as she had so many times before.

Drew found a freshly laundered handkerchief and handed it to her. "Perhaps you do need to explain."

The words tumbled out of Amanda, who seemed helpless to stop them. "The last few weeks have been difficult. You know that. But I would not change anything that happened." She stopped short and looked at him, horror in every line of her face. "Oh, not your accident. I would change that. Please, believe me I would. I'd never want anything like—"

"Amanda, I understand! Continue." He smiled at her, and she felt warm all over in a new, strange way.

"The measles have given me more time."

"What? If anything, you have less time to yourself."

"Not during the day. More time to cope with this, . . . this difficulty." She rose from the chair and began to walk around the room, her skirts swishing as she moved.

"But you didn't solve it?" Drew asked.

"No, and now he will be here in a sennight!"

"He? Who are you talking about? Amanda, what have you gotten yourself involved in?"

"Major Besley."

"Who?"

"Robert's other guardian." Her eyes grew wide as she realized what she had said. She stood half-hidden by the draperies at the corner of the bed, hoping that Drew would ignore what she had said.

"What do you mean Robert's other guardian? Jeremy

told me that you have had the boy since he was born."

"I have." Amanda drifted toward the door as if to make her escape.

"If you leave now, I will follow you," he promised, struggling up as if he were getting out of bed.

"No. Don't! Get back up there, this minute," Amanda demanded as she hurried to his bedside.

"Are you going to stay?"

She flounced down in her chair again, folded her hands primly, and said in icy tones, "Yes."

Drew waited for a moment. Then he asked through clenched teeth, "Are you going to tell me, Amanda, what this this is all about?"

"No."

Drew rolled his eyes heavenward and clenched his fists. When he had himself under control again, he leaned over the side of the bed, getting as close to her as he could and still remain in bed. "I meant what I said," he said coldly, glaring at her.

"This is not your problem," she told Drew firmly, feeling herself weaken under the glare of his blue eyes.

"Neither was my leg your problem. But you took me in. Amanda, maybe there is nothing I can do to help. At least let me try. Sometimes a new person can offer a fresh perspective."

"I had the fresh perspective, but Jeremy took one look at him and vetoed him."

"Him?"

"A husband."

Drew felt as though his horse had just kicked him in the stomach. He had to clear his voice several times before he could ask, "Husband?" Even then, the word sounded like a croak.

"Only a temporary one," she assured him.

Drew gulped. He lay back on his pillows and closed his eyes for a moment. When he had himself completely in hand, he asked, "Amanda, could you begin at the beginning? I don't think I understand."

"It's not right. If I were a man, no one would think it

wrong of me to be made guardian of a child — even a girl. Now, because I'm not married, Robert will be taken away from me — taken to India. I shall never see him again. He will probably die of a fever. Jeremy should not have sent that man away." Her voice shook and one or two tears trickled down her face. Angrily she brushed at them.

Drew searched fruitlessly for the discarded handkerchief for a few moments. As Amanda pulled it from under her and scrubbed at her cheeks, he sighed deeply. Then her words seemed to echo around him. He asked, "Robert? This man has threatened to take Robert to India?"

"Yes."

"We must write your lawyer immediately."

"He . . ." She forced herself to take a deep breath to still the quaver in her voice and then began again. "He said as long as I'm not married, there is nothing he can do." Drew stared at her as if stunned. "He thought my suggestion of a temporary husband might be my only salvation."

"Humph!"

She raised her head and glared at him "I suppose you think it foolish beyond belief too."

"Yes, especially for a lady as lovely as you."

"What does my appearance have to do with it?"

"You have had offers, haven't you?" he asked pointedly.

"Of course. But Grandfather refused them all." Her trembling stopped. She smoothed her dress and hair.

"You never thought of accepting one of them when this problem presented itself?"

"No." Amanda shuddered and she clasped her hands together to keep them from shaking once again. "How would you like to be pursued openly for your fortune?" she asked bitterly.

"Why do you think I was in Bristol?" Drew said sharply. Realizing what he had said, he hesitated and then asked, "But what caused this situation in the first place? I thought a child usually had only one guardian."

Amanda looked at him curiously, noting not for the first time his breadth of shoulders and blue eyes. Even in bed he had a commanding appearance, one she could spend hours viewing if she were honest enough to admit it. For the first time since she had received the letter, she smiled. "So, Drew, you have been the focus of some lady's attention. You do not have an heir. Shouldn't you be thinking of one?"

"Thinking, maybe. But I'll marry to please myself, not anyone else," he said firmly, eyeing her warily and wishing that she were ready to listen to him.

"So you didn't like the pursuit and ran away." She laughed bitterly. "You still have a choice. If I am to keep Robert, I must give mine up."

"Why? How did this happen?" Slowly, he pried the information from her.

"My cousin Alice and her husband lived nearby for a time. Then Robert, her husband, was posted to India. Alice was devastated." Drew looked at her, puzzled. Amanda explained that her cousin had been in the family way and very ill. Following her doctor's orders, she had remained behind, taking up residence at Hedgefield at Amanda's insistence. Alice's parents had died of influenza some time earlier, and her brother, with a growing family of his own, was not at all welcoming.

In spite of Alice's poor health, those months had been happy ones. "Even Jeremy and Grandfather said they would miss her when she left to join Robert," Amanda said softly.

"And?" Drew nudged her on.

"She never left. The confinement was a difficult one. Although Robert was a healthy baby, something went wrong. Alice died." If Drew had not been watching her face, he would have believed that she felt nothing for her cousin. But on her face the remembered sorrow was all too evident. "To our surprise, Alice was prepared. Grandfather and Jeremy were to be the child's financial advisers, but he was to be mine until his father came home." Her face was stern.

"I don't understand. Did his father send Major Besley to escort him to India?"

"His father? His father is also dead."

"Stop! When did he die? Explain."

"He died a short time after he arrived in India in an uprising of some sort. On his deathbed, he wrote his will, directing that his commanding officer take charge of his child. The man probably despises children. Goodness knows he has had little interest in Robert over the first years of his life."

"Then this man has never seen the lad?"

"Never. And he has the audacity to tell me that because I am not married I am not a wholesome influence on Robert. And my lawyer says there is nothing I can do but marry some man. Marriage!" She stood up and stalked to the end of the bed. "Do you know what happens when a woman marries? All her possessions belong to her husband."

"But he usually is the one with the training—"

"Training? Those pampered dandies who courted me knew nothing of money but spending it. All they could see were those lovely golden guineas. Am I to turn over my fortune, myself, to some man who will then have the right to refuse me the option of keeping my ward? No!" Her eyes storming, her breasts heaving, Amanda pounded the end of the bed, her fists sinking into the feather mattress.

Drew simply sat there and stared at her as she paced back and forth from one corner of the bed and back again; her words seemed the end of his dreams. The gray silk bed hangings embroidered in red and blue like the draperies created a frame for her much like the curtains of a theater.

When her movements grew less frenetic, he asked quietly, "If you don't plan to marry, then why did you arrange for a temporary husband?"

Although he tried hard to hide his cynicism, Amanda quickly caught the edge in his voice. "It would have worked. Jeremy should have given it a chance."

"No, please," Drew said. "This is where our conversation began. Send for our tea, and then you are going to answer some questions."

Amanda's knuckles turned white as she clutched the hangings. Suddenly Drew realized that he had just lived up to her expectations of men. He watched her cautiously. She took deep breaths and muttered under her breath.

Realizing his mistake, he assumed his helpless pose. "I'd ask Jeremy, but I cannot get out of bed," he reminded her, his voice as sticky sweet as honey.

The next few minutes were not the most comfortable Drew had ever lived through. Facing Amanda was almost as hard as facing Wellington when he had brought bad news. She looked at him, her face pale but blank. Then she took a breath so deep that releasing it quietly took all her efforts. She walked through the open door of the sitting room. A few minutes later the door to the hallway opened. Drew stretched up and tried to see what was happening, but the bed hangings were in his way.

Finally Amanda reappeared. This time it was he who sighed in relief. At least he had not driven her away. She sat primly once more, her feet lined up neatly, her hands folded. Her eyes still flashed fire, though. When the tension between them was almost too much to bear, Amanda said so softly that Drew could hardly hear her, "What happened proved my point. I may owe you an explanation, Drew, but if you take that tone with me again . . ." Her voice had grown louder with every word. Suddenly she stopped. "Robert will have his tea with Cook today. Ours wll be up shortly."

The tightness in his chest kept Drew quiet. He reviewed what he had said, trying to determine his next move, wondering at his own stupidity and trying to convince himself that he still had a chance with her.

After the teatray had arrived and she had poured, Amanda resumed her story. "After my lawyer gave me his opinion, I consulted others. The reply was the same. One, however, reminded me that all marriages are not permanent. The man could die." Her cup clinked against her saucer. "But not even for Robert would I enter a Newgate marriage."

"I should think not."

She raised her eyebrows and continued. "When the lawyer understood my objection, he suggested an alternative."

"What?"

"He would find a gentleman who would agree to annulment—for a fee, of course. The man would be willing to put his intentions in writing."

"And?"

"Jeremy ruined it. He sent the man away without even talking to him." Amanda was once more filled with indignation. She hit the arm of the chair for emphasis.

Considering the angry thoughts running through his head, Drew was remarkably calm. He asked, "Did you know the man well?"

"No. I had never met him."

He gulped, but his voice stayed level. "Amanda, how did you know he would keep his word?"

"That's what the papers were for." The tone of her voice implied that perhaps he had not been listening well. "And my lawyer would hold most of his money until I was ready for the annulment."

"This is the same lawyer that suggested you go through a Newgate marriage?"

She nodded, rather annoyed at the direction his questions were going.

Silently, Drew gave thanks for the measles and his accident. He finished his tea and held out his cup for more. When he had taken another gulp, he went on. "Had you considered that the two men might be in league with each other?" She looked up from her cup, startled. "Once you were married, you would have been at their mercy. And if your 'husband' and his lawyer friend had insisted, you would have been his wife—perhaps permanently."

"But the papers?"

"Illegal at best. And if they were destroyed? And in an annulment, one fact must be proved. If he had chosen to . . ." Drew paused.

As Amanda realized what he was saying, her heart beat erratically. She began to tremble. She felt as though she were choking. She paled alarmingly. Struggling to rise, she hesitated for a moment and then crumpled to the floor.

Cursing his helplessness, Drew struggled to get out of bed for a few moments. Realizing the impossibility of the task, he shouted in his best battle voice, "Jennings! Thompson! Huttle! Someone! Come here immediately!"

Before he could get the last word out, Jennings was beside his bed. In a few minutes any servant within hearing distance—and some said later that his shout carried to the stables—was outside his room. It was only with difficulty that the maid in charge of the sickroom kept her only charge in bed. The nursery maid was certain that something had happened to Master Robert.

As soon as Jennings had a chance to look at her mistress, Drew asked, "What's wrong? What happened? Should you send for the doctor?"

Jennings looked at the assembled servants carefully, finally signaling for the stoutest footman. "Put her in her bedroom," she directed. Her mistress taken care of, she answered Drew. "It seems a simple faint to me, Lord Mainwaring. Miss Desmond has a history of them. She usually recovers on her own."

"I still think . . ." He looked at the crowd outside the room and then at the butler. "Don't you think we should send for the doctor, Thompson?"

The man looked at Amanda's maid. Although it had not happened for several years, Miss Amanda had at one time fainted regularly. As formally as if he had been asked to announce the Regent, he said, "Jennings usually is right, your lordship." The maid slipped from the room. "Now, I believe I need to direct these people." He waved at the crowd outside the door, and it began to disappear.

Before he too could vanish, Drew stopped him.

"Thompson, you will keep me informed?" The man nodded.

The silence in the room seemed to echo in Drew's mind. He saw once again the way Amanda paled. Just when he was reaching for the bell beside his bed to call for Thompson, a cough from the doorway startled him. There leaning on the door frame and Huttle was Jeremy. Wrapped in an elegant dressing gown, now too large for him, the man said, "You must tell me how to create all this excitement. It's devilish dull in my room."

6

"Jeremy! Gad, man, you'd best sit down. Are you certain you are allowed out of bed?" Drew asked, noting his friend's pallor.

"After the brouhaha in here, I couldn't stay away." Jeremy sat in the red chair, his long bony legs sticking out on his robe like sticks. "What happened? Has there been a robbery?"

Drew actually blushed. As if to hide his flaming face, he brushed back his hair from his forehead, trying to explain without giving his friend the wrong idea. Then, deciding honesty probably was best, he blurted out, "Amanda fainted."

Jeremy leaned back and took the glass of port Huttle handed him. "Have I cause to call you out?" His voice seemed casual, but he was deadly serious.

Drew did not make the mistake of misreading him. "Blast it, Jeremy. Nothing happened."

"She fainted because nothing happened? Did you try to kiss her, touch her?" His tone was sharper.

"No! All I did was tell her — delicately, of course — that her 'temporary' husband might have decided to make the marriage permanent. Good Gad, Jeremy, why hadn't you pointed it out to her before?"

"You told Amanda that and she fainted." Jeremy's voice was flat. He drained his glass of port and held it out for a refill. His face was thoughtful. Amanda had been in Drew's bedroom. And his friend had felt free to tell her what he really thought. His free hand tapped the chair arm slowly as if Jeremy were measuring time, time that seemed to be giving his idea a chance to develop.

Just when Drew was about to shout at him to stop, the door flew open and Robert ran in. "No, Thompson, Drew likes me here. Besides, I want to see Manda," he called to the butler, who was on his heels. Catching sight of Jeremy, both the butler and the child stopped. Robert was the first to recover. "Are you well, Cousin Jeremy? The cat in the stables had kittens. I will take you to see them if you like." Remembering Drew, he added, "You too, Drew."

"I think I'll need to wait a while, halfling," Drew said with a laugh.

Jeremy looked from the child to his friend and back. "I'll wait a while also." He watched in satisfaction as Amanda's ward climbed up on the high bed, claiming a spot at Drew's side as though this were his bedroom.

Settled comfortably with his favorite toys close at hand, Robert looked around curiously. "Where's Manda?"

In the suite next door Amanda opened her eyes slowly, wondering much the same question. As she looked at the hangings above her, hangings that she had picked out to please herself, she shivered as she thought of what Drew had said. What if she had married the man only to have him turn on her? She shuddered.

Noticing the movement, Jennings hurried to the bed with a blanket. "You just lie there and get warm. Tea will be here shortly," she said, her voice soothing.

Emotionally drained, Amanda did just that, reviewing time after time the picture Drew had painted. Each vision brought back memories Amanda had thought long buried.

On his way back to his room after soothing both Drew and Robert, Jeremy stopped to see her. His voice husky from his exertions, he asked Jennings, "How is she?" He was certain he knew the answer. In spite of the maid's protests, he crossed to the bed. "Amanda?"

She jumped and turned over on her back, her face ashen and her eyes haunted. Carefully so that he did not frighten her, Jeremy covered her hand with his. Her fingers closed convulsively around his. For a moment there was only silence. Then she looked at him and asked, "Why didn't you tell me what could happen?"

"There was no need. I planned to question him closely. As it happened, he revealed his character to me by his actions immediately."

"But I was so angry and hurt."

"Neither are new to our relationship." He squeezed her hand and laughed weakly. "I'm sorry Drew frightened you," he said, his voice growing weaker.

Amanda took a closer look at him. Putting her own fears to one side, she called, "Jennings, get a chair. And pour him some tea."

By the time Jeremy's face regained some of his color, Amanda had recovered enough to scold him. "What are you doing out of bed?"

"I heard Drew's bellow."

"What?"

Jennings covered her smile quickly. Jeremy made no such attempt. He laughed. "When you fainted, Drew became excited." Jennings twittered.

Amanda looked at her maid and back at her cousin. "What did he do?"

Jeremy smiled sweetly. "He called for help." He paused and then added, "Very loudly."

Amanda gulped and closed her eyes. "Is it too much to hope that only you and Jennings heard him?" she asked, thinking about what the vicar's wife would say about this incident.

"Oh, yes." His worry about her eased, Jeremy was enjoying the situation. He grinned. "I think everyone in the house heard. Don't you think, Jennings?"

The maid nodded. Amanda groaned.

"The footman who brought the teatray said two of the grooms were asking what had happened," the maid added. It was better that her mistress hear the news from them than from strangers.

A slow blush crept up Amanda's neck, washing her

face with crimson. "If you will stay in bed the rest of today and tomorrow, we may brush through this fairly well. The strain of caring for so many people caused nervous exhaustion. I think that's the thing. What do you say, Jennings?" Jeremy asked, completely ignoring his cousin's furious denials.

"In bed? All day? But Major Besley . . ."

"What about him?"

"He'll be here in a few days."

"All the more reason to stay in bed. You were devastated by the news. It and the sickness in the house were too much for you." Jeremy stood up carefully, keeping a firm hand on the back of the chair. He smiled at her. "Cousin, if you want to avoid gossip and relieve Drew of his guilt, you will remain in bed." He held up a hand as she started to protest. "I will tell Thompson to send Robert in to see you." He looked at her curiously. "I left him with Drew. That is a situation I think we need to discuss later."

Amanda held her breath as she watched him move slowly toward the door. When his hand reached for the latch, she called, "Jeremy?" He turned slightly, propping himself up with the door frame. "I'll do as you suggest." He smiled and left, far weaker than he wanted anyone to know.

Amanda lay in her bed staring at the ceiling. Loath to ask questions, yet knowing how important the answers were, she turned to her maid. "When Lord Mainwaring called for help and I was discovered on the floor, what was said?"

Jennings' face and voice were soothing. "Miss Amanda, there was great concern."

"And what was said?" Amanda's voice lost its softness, taking on a flintlike quality as her worst fears surfaced.

"I'm sure I couldn't say. I was in attendance on you."

Her mistress sat up in bed and stared at her, willing the woman to answer her questions. When the silence grew heavy, Amanda said as quietly as she could, "Jennings . . ."

The maid put down the fine lawn chemise she was folding and looked at Amanda sternly. "Mrs. Thompson tried to tell you how it would be, Miss Amanda. Spending so much time in Lord Mainwaring's room, even with Master Robert there. And him such a handsome man." She closed her lips tightly and turned her back, disapproval in every line.

Sinking back into her pillows, Amanda closed her eyes, frustration written on her face. What did Drew think of her? What had she done to his reputation as well as her own?

Unable to bear the silence, the maid crossed to the bed. "Perhaps if you follow Master Desmond's suggestions?" the woman said hesitantly, wanting to erase the pain she saw. And she would have a word with the housekeeper and her husband.

Before Amanda had a chance to respond, the door to the hallway flew open and a small boy flew in. "Master Robert!" The stern voice of Jeremy's valet, who stood just outside the door, stopped the child in his mad rush to Amanda. "Apologize immediately for your ungentlemanly entrance."

The boy hung his head, bowed politely, and said, "I'm sorry." As soon as the words were out of his mouth, his head came up and he ran toward the bed. "Manda, what does fainted mean? Drew said you fainted. Was that why Cook was talking behind her hand?"

Jennings exchanged a rueful glance with Huttle and shut the door. "Talking behind her hand? When?" Amanda asked, reaching down to pull Robert up on the bed with her. He had that fresh-washed scent that little boys found so hard to maintain.

"Just before I came upstairs to join you and Drew." He settled down beside her, looking around as if he had never seen the room before. "I like this bed better than Drew's," he said with a bounce.

"You do?"

"Yes, I can get up here without steps." He bounced again.

The two women smiled.

"What have you been doing?" Amanda asked. "Did Huttle bathe you?"

"Yes. He said, 'No gentleman goes to see a lady reeking of the stables as you do, Master Robert,' " said Robert, his sweet voice mimicking Huttle's deeper one. "What does 'reek' mean?"

Amanda hugged him and then explained.

"If I 'reeked,' why didn't Drew say anything?" the boy asked, his face twisted as he tried to understand.

"When?"

"When I climbed up on his bed."

Amanda and Jennings exchanged glances.

"You had better tell Mrs. Thompson to have those sheets changed," Amanda told her maid, thinking of the effort it took. "At least now it will be easier to lift Lord Mainwaring," she added quietly.

The maid nodded and left.

"Why is Drew being lifted? Where is he going? Manda, I don't want him to go anywhere," Robert said firmly.

"Hush. He is not leaving." At least not yet, she added silently. But he would go and she would miss him. Remembering the letter she had received, she hugged Robert so tightly he protested. Her voice trembling only slightly, she said, "A friend of your father's, Major Besley, is coming to see us soon."

"He is? He wants to see me?" The excited tones in the boy's voice sent shards of pain lancing through Amanda.

Controlling her emotions the best she could, she explained. "Your father asked him to watch over you."

"Like you and Cousin Jeremy do?"

"Something like that."

He sat still for a moment, a frown crossing his brow. "Then why hasn't he come to see me before?"

"He was in India."

"Like my father? Do you think he has seen a tiger or an elephant?" Robert's tone was filled with awe.

"He could have. You can ask him when he arrives," she said, her voice almost breaking. Robert, caught up in his excitement, never noticed. Amanda ran her hand lightly over his curls, smoothing them back, adding a word now and then when Robert expected one. She had no idea what she said. One thought kept running through her head: I am going to lose him.

Except for times when Robert was with her, Amanda lay in bed quietly, so quietly that Jennings asked Huttle to talk to his master.

That afternoon the doctor made one of his increasingly infrequent visits. After visiting his other patients, he stopped to see Amanda. Only his training kept him composed when he saw her. He had seen that look before on old women who had decided that they had lived long enough. Masking his apprehension, he said cheerfully, "Hello, Miss Desmond, I see you have finally taken my advice."

"Advice?"

"To rest. With our last patient coming along nicely, you have nothing to worry about." Her eyes seemed to mock him. "I am removing the quarantine. By the end of next week even Lord Mainwaring and Master Desmond have permission to move to Hedgefield." She looked at him blankly. "I imagine that you will find youself with many visitors. I understand at least one of your neighbors delayed her departure to London when she heard Mainwaring was staying in the area. He must be considered one of the prizes of the marriage mart."

Focused only on the possibility of losing Robert, Amanda had forgotten her original plan to find a husband. Now it returned. A smile broke across her face, startling the doctor. He took her hand and noted the way her color was returning. Her voice had lost its flatness when she asked, "So my household can return to normal?"

"Except for the nursery maid, everyone is recovered," he assured her. "Send the child home for a short stay with her family at the end of the week. Nurse has informed me that since she is no longer needed with Master Desmond, she is ready to resume her duties with Master Robert.

And, you . . . " Dr. Weston paused and looked at her
sternly. "You are to spend more time outside." She
nodded. Having heard the story of what happened from
both Drew and Jeremy, he opened the door and said
clearly, "Stay in bed the rest of today, Miss Desmond. I
am certain it is nothing more than nervous exhaustion.
Please send for me if you need me further."

Behind the door the doctor had shut so firmly,
Amanda was reviewing the eligible men of the area. She
had had offers—some even as late as the winter—but she
had never taken any seriously. Making her list, she
considered each one but carefully avoided thinking of
Drew. That one was really too old, and Robert did not
like him. Another she had seen kick a dog, while a third
was known for his extravagances. Maybe she could
persuade Jeremy.

While Amanda was reviewing her prospects and
marshalling her plans, an ever stronger Jeremy spent part
of the day with Drew. With Robert back under the care
of Nurse, Drew was once again suffering from ennui.
That morning his restlessness had driven him to write for
his valet. With the quarantine lifted, he decided he
needed Gilbert's way with his boots. With luck the man
would arrive before the Indian major appeared. Drew
stretched and sealed the letter. Feeling guilty, he quickly
penned a letter to his mother, simply telling her his stay
in the country had lengthened.

As the servant left to see to the notes' dispatch, Jeremy
walked in, moving slowly but without Huttle's support,
although the valet hovered behind him carefully. Drew
almost laughed as he watched his lanky friend falter and
stumble. Huttle, a foot shorter than his master, reached
out as if to catch him.

"You had best sit down before both you and Huttle
come to grief," Drew suggested.

Jeremy looked over his shoulder and frowned. He said,
"I told you I did not need your help. Why are you
following me?" The valet ignored him and moved the
chair closer to the bed. "Not that one. I'll sit over there."

Jeremy pointed to a chair covered in vivid-blue figured silk. Huttle looked at him, his face impassive, and brought it closer to the bed. "You may go."

Recognizing the hopelessness of arguing with his master when he had that tone in his voice, the man bowed and left.

"Servants!" Jeremy added a wealth of feeling to the word. He sank down on the chair, but his sigh of satisfaction was interrupted. He shifted restlessly and looked longingly at the red one. He stretched his back, though, and refused to move.

"How is she?"

"Amanda?" Jeremy noticed how worried his friend looked. He settled in the chair more comfortably.

"You know I mean Amanda. How is she? What did the doctor say?" Drew asked, his voice impatient.

"She is resting comfortably," Jeremy said as if quoting the man. "Stop grinding your teeth."

"Then tell me everything the doctor said. How did she look?" Drew's voice was as eager as his face was anxious.

Jeremy relayed the doctor's words, rebelling only when Drew bombarded him with questions he couldn't answer. "Oh, another thing . . ." Jeremy paused effectively. "We can move to Hedgefield next week." He waited for Drew's reaction, hoping it would tell him more about Drew's feelings for Amanda. But it was not as emphatic as he thought it would be.

"You don't think we should stay here until the major arrives?" Drew asked, his voice more tentative than Jeremy had ever heard it.

"No. If he arrived with us here, he would expect an invitation to stay. And that I won't have."

"Why?"

Jeremy turned his chair so it faced the bed. His burgundy dressing gown caught on one leg and he was forced to yank it free. At school the expression he wore had been called "Jeremy's fighting face."

Drew ignored it. "Why?" he asked again.

"Amanda will not stay in a house with an unmarried man."

"She has with you and me," his friend reminded him jokingly.

"You were immobilized in bed. I . . . I do not count," Jeremy said, his voice as cutting as his eyes were cold.

Had it been any woman but Amanda, Drew would have halted his questions. "Jeremy, stop playing 'keep the secrets from Drew' and tell me."

Jeremy looked at him, renewed anger simmering just below his surface calm. The burden of protecting his cousin had weighed heavily on him since she returned home from Brighton. It had been easier with someone to help. If the major proved a rotter, he would need a reliable witness. And Drew seemed to care. Slowly, carefully he weighed the advantages and disadvantages of an explanation. Besides, if his plans worked out, Drew would need to know.

Knowing that he could not rush Jeremy, who moved to his own rhythms, Drew watched his friend's face carefully. Noting the frowns and anger give way to a more serene look, he was ready when Jeremy said quietly, "On your honor, Drew. Swear on your honor!"

Drew looked at him puzzled. Then he nodded.

"It began when Amanda was sent to Brighton after our little 'escapade.' " Jeremy grabbed the arm of the chair and held on tight. "If we had not been so headstrong, so determined . . ."

"What are you talking about?"

"Amanda's exile to Brighton." Jeremy looked at Drew, now sitting upright in bed. "You remember. Aunt Elizabeth had decided to remain at Hedgefield for the summer. Lord Ainsworth, one of our ambassadors to Portugal, had been most attentive."

"Didn't she marry him later that year?"

Jeremy nodded. "They spent several years in Brazil with the court." He cleared his throat. "Trying to prevent more unpleasantness and still some gossip, Aunt Elizabeth shipped Amanda to her cousin in Brighton. You know, the one with the pug dogs and the daughter in Canada."

Drew thought for a moment and then nodded.

Jeremy cleared his throat. Then he said, "I don't really know what happened. Grandfather kept most of it from us."

Drew looked at him, willing him to go on but not really ready to hear the words. He swallowed.

His friend rushed on, his fists clenching and unclenching. "It seems the husband had a brother, not quite suitable for company, who was kept in the attic." Jeremy's voice was as flat as he could make it. Drew shuddered. "One night he eluded his jailer, no one ever said how, and ended the evening locked in a room with Amanda and her cousin."

Drew moaned. Then his eyes darkened with anger. "Did he?"

"No. She was mauled badly, but he did not touch them otherwise. Since then, Amanda has been afraid of strange men."

Drew let out the breath he had been holding, and slipped down in bed. He closed his eyes briefly, picturing her alone with a madman. "She'll have to meet the major," he reminded Jeremy, his voice harsh.

"But if the man has to stay at the inn, he will not expect to stay for supper each evening. Maybe this way, Amanda can control those faints."

"Her what?" Drew sat up in bed again.

"Her faints. That's why she retired from society. Any time a man touched her, she fainted. She even did it to me a few times. Have you ever tried to dance with deadweight in your arms? Aunt Elizabeth thought she did it deliberately, but she didn't."

"She faints," Drew said, his tone very surprised. "At the thought of a man touching her?" He remembered all those days in the last week they had argued over cards or over Robert, their fingers intertwined. He started to tell Jeremy about it then. Then he stopped. He smiled. "She faints."

7

Her prospects considered and rejected as they had been weeks earlier, Amanda sank once more into despair. Her mother's letter, with its monthly reminder that there were eligible men in Vienna and that she wanted to be a grandmother, cast her deeper into gloom.

As soon as she recovered, Amanda threw herself into work. The entire house was scrubbed and polished. Jeremy, who was one of the first to be moved out of his room for the cleaning brigade, asked, "Why don't you wait until Drew and I move to Hedgefield?" He added plaintively, "I'm still not strong enough to go through this." His protests did no good.

Amanda sent him to an empty bedroom that had already been cleaned, and she, Mrs. Thompson, and their team of maids and footmen stripped the room, replacing not only the heavy green velvet drapes and bed hangings for ones in lawn but also the mattress and pillows. By the time he was allowed to return, grumbling, hours later, the room reeked of wax, the rich rosewood of its furniture gleaming brightly. The sweet scent of spring breezes and flowers lingered in the fine white linen. The new mattress, freshly stuffed with feathers, was so fluffy that he sank into it happily, breathing a sigh of satisfaction.

"Smells good," he mumbled as he allowed his valet to smooth his bed covers around him. Unwilling to give into his "weakness," as he called it, he had refused to rest in the bedroom where he had been sent, choosing instead to visit Drew and spend the time playing cards.

Amanda, her conscience reminding her of how sick he had been, opened the door quietly. She paused on the sill, her eyes asking Huttle's approval. At his nod, she approached the bed, her face concerned. He still had blue circles under his eyes, she noted. His face, too, was pale, its customary brown replaced by a sickly pallor. She sat in a chair beside the bed, afraid as she had been so often the last few weeks. She asked in a low voice. "He is better, isn't he, Huttle?" If she lost both Robert and Jeremy, she would not want to go on living. "He hasn't been doing too much?"

Huttle hurried to her side. "He is much stronger than he looks, Miss Desmond. The doctor is pleased with his progress," the valet said, his voice reassuring. "As soon as he returns to his outside activities, you will see a return to his former self."

Amanda sat at her cousin's bedside for some time longer. As she watched him sleep, she considered him carefully. Several girls she had known at school in Bath had married cousins. Would it work for Jeremy and her? Her grandfather had considered the idea for a time and then discarded it. As she weighed the possibilities, Amanda had the same reaction she always had. It would be impossible. She knew him too well. Besides, he needed someone far different than she. And far different from those light-skirts he favored, she added. As she tried to visualize the perfect wife for her cousin, he stretched and opened his eyes.

Startled to see her sitting beside his bed, her dress covered by a voluminous apron, Jeremy sat up. He asked, "Have you come to toss me out of the room again?" His voice was very dry.

Amanda gasped and paled alarmingly.

"None of that, miss," Jeremy said sternly. "Huttle, get her a glass of port." He watched as his valet handed one over. He waited patiently for an explanation.

Getting herself under control, Amanda took a sip or

two of the wine. Then she said, "I'm all right now." Her voice still contained a suspicious quaver.

"Want to tell me what that was about?" he asked, running a hand over his disheveled blond hair.

"Jeremy, have we, Robert and I, kept you from marrying?"

"What?"

"You should have a family of your own. Has helping me take care of Robert kept you from setting up your own family?"

Jeremy looked at her in amazement. For a few minutes he said nothing. Just as she was becoming restless, he asked, "Amanda, are you sickening for something?"

"No."

"Then you must be mutton-headed to think of such a thing. Remember how I begged you to help me avoid marriage not three months ago? Amanda, I've been busy staying out of the parson's mousetrap. If—no, *when* I decide to marry, neither you nor Robert will cause the least difficulty. What gave you such an idea?"

After a few attempts to evade the issue, she said, "Doctor Weston mentioned that Drew is considered quite a catch. You must be, too."

Jeremy laughed dryly. "So much a prize that neither of us wants to face this Season in London. You only gave me a good excuse." He watched her closely, noting in satisfaction how her face lost some of its tension. Then she looked at him, a mischievous gleam in her eyes. Quickly reading that look as dangerous, he said, "No!"

She just looked at him, her face a model of confusion. "What do you mean?"

"It will not work, Amanda. I will not agree with whatever you are planning. Just take that expression off your face." His voice was determined, but he was worried.

"Well, I suppose you are right."

"You suppose right."

"You would not be my first choice."

"Choice for what?" Immediately, he realized he had

fallen into her trap and tried to retreat. "No, I don't want to know."

"But, Jeremy, it would be the perfect solution. But, of course, you are right."

"To what?" He knew he should not ask, but her look told him she was determined. And to Amanda, determination was the key to getting things done.

She looked at him carefully, noting the firm set of his mouth. "You are right. It is a silly idea." She waited for a count of three.

He did not disappoint her. "Amanda, you will tell me at once."

"We could get married just until—"

"No! Amanda, we have discussed this before. Who would believe that a marriage between us would need to be annulled?"

She glared at him, her face losing its glow of anticipation.

He hurried on, adding a new argument, "Besides, it would destroy our relationship."

She looked up in amazement. "Why?"

He thought quickly. "Can you imagine how the tongues would wag? We would never be invited anywhere together again. Nor could we visit each other." He paused to let his ideas sink in. "One of us would be a social outcast. Think what that would do to Robert."

Amanda sat back in her chair to consider what he had said. She started to curl her legs beneath her, but the chair, with its green-and-gold-striped damask, was not as comfortable as the one in her study or even the one in Drew's bedroom. She stood up finally and crossed to the window, holding the fresh curtains to one side in order to look out over the herb garden on that side of the manor. As she watched, Robert ran across the area, looking backward as if escaping from someone. She bit her lips and turned, agony turning her eyes a dark green-gray.

Hesitantly, as if just thinking of the idea, Jeremy said, "It would be more practical to marry Drew." Amanda turned red and had a hard time catching her breath. "Do you want me to talk to him for you?"

"No." Amanda cleared her throat and shook her head.

"All right. I will leave it to you. But I thought . . ."

Amanda cleared her throat again and said, "Not Drew. I don't think he would agree."

"Nonsense. I will talk to him shortly."

"No. You are to say nothing, Jeremy. Do you understand? Nothing!" She turned pale.

His face carefully hiding his delight, he asked, "Why? Amanda, I should have thought of it sooner. You can trust Drew to keep his word. It would be the perfect solution."

"No. He might feel compelled to agree simply because of the situation." She crossed to stand beside the bed, refusing to admit even to herself how unhappy a temporary marriage to Drew would make her. "Jeremy, promise me you will say nothing."

He lay back on his pillows and closed his eyes. He said sadly, "I was just trying to help." He opened his eyes and looked up, a wistful expression on his face. "But if you feel so strongly about it . . ." He paused and took a deep breath. "I promise."

Amanda let out the breath she had been holding. She bent, kissed his cheek, and then crossed to the door.

"He has been asking about you and Robert," Jeremy said quietly.

She turned. "He has?"

"See him." She nodded and reached for the latch. "But take Jennings and Robert with you," he said.

Her eyes flashing and her mouth set at his implication, she nodded. She swept out of the room. The door slammed behind her.

Jeremy laughed quietly to himself.

Later that afternoon Amanda and Robert followed the footman into Drew's bedroom. Amanda smiled broadly and looked at the bed. It was empty. Her heart almost stopped. Startled, she stopped and dropped Robert's hand. He was the first to spy Drew, seated in the chair beside the bed, his leg propped on a low stool. His dark-blue robe made his eyes seem bluer than ever.

"Drew," Robert shouted, and ran toward him. He slid

to a stop only inches from the still-splinted leg. "Are you all better? Do you want to see the kittens now? Their eyes still are not open. One is all white. Manda said it could be my very own. But it has to stay with its mother for a while longer. I can take you to see it, though."

Drew smiled at Amanda over Robert's head. She was wearing a soft butter-yellow muslin dress with a rounded decolletage trimmed with deeper yellow, the sleeves puffed and caught with the darker ribbons. Her curls were bound by matching ribbons.

When Robert had finished, Drew said, "I think I will need more time, halfling." Robert's face fell. Drew patted a spot beside him on the chair. "Come tell me how you have been spending your time."

Before the last word was finished, Robert was there. "I got to ride my pony. But Manda wasn't with me; I had to go with a groom. She was cleaning."

Amanda smiled and took a seat near the table where the teatray had been set. "Come and get Drew's tea," she said softly, adding a drop of cream just the way her guest liked. Carefully, the child carried it back, not spilling a single drop. "You may also pass the cakes."

"I told Cook we like strawberry tarts, Drew. They are very good." Robert offered the plate to his friend, watching in satisfaction as he took one of the tarts. He took the plate back to Amanda and chose his own carefully. Skipping happily, he sat down beside Drew again.

Amanda had just picked up her own tea when Robert asked, "Do you think Major, Major . . . ?" He looked at Amanda as if asking a question.

"Besley." Her hand trembled. She put her cup down with a small sound.

". . . Major Besley likes strawberry tarts?"

"We will have to ask him," Amanda said, controlling her voice with effort.

Drew frowned to see how distressed she was. He raised his eyebrows questioningly.

"I told Robert about our visitor a few days ago," she told him quietly.

"He knew my father. And he's lived in India. I think he has seen tigers and elephants. Don't you think so?" Robert asked Drew. "Manda said we'd have to ask when he gets here. He promised to help look after me." He frowned. "Would you wait six years to see a boy you'd promised to look after, Drew?"

Amanda closed her eyes as if she had been struck.

Drew said quickly, "No, halfling, not if I could help it."

"Manda says he's a soldier and that's why he hasn't seen me."

"She is right. India is very far away." The more the boy chattered, the more somber Amanda became. "Tell me about your ride," Drew said, trying to bring their talk to more pleasant subjects. He noted with satisfaction the way the color returned to Amanda's face as Robert mentioned the sights that had caught his attention. His tea and Robert's story finished, he handed his cup to the boy so he could return it to the tray.

Amanda had forced herself to take part in the conversation, but when Robert returned to her side, she reached out to hold him next to her for a moment, hugging him tightly.

"Manda," he protested, and wiggled free, "I'm not a baby."

"You will appreciate those hugs when you are my age, halfling," Drew said, laughing, though he longed to hold her close himself.

"Why?" Robert stood facing Drew, his hands on his hips.

Amanda smothered a laugh. "Yes, Lord Mainwaring, why?" she asked, giggling at the look on his face.

The look he sent her made her catch her breath. Her heart raced. She felt breathless. "That is a question to be discussed between men. I'll tell you later," he promised Robert.

Their tea finished, Amanda drew a protesting child from the room, one arm around his shoulders and the other brushing his hair back from his forehead. As the door closed behind them, Drew lost the pleasant look he had so carefully maintained. He frowned. Reaching for the paper and pen on the table beside him, he began a letter to a friend in the Foreign Office. Maybe Major Besley had a flaw or two he could find. The pen sputtered and he cursed. Pulling the penknife closer, he sharpened the pen and began again.

The next day both Drew and Jeremy were allowed tea downstairs. Sweating profusely from the strain, he sank onto Amanda's ivory-and-red-figured settee. He took several deep breaths.

"Have a brandy, Drew," Jeremy suggested, waving the glass in his own hand. "Never felt so weak in my life, I assure you. Rather feel foolish to be laid low by a childish complaint."

Drew mopped his brow and waved away the brandy. "On one leg I can't afford to be wobbly," he said regretfully. He took a cup of tea the butler offered instead. "Where's Amanda?"

"One of her tenants has a problem with his roof. She, Robert, and her agent rode over to have a look. Should be doing the same thing myself," he muttered.

"What?"

"Nothing. Just complaining about staying in."

"I know. I'll be glad to get on horseback again. I've had more bed rest than I can take." Drew shifted restlessly, finally lifting his leg to the settee and propping himself up in the corner. He cleared his throat. "Don't tell Amanda, but I sent my groom to London with a letter about that major."

Jeremy sat up straighter. "When?"

"Yesterday. It may produce nothing," Drew said quietly.

His friend nodded solemnly. "I appreciate it." He got up, stretching his lanky body to its full height. He looked at Drew carefully, pleased at the way he had taken on Amanda's problems as his own. "Grandfather's lawyer said we could tie the case up in court for a time. After that?" He shrugged.

"How will Amanda take it if she loses him?"

"You've seen her. In her mind he's as good as gone. She says good-bye each time she touches him." Jeremy put his glass down so hard it cracked. "Except for checking on her tenants here on the estate, she will probably isolate herself."

"She must not." Drew stopped, his face slightly red. "I mean, she is such a lively person, or she was," he added truthfully.

"I only hope the man hates children."

"Perhaps we could help that impression?" Drew raised one eyebrow suggestively.

"No, Amanda has worked too hard to get the boy ready for this visit." Jeremy sighed and sat down again, his shoulders slumped, dejected. "Besides, if he does have to go with him, such action will make it harder on Robert." He pulled the tawny-brown worsted of his sleeve down and arranged his cuffs precisely. He raised his eyeglass and stared at Drew, finally noticing his apparel. "A trifle formal, aren't you, Drew?"

"Huttle assured me no one would notice," Drew told him, assuming a hurt expression.

"Kneebreeches at tea? Gad, Drew, they are hard not to notice. Not the thing at all."

"Have you ever tried to get pantaloons over this?" his friend asked, pointing to his leg, still encased in splints.

Jeremy shook his head and considered the problem. "Too difficult for me." He yawned and stretched.

A quiet silence fell over the room. A short time later both men dozed off.

Then the door flew open. "See, Manda. They are here. Oh," Robert said, running into the room.

"Shh! You'll wake them up," she said, trying to silence him.

"Already has." Jeremy stretched. "Well, brat, nothing to say? Come here." He held out his arms.

Amanda, who was holding Robert's hand, released it, and Robert dashed into Jeremy's arms. Amanda bit her lip. Drew, his eyes a deep midnight blue, watched, his face impassive. He wished he could hold out his arms to her as Jeremy had done with Robert.

The next day Drew's valet arrived with a carriage, trunks, and a sheaf of mail. He took one look at the room, surveyed his master, and set to work. A short time later Drew was once more correctly attired for the daytime, his pantaloons cut at the seam and laced over the splints. The valet allowed him only one concession: soft slippers instead of his Hessians. The man bustled about the room, putting out brushes and mumbling under his breath about the condition of the clothes in the wardrobe.

"Gilbert?" Drew asked. "When did this come?" He held up a letter.

"I really could not say, your lordship. It was part of a packet I was told to bring you."

Drew frowned. He turned back to the letter. The major was highly regarded in his profession, according to his friend. Why couldn't the major have been a rotter? Drew crumpled the letter and then said, "Call the footman, Gilbert. I'm going down for tea."

That afternoon Amanda was alone in her sitting room when Drew entered, her face sad and her hands folded loosely in her lap. She jumped off the settee and moved to another chair when she saw him. She smiled at him, her eyes lit by an emotion she still hid even from herself.

Protesting, he took her place. "You won't even let me act the gentleman."

"Your leg is more important than your manners, sir."

"That is not what I heard you tell Robert." He sighed as he took his place.

"Robert does not have a broken leg," she said primly, settling herself in a chair that set off the red print in her dress perfectly.

"Where is he?" Drew asked.

"Upstairs. He had choir practice this afternoon, the first since the measles. He was sleepy when he arrived home."

"And Jeremy?"

"He has deserted us." Drew raised his eyebrow. "Just temporarily. He has gone to Hedgefield for the afternoon. Something about needing to get out."

Drew nodded and laughed. He cleared his throat and started to speak. The door opened. Thompson entered, the teatray gleaming in the soft afternoon light. Drew waited impatiently as the butler passed the teacup to him and then the tray of sandwiches. Finally the servant retreated. Drew began again. "Amanda?"

She looked up, startled by the note in Drew's voice.

"Amanda," Drew stopped. She waited. "I asked a friend to make some inquiries about the major." Her face flushed and her eyes flashed. "I know that this is not my concern, but I was worried."

"And?" Amanda's voice dripped with anger and sarcasm.

"He has an outstanding record. His superiors and his men speak of him highly."

"I thought as much. Robert's father was a good judge of character. He would hardly entrust his child to someone he could not respect." She looked at Drew, her brow creased in a frown. She smoothed her skirts and began twisting one of her ribbons in her fingers. Then she picked up a piece of thinly sliced bread and butter and began to crumble it. "But I do thank you."

"For what?"

"For trying to help me." She realized what she was doing and put the rest of the bread back on her plate. "I haven't told Robert that he might be leaving for India," she said quietly, her voice shaking.

"Don't. Something may happen to prevent it."

"And perhaps it won't," she whispered. She shook herself slightly and sat up straight, an obviously false smile plastered to her face. "Jeremy tells me that you and he will be leaving us tomorrow."

"Yes. I'm certain you will be happy to see our backs." Drew put his cup on the table in front of the settee and sat up straighter. "I can never thank you enough for all you have done for me."

"Nonsense. Anyone would have done as much," Amanda assured him, pain lancing through her at his carefully polite and formal words and a hidden, not quite realized hope dying.

"Amanda."

She looked up to find his blue eyes staring at her. Suddenly the hope was back. Her heart beat faster.

"Amanda, you have been more than kind. You and Robert are very special people."

She blushed. Forgetting that the tea had grown cold, she picked up her cup and took a sip. She grimaced and rang for a fresh pot. "You certainly did your share with Robert," she reminded him.

"He's a very likable little boy."

Amanda smiled politely.

Drew waited impatiently while the butler brought fresh tea. Then he took a deep breath. He squared his shoulders, an action that made his dark-blue coat with gold buttons ripple. He pulled his sleeves down carefully, aligning them precisely over his cuffs. As soon as Amanda and he were alone again, he cleared his throat and said, "Amanda, I have been thinking about that plan you told me about. About your arranging a temporary marriage."

She looked up startled. Her heart raced and then slowed. "A temporary marriage?"

"Like the one that lawyer tried to arrange. With legal documents to protect you." She nodded. He took a deep breath and continued, "I would be willing to help you keep Robert."

"How?" Amanda simply stared at him.

"I'll marry you." Watching her face, he hurried on. "Just temporarily, of course."

"What?"

"I said we could get married. Then you could keep Robert."

Once again the door opened. Drew looked up in annoyance. Jeremy walked in. He threw his coat to Thompson, who had followed him, and took his seat. He accepted a cup of tea from Amanda, who struggled to keep her hands steady. After taking a swallow, he became aware of the tension in the air. He looked from one to another curiously. "Are you planning to tell me what is going on?" he asked, looking at Drew pointedly.

"I've asked Amanda to marry me."

Jeremy dropped his cup on his saucer and pounded Drew on the back, his face beaming with satisfaction.

Amanda brought him back to earth. "But I haven't said yes."

8

Silence fell in the room. Jeremy stood up and crossed to the fireplace. He leaned on the mantel, a quiet figure dressed in dark-brown worsted and buff riding pants. He stared at his cousin and then at his friend. "Well?"

"I've offered to sign an agreement much as Amanda had arranged to do with that other man," Drew said quietly.

"You've what?" Jeremy turned on Drew, his hopes dashed. He opened his mouth to continue, but Drew shook his head slightly. He turned back to his cousin. "Well, Amanda? This is what you wanted. Have you changed your mind?"

Unable to sit quietly one moment longer, Amanda stood up. She began walking around the room, wringing her hands. Finally she turned to Drew. "It isn't fair. I was going to pay that other man. What can you hope to gain?" She took a few more turns around the room.

Jeremy considered Drew carefully, weighing the same question in his mind. Two pairs of blue eyes stared into each other.

"I won't let you do this simply to repay me for taking care of you," Amanda said angrily, ignoring the looks her cousin was giving his friend.

"Repay you?" Drew laughed harshly. "My dear Miss Desmond, it will be as much to my advantage as to yours."

They stared at each other for a moment. Then she asked as if the words had been forced from her, "How?"

"How what?"

"How will this be an advantage to you?"

Drew ran a hand through his carefully tamed locks, disarranging the style his valet had worked so long to perfect. He looked at Jeremy, who had his mouth pressed tightly shut, disapproval in every line of his face. "Jeremy, tell her why I accepted your invitation."

His friend started. He looked at Drew. Then, as if he had read something from Drew's face, Jeremy smiled. It barely caused his lips to move, but his eyes sparkled. "Are you sure?" he asked. Drew looked into his eyes and nodded. Jeremy's smile grew. "Drew was running away from home. His mother and several of the matchmaking mothers were trying to trap him into marriage. He had had enough. So he ran."

Amanda looked from one man to the other as if weighing the information she had been given. She turned to Drew, "Is he right?"

"Yes."

She considered his answer carefully.

Jeremy, realizing from the look on her face her confusion, gave her a push. "Amanda, I hope you consider this carefully. I think you will be making a mistake if you agree."

"Amanda, please think what it will do for you and for Robert. Also, it will give me a chance to live normally again," Drew said.

Amanda's eyes changed colors. She glanced at her cousin thoughtfully. Then she looked back at Drew. She took a deep breath and asked, her voice almost a whisper, "Do you insist on an answer immediately?"

Drew smiled. "No." At least she had not refused him. He exchanged a glance with Jeremy, who shrugged as if refusing to guess what her answer would be.

"I'll give you my answer this evening," Amanda promised. She crossed to the door and paused, her hand on the latch. "Drew . . ." He looked at her and smiled. "Thank you."

No sooner had the door closed behind her than Drew

turned to Jeremy. "What were you doing? As hard as I've worked to get her to agree, and then you tell her to refuse me. Are you insane?"

Jeremy just smiled at him. "You will see. Opposition has always had a curious effect on Amanda." He crossed to the door. "I'll send someone to help you upstairs. Unless I miss my guess, we will be celebrating your betrothal by dinner."

While the two men were resting, Amanda had retreated to her bedroom and her chaise. As she sat with her legs curled under her, she wondered why she had not accepted Drew's offer immediately. "It is what I planned," she whispered to herself. "But . . ." She shifted restlessly, afraid to admit even to herself that she wanted more than Drew was offering. He had said he was willing to sign the documents. She had to agree. She picked up her embroidery, no longer satisfied simply to curl up on the chaise. As she jabbed the needle into the fabric, she told herself over and over again that this was what she had wanted, what she had grown so angry about when Jeremy had thwarted her. The once-neat stitches of the pillow cover grew longer and longer. Finally she flung her sewing to one side and stood up. Too restless to sit still any longer, she reviewed Drew's offer. "I have to agree," she said firmly. Then her conscience reminded her of the consequences. This marriage was only temporary. How long did he plan for it to last? If it were over too soon, the major would have a further reason to take Robert. "And just think of what the vicar's wife will say," she said quietly.

When her maid entered a few minutes later at the head of a line of servants bearing a tub and hot water, Amanda was still wandering restlessly around the room. Even sitting to have her curls swept up away from her neck and ears was almost more than she could bear. Only in the tub did she relax, soothed by Jennings' massage.

As soon as she emerged, the problem rose to the surface again. "I have to," she said, her voice determined.

Jennings started. "Yes, miss?" She paused and allowed Amanda's curls to drift waywardly about her face.

"Go on, Jennings," her mistress said impatiently, tapping her fingernail against the dressing table. Drew had said that the marriage would benefit him also. Could she believe him? She waved away Jennings' first choice of a dress for this evening—a green newly arrived from Madame Camilla. "The blue with the vandyking," she suggested. Her maid looked at her strangely and then hurried to get the more formal dress from the wardrobe.

A few minutes later Amanda was dressed, the deep v-necked dress plunging farther than she remembered it. She glanced in the mirror at her hemline, fashionably raised to her ankles. She considered herself, checking carefully that the points of the lace were long enough. Jennings twisted one curl over her forehead and stood back proudly. "I'm going to refuse him," she said clearly, her heart sinking as she realized what she had said.

Jennings looked up startled. "What, Miss Amanda?"

Amanda ignored her. "He is just making the offer to be kind." She squared her shoulders and left the room.

In the red sitting room below, Drew waited impatiently. His valet had done his best. His hair shone; his linen was impeccably white. Only his constant fingering of his fob revealed his nervousness.

Amanda entered and he caught his breath. Her gown, caught under her bust line by a band of lace, was the most fashionable he had seen her wear, emphasizing her beauty and her charms. He gasped when he noticed the neckline and bit back a command that she return to her room to change her gown. She came to stand in front of him, her face serious. The candlelight at her back created interesting shadows. Drew took a deep breath and tried to look anywhere but at her breasts right in front of him.

She took a deep breath, and Drew held his. To her own amazement, she said, "I would be pleased to accept your offer, Lord Mainwaring."

The breath he had been holding exploded from Drew. He smiled and held out his hand to her, settling her beside him. "Thank you," he said quietly.

Amanda shook her head. "No."

"There is no need to agree who is the most grateful. We are both satisfied with the arrangement." The door opened to admit Jeremy. "Wish us happy, my friend," Drew said, his smile bursting across his face.

Reluctantly, Jeremy took their hands, looking both of them over carefully. Amanda, startled by her answer, held her breath as he inspected her face. He frowned and then nodded, "I suppose there is nothing more to be done."

"Nonsense. There is much to do if this is to proceed smoothly," Drew said heartily.

Amanda looked at him warily. "What do you mean?"

"Why, we must make plans for our marriage."

"But I thought we would get a special license and be married quietly here," Amanda said, her voice trembling.

"And what would that do? A hole-in-the-corner marriage is not likely to satisfy the major. Besides, I need everyone to know about it if it is to help me."

"But Drew . . . ?" Amanda looked at him in amazement. "The major is supposed to be here tomorrow."

Jeremy, an interested spectator, nodded gravely. "She is right."

"And if we married tonight—even if we could find the bishop—think what kind of impression that would make. Better to have him see us going through all the formalities."

Amanda's face brightened. "Maybe he will return to India and we can call this marriage off."

Drew threw his hand across his forehead. "I'm wounded. The heartless wretch plans to use me and throw me to one side," he said dramatically; it was the only way he knew to hide his true hurt. She could not refuse him.

"Amanda!" her cousin shouted. "This marriage is bad enough as it is, but I thought you were less selfish than that."

"I am," she said, regretting her hasty words. "We will do just as you suggest."

Her guilty agreement was tested not too many minutes later when Jeremy pulled the bellpull. "Champagne, Thompson. My cousin has just promised to marry Lord Mainwaring."

The butler stopped. Then he approached his mistress. "May I extend the good wishes of the staff?" he said proudly, and bowed.

Drew smiled broadly. Amanda, still slightly confused, nodded formally. She reminded herself that the marriage was merely a prelude to an annulment. She took a deep breath, wondering at her heartache.

The butler inspected them carefully, trying to determine if this were part of his mistress's plan. The look in his lordship's eyes when he watched her gave him hope that it was not. He bowed once more and hurried from the room.

"Why did you tell him?" Amanda asked. "It will be all over the county by morning." She glared at both men.

"Good! What better way to convince the major that the marriage is a legitimate one," her cousin reminded her, grinning broadly. And what better way to ensure that it lasts, he added silently.

"I thought you were against the match," she said stormily.

"I am, but if you are determined to proceed, you might as well do it up right." He chuckled. "Lud, I would give a monkey to see some of their faces when those society ladies open their newspapers a few days hence." He looked at Drew, raised one eyebrow, and they both burst into laughter.

Amanda rose angrily. She crossed between them, her arms folded about her. She tapped her foot impatiently, waiting for their laughter to cease. When it had subsided to mere chuckles, she said frostily, "There has been quite enough said already."

"No, there hasn't," Drew said, his tones firm beneath the laughter. "Later this evening we will both write our mothers."

"My mother? Never!" Amanda quivered with indignation, wondering how the situation had gotten so far out of hand.

After the champagne, the roasted pigeon, a stuffed sole, green peas, and a syllabub she refused to touch, she was still protesting.

"Amanda, did you or did you not accept my offer?" Drew finally asked, his voice cold.

"I did. But I didn't know—"

"Do you mean to keep your word?"

"Yes! I never go back—"

"Then write your mother," he said quietly, breathing a sigh of relief. "She will need time to arrange her trip home. Will six weeks be enough?" He lifted his leg up on the settee and winced as his muscles protested.

"Enough of what?"

"Enough for her to get here," Jeremy said impatiently. "Cousin, pay attention." He leaned back to enjoy their sparring.

Drew, however, looked at him coolly. He asked, "May my intended and I have some time alone?" He glared at Jeremy. Amanda, too, turned her icy stare upon him.

"My apologies. I will remove my unwelcome presence from your midst." Jeremy stood up, an injured expression on his face. "I would have thought that a couple planning a temporary marriage would avoid any suggestion of . . ." He let his voice trail away as he opened the door. "You will let me know your plans?" He paused, one pale hand against the door frame.

Drew and Amanda exchanged rueful glances. They nodded. After the door had closed, they sat in silence for a few minutes. Amanda shifted restlessly, her heart beating as rapidly as it always did when she was alone with him. Drew moved his leg from the settee to a low table in front of it. He cleared his throat. She looked up expectantly. He looked away and cleared his throat again.

"Oh, hmm, if your mother can arrive by then, I hope that we can be married in June," Drew said nervously.

"That is two months from now," Amanda said sharply.

"We could make it July if you think she will need more time."

"No." Amanda's voice was almost a whisper.

Drew leaned back and straightened his neckcloth. It had grown tighter throughout the evening. "Do you wish to be married in London?"

Amanda dropped the fringe she had been playing with and looked up, startled. "No. I had rather hoped to have a private service here," she said firmly.

"We have already discussed that."

"You stated your opinions. We did not discuss it."

"Remember why I am doing this," he said firmly. "My marriage needs to be as public as I can make it."

"What do you plan to do? Have it at Westminster Abbey?"

"You said you did not want to be married in London," Drew reminded her.

"I was only joking." She turned to look at him, her eyes wide. "Just how big do you plan on making this wedding?"

He thought for a moment. "With my family and closest friends, I plan to invite about two hundred."

"Two hundred? People? Just where do you plan to hold this affair? The parish church is rather small."

"Bath is nearby. The abbey will do nicely."

She closed her eyes briefly, thinking of the long walk she would have to make up that aisle toward him. "I suppose you have plans for a wedding breakfast too?" she said faintly.

He nodded. "My house in Lansdowne Crescent should do nicely. My mother keeps it staffed, as she spends most of her summers here. Yes, that's it. Amanda, pull the bellpull."

"Why?"

"To get someone to help me to my room. I want my letters to go off as soon as possible tomorrow." Amanda stared at him, wondering how an answer to one question could have caused so much commotion. "Amanda?" She crossed to the bellpull and pulled it. She stood there as if in a daze until he asked, "Is there anything else we need to discuss?" She shook her head.

That night as she sat in front of her desk, her pen in hand, she thought about the evening's events. It was as if she had plunged into a swiftly moving river and could hardly keep her head above water. She gritted her teeth, dipped the pen in the inkwell, and stopped. This whole situation had been her idea. How had Drew taken charge? She dipped her pen again, this time putting the facts on paper as fast as she could. Reading back over what she had written, she paused. She was marrying Drew. She smiled. Then she gave herself a mental shake, reminding herself of his promise — an annulment anytime before six months were up. She ignored the nagging voice that kept saying, "Don't let him go."

The next morning she could not ignore Robert's reaction. "You mean you and Manda and me will be a family?"

Drew smiled at the boy and nodded. He spread his arms to catch Robert as the boy threw himself into his arms. "A family," the child repeated happily, and hugged Drew's neck tighter.

Amanda's throat tightened. How would he react when the marriage was over? "Drew . . ." she said huskily. He looked up, a smile on his face and in his eyes. "This has gotten out of hand. I think . . ."

"I think you are having second thoughts, my lady. Remember why we are doing this," he said, cutting her speech off. He nodded at Robert, who was sitting by the table putting one of his puzzles together.

Amanda looked sad. Then she nodded. "Come, Robert," she said firmly. He started to complain. "Remember Drew and Cousin Jeremy are moving to Hedgefield today."

The boy's face grew stormy. "No. I won't let them." Amanda merely looked at him sternly, and he hung his head.

"And you will be having company soon," Drew added quietly. "Major Besley." For the first time since she received the major's first letter, Amanda heard the words without flinching. "And your Cousin Jeremy has invited you to luncheon tomorrow."

Robert's face regained its sunny expression. "Can Amanda come too?"

"May, Robert," Amanda said gently.

"Well, may she come?"

The adults broke into laughter.

"Of course, halfling. And the major too, if he is here."

To Amanda's surprise, the time between Jeremy's and Drew's departure and the major's arrival dragged. After dealing with the housekeeping and talking to her agent, she had hours to herself. Even Robert was busy with his lessons. She picked up a novel she had had to lay aside until the crises were over. Even that failed to hold her interest. The hero, with his dark hair and blue eyes, reminded her too much of Drew. Finally, she walked out into the garden, a basket for flowers on her arm. She stopped occasionally to inspect one bloom or another, but her basket was still empty when she returned.

She sat down to a solitary luncheon of a fluffy mushroom omelette and a clear soup followed by a salad of oranges and almonds. For the first time in days she picked at her food. "Missing his lordship already," Cook sighed romantically.

To her dismay that was exactly what Amanda was doing. Even when she and Robert had moved to Applecroft Manor, she had not been as lonely as she was now. Of course, then everything had been new and so exciting. She straightened and picked up her book again, determination in every movement.

Fortunately for that determination, Thompson entered. "Major Besley has arrived."

Amanda put a hand over her heart to stop its racing. "Show him in, Thompson. Then send Nurse word that she is to bring Master Robert down in half an hour." Her voice was breathy but controlled. The butler bowed and left.

A short time later the door opened again. "Major Besley," Thompson said in his most stentorian tones.

Amanda stood, the very simple yet expensive afternoon

gown in a soft violet providing a contrast to the heavy
books behind her. She had purposely chosen to receive
the man in the library, instinctively realizing that she
would have more control of the situation in a more
businesslike setting.

The major was a stocky man, about five feet eight, his
thinning sandy hair brushed forward and his skin
bronzed by the sun. He stopped in the doorway. Miss
Desmond was as lovely as everyone had said she was. He
hurried forward and bowed formally.

Amanda inspected him from his sandy-brown hair to
the tips of his gleaming Hessians. Accustomed as she was
to her cousin's and Drew's height, he seemed short,
almost squat. She waved him to a seat. "May I offer you
some tea?" she asked, relying on manners learned as a
child to carry her through.

He agreed. Then he said with a smile, "I cannot begin
to express how I have been longing to meet you." His
voice was surprisingly light.

"Oh?"

"Robert, Lieutenant Shilling, was very complimentary.
He talked about you almost as much as he talked about
his wife." He smiled broadly. "I feel that we are already
the best of friends."

Amanda could feel the hairs on the back of her neck
quiver. Although she knew she had to face him and that
Jeremy had volunteered to stay, she felt brief anger with
her cousin for leaving her alone to meet this man. Before
that anger could grow, however, Thompson appeared
with the teatray. Carefully, Amanda signaled him to
remain.

His presence did little to discourage her guest. "Everyone in London told me how lovely you were, but I now
find that they failed to do you justice," he began again,
taking his tea from the butler. He sat back casually in his
chair.

Suddenly the door flew open and Robert ran in.
"Nurse said he's come. Manda, where is he?"

She smiled at him and indicated their guest. Robert

made a sketchy bow that brought a frown to the major's face, and then he started asking questions. "Have you ever seen a tiger or an elephant?"

"Robert," Amanda said quietly, noting the major's disapproval, "let our guest have a chance to finish his tea. Then, if you are good, he may answer your questions."

"Humph!" The major put his cup down with a sharp click. "So this is the lad. I might have known." He looked at Robert, noting with disfavor the less-than-spotless hands—Nurse had washed them before they left the schoolroom—and his wrinkled clothing. "Hmm. Yes, I see the need of a man in charge here."

Robert took a gulp of tea, blowing on it first to cool it. The major frowned. Amanda's heart sank. "I think I arrived just in time, Miss Desmond. A few days with me and those disgusting manners will disappear."

Robert heard only the last few words. He turned to Amanda uncertainly. "What is he talking about, Manda? I'm not going anywhere with him even if he did know my father."

The major stood up and crossed to stand beside Robert's chair. "It is a good thing I arrived when I did. I told my lawyer what would happen to a boy left in a household without a man at its head." He paused and inspected Robert once again. "Finish your tea, boy; then leave."

Amanda forced herself to count to ten, double the number she used when she was arguing with Jeremy. Before she had finished, Robert stood up. He glared at the major. Then he said, "I'm leaving. But I won't go with you." He ran over to Amanda and grabbed her, hugging her tightly. "You won't let him take me away, will you? You and me and Drew are going to be a family." His blue eyes filled with tears.

The major snorted in disgust. "Soft. I knew it."

Amanda hugged the child. "You run to Nurse. The major and I need to talk." She hugged him again. "Remember we're a family now," she told him quietly.

"You and me and Drew?"

Amanda nodded.

Robert stepped out of her arms. He turned toward the major and bowed before running to the door. Just before he slipped through it, he turned around and stuck out his tongue.

Amanda coughed discreetly to hide her laughter.

The major missed the action. "Who is this Drew the lad was talking about?" he demanded.

"My fiancé, Lord Mainwaring." Amanda's voice was full of pride.

9

Later that afternoon Amanda was still laughing as she wrote a note to her cousin and Drew. She had seldom seen a man react so strangely. Quickly trying to capture the flavor, she jotted down the details of the rest of their meeting.

"Your fiancé? No one mentioned him before," the major had said suspiciously. He rose to stand behind her, an action that made her slide farther forward in her chair. Thompson, realizing what had happened, walked over to offer the man a cake.

"The engagement is rather recent," she said primly.

"Oh? And when do you plan to marry? Perhaps the boy should stay with me until then."

For the first time Amanda acknowledged the wisdom in Drew's planning. "We plan to marry in June. And Robert is to take part in the ceremony. I think it would be best if he remain with me."

"You will be married here?" The man's voice dripped with suspicion.

Amanda deliberately assumed a look of astonishment. "Here? I am afraid that our parish church is too small. Lord Mainwaring has asked his mother's dear friend, the Bishop of Bath and Wells, to officiate at the abbey," she said smugly. "If you will give me your direction, we will send you an invitation. Your lawyer has been rather secretive about where we could contact you."

The major took his seat once again. "You have been rather secretive yourself," he said, his voice snappish. "If

I had known about your engagement, we could have discussed the situation with your fiancé and his lawyer." He glanced at her once again, bidding farewell to the fortune and the beauty he had seen within his grasp. "I would like to meet this man," he suggested, his tone questioning Lord Mainwaring's existence.

"Certainly. He is staying with my cousin. They went to school together. Jeremy suggested that you take luncheon with us. Anyone in the village can give you directions. Tomorrow at one, then?" She stood, forcing the major to stand also. She held out her hand, giving him no choice but to make his bow and leave.

As the door had closed behind him, she had sighed in relief. Then she hurried up to the schoolroom to see Robert, to reassure herself that he was still in her care. Immersed in the difficulties of his sums, at first he did not notice her. But when he did, he stood up and crossed to her side. He pulled her over to a chair, and when she was seated, he whispered in her ear, "I do not like that man."

Amanda smiled at him, whispering back, "I know."

"I did not mean to be rude, though," the boy assured her, already having endured a lecture from Nurse, who had heard of his behavior from Thompson.

"Then you must apologize to the major personally when you see him tomorrow." Robert backed up, a mutinous look on his face. "You will see him at luncheon tomorrow. The major was a friend of your father's," she reminded him.

Robert glared at her. "I don't believe that."

"Why not?"

"My papa would not like someone who did not like little boys."

Amanda laughed softly. "Robert, I am certain there were few little boys in India for the major to get to know. We must give him the chance to get to know you."

"Do I have to?"

"You do." He glared at her. "Robert." Her voice told him that he had better agree and right away.

"All right. But if he doesn't like me, I won't like him," he said, his voice determined.

Amanda nodded, carefully hiding her amusement. Sending him back to his sums, she watched for a few minutes and then left.

The next day she and Robert left the manor shortly after breakfast, choosing to ride the short distance between the two estates. The morning was a pleasant one, cool but clear. The fields, newly planted, showed only faint touches of green. The air was fragrant with the scent of freshly washed air and recently turned dirt. Somewhere in the distance a lark sang.

Robert laughed and spurred his pony. "Hurry, Manda. Cousin Jeremy and Drew are probably wondering where we are."

"They will wait, pixie. Do you remember what I told you about calling Drew by his first name?"

He pulled his pony up beside her. "Yes. But Drew told me I—"

"The major expects good behavior. Besides, while calling Lord Mainwaring Drew in private is acceptable, you must address him by his title in public."

Robert nodded. For the next few minutes Amanda had to hide her smile as she heard him whispering to himself, "Lord Mainwaring, Lord Mainwaring . . ."

The gentlemen had obviously been watching for them. No sooner had they dismounted than both Drew and Jeremy walked out the front door. Amanda stopped short, confused by the difference between Drew seated and standing. He was an inch or two taller than Jeremy. Even with the weight he had lost and his still-pale skin, he was an imposing, powerful figure. For a moment all of Amanda's fears returned. She hesitated. Then he smiled at her, the same boyish smile he had used to convince her that Robert could climb on his bed. She took a deep breath and hurried forward.

Of course, Robert reached the two men first. He stopped short and said accusingly, "You are taller than Cousin Jeremy."

Drew leaned heavily on his gold-headed walking stick and said, very seriously, "So I am, halfling. So I am." Then he laughed and ruffled Robert's hair. In spite of his

words, most of his attention was on Amanda. Her habit
was a rich burgundy worsted, its shoulders trimmed with
epaulets and silver braid. Her bodice outlined her figure
and was embellished with brandenburg fastenings of
matching silver braid. Her habit shirt and stock were a
gray so pale that they did not go beyond what was
fashionable. Her hat in the Wellington style was also pale
gray, with burgundy plumes.

Before he could do more than smile his welcome,
Robert tugged on Drew's coattails. "What is it, brat?" he
asked, his tone at odds with his words.

"That Major Besley is coming to lunch today." Drew
nodded and followed the others into the entranceway, his
steps still slower than he would have liked. "I asked him
about tigers and elephants, and he did not even answer
me."

"He didn't?"

"No, and he told me I had bad manners." Although
Drew listened as Robert recounted in detail his meeting
with the major, he was more interested in the low-voiced
conversation between Amanda and Jeremy. Had he
realized that he was the subject of it he would have felt
more confident.

"When did the splints come off?" Amanda asked, her
hazel eyes worried.

"Late yesterday. Doctor Weston said he wanted to
make certain Drew was protected on the ride here, or he
would have taken them off earlier." Jeremy led his cousin
toward a small sitting room, chosen more for the fact that
it was convenient than for its fashion.

"But Drew is limping. I thought the doctor had
prevented that."

"According to Weston, the limp is much less than it
could have been, and it may still improve. Drew will still
be able to ride, to dance." Jeremy seated her beside the
window. 'Now, tell me about this major.''

"Yes, do. Robert thinks he was rude," Drew said,
taking his own seat and propping his leg up on the
footstool Robert so carefully provided.

The three adults exchanged rueful glances. Then Jeremy suggested, "There are puppies in the stables, Robert. Tell the head groom I said you might play with them."

Knowing that they were trying to get rid of him and yet unable to resist the lure, Robert hesitated for a moment and then dashed for the door.

"Robert," Amanda said firmly. He stopped, his hand on the latch. "Remember to allow time before luncheon to make yourself presentable." He nodded and hurried out the door.

"Presentable?" Jeremy asked quizzically.

"The major was less than pleased with his appearance and manners yesterday. Only the fact that we are engaged kept him from ordering me to have Robert ready to leave immediately."

Determined to have all the facts, the two men kept asking questions, trying to supplement her letter. By the time she had finished, they were grim. Although Amanda did not mention her own uneasiness in the major's presence, they knew from her words that she was keeping something from them.

When the major entered later that morning, her discomfort was apparent from the first moment the man bowed and took her hand. Drew and Jeremy exchanged glances and took up their positions beside her.

After making his bow, the major took his seat, raising his glass to his eye to inspect Drew carefully. "So you are the man who is to take charge of my ward? He will need a firm hand. I fear he lacks discipline."

Amanda bit her lip to prevent her angry words from spilling out. Drew merely smiled.

"Have you any experience?" Besley asked, his face wearing a rather contemptuous expression as he noted Drew's soft shoes and walking stick.

"Lord Mainwaring was on Wellington's staff and was frequently mentioned in the dispatches," Jeremy said, enjoying the look of discomfort that flooded the major's face.

Just then the door opened and Robert appeared, closely followed by the butler. Immediately the major's face hardened. When he discovered a few minutes later that Robert was to share their meal, his disapproval became too much for him to contain. "I must protest."

"About what?" Jeremy asked, his voice revealing his utter indifference.

"The lad is too young to have his meals with us."

Robert's frown was erased by one word. "No," Amanda said firmly. Drew smiled at her and nodded. Jeremy, incensed at being told whom he could entertain at his table, bit back his angry words. Quickly the butler announced luncheon.

The meal, although delicious enough to satisfy even the most discerning tastes, was not a pleasant one. With the numbers uneven, it was difficult to converse as society demanded. Seated at the foot of the table, Amanda had Drew on her right and the major on her left. During the soup à la Monglas, she was able to relax, as Drew kept her talking about Robert or about the latest information he had discovered in the mounds of papers waiting at Hedgefield. As he watched her and kept her occupied, she sipped the soup.

When she turned to talk to Major Besley during the second course—a turbot in lemon and herb sauce—her appetite disappeared. "I heard you speaking of that bounder, Byron," he said pompously. "The fellow deserves all our disapproval. He should have considered his actions if he wanted to remain in society."

"You have met Lord Byron?" The major shook his head. "Then I suppose you disapprove of his poetry."

"Poetry, ha! That is no fit occupation for a gentleman. No, Miss Desmond, that is not why I disapprove. My cousin lives near the Milbanks. I only wonder that Lady Byron waited so long to leave him."

"Then you advocate the dissolving of marriage vows when partners do not suit?" Amanda waited for his answer, hiding her nervousness. Drew leaned closer to hear the man's answer.

"Nonsense! But it is evident the man is vile. Lady Byron has every right to return to her parents."

Drew breathed a sigh of relief while Amanda bit the inside of her lip. Fortunately the footman appeared with the next course, a ham in Madeira sauce, and it was time to return to Drew. By the time the savories and the gâteau glacé àu l'abricot were served, Amanda was having a difficult time hiding her trembling as the major leaned closer to her to give her more of his wisdom. As soon as the port was put out, she made her escape with Robert, insisting that he have a short rest.

By the time she returned from tucking him in, the men were once again in the sitting room, and her rest was over.

Noticing that the child had indeed been sent off to rest, Major Besley, no longer quite as intimidated by Drew as he had been earlier, opened his campaign for information. "Miss Desmond tells me, Lord Mainwaring, that your engagement is fairly recent. It is rather remarkable that you should choose to marry just when I announce my visit." He looked from one to another suspiciously.

Amanda had to keep a firm control on her emotions to prevent herself from snapping at him or shaking so much he would be suspicious.

Drew, however, seemed to have no trouble. He smiled broadly and winked at Amanda. "Since she refused my very first offer eight years ago, I would hardly call this sudden. Persistent, perhaps."

Amanda blushed and then held her breath. Jeremy chuckled.

"Eight years ago? Why, she would have been . . ."

"Eighteen, Major Besley. Of course, I did not take him seriously."

"I had the devil of a time persuading her this time. I even fell off my horse to get her attention."

"Drew." Amanda blushed again.

"Fell off your horse? I do not understand." The major turned to Jeremy in confusion.

"He is only teasing Amanda," Jeremy said. "Will you be free to attend the ceremony?"

"If it does not interfere with the festivities in London. My cousin has hired windows along Prince Leopold's route to Carlton House." He turned to the others. "Miss Desmond mentioned June. Have you set the date?"

"We must wait to hear from our mothers and the bishop to be certain, but we hope that June second will be acceptable to everyone." Drew pressed Amanda's hand hard to keep her from from speaking. She glared at him and shut her lips tightly. "Amanda is still rather hesitant. She feels that it would be better to wait longer after the princess's marriage. What do you think?"

Besley thought for a moment, a frown creasing his forehead. "She may be right." Jeremy bit back a bark of laughter. "However, since your marriage will be performed in Bath . . ." He paused again thoughtfully. "Of course, I am no arbiter of fashion, but I believe it will be acceptable. And it does solve a problem for me."

Amanda, who had been deliberately daydreaming, sat up straighter. "What do you mean?" she asked quickly.

"I leave again for India in August. I had thought to marry and take Robert with me. Now there is no need. He can remain with you. If the marriage does indeed take place and Lord Mainwaring agrees." He smiled at Amanda as though he were bestowing on her the highest medal of the land.

"How disappointing for your betrothed," Jeremy said in a faintly mocking tone.

"Oh, I am not engaged."

The other three people stared at the major in astonishment.

"But you said . . ." Amanda said breathlessly.

"I planned to meet the lad and then find someone suitable."

Drew and Jeremy exchanged glances and almost choked as they tried to hold back their laughter. Amanda, on the other hand, saw herself in his actions and blanched.

Catching a glimpse of her face from the corner of his

eye, Drew turned toward her. "May I get you something to drink? Jeremy, call for some wine."

"No, no. I will be fine momentarily." Amanda waved away their protests.

Horrified at the thought that his words had brought embarrassment to a lady, for he could find no other reason for her actions, the major quickly apologized. He made his excuses and left after scheduling another meeting with Amanda on the morrow.

When Robert came in a short time later, he found the two men laughing helplessly. Eventually Amanda joined in. Although Drew and Jeremy truly found the situation funny, for Amanda her laughter was merely nervous reaction.

August, she thought. Then her marriage to Drew could be annulled. For some reason the thought sent a shiver of fear through her. Carefully, she brought her feelings under control. She stood up and swept her long skirt over her arm. She collected her ward. "Make your good-byes and remember to say thank you," she whispered. She pushed him toward Jeremy. The two men protested their leaving, but she insisted.

"May I call on you tomorrow?" Drew asked formally as he walked her to her mount, a beautiful gray mare she had named Mist.

Amanda frowned as she noticed that his limp was more pronounced than it had been earlier. "You may, sir." She allowed a groom to throw her into the saddle. Then she bent down and told Drew, "But you must promise to rest." His nod made her frown disappear.

Later that afternoon as she read the papers that Jeremy had sent home with her, she made careful note of every detail of the princess's wardrobe, passing the fashion notes on to her maid as she finished with them.

Jennings was much more critical of the royal wardrobe than she. "No matter what her royal highness chooses to do, I believe that a white wardrobe is both impractical and unimaginative," she said firmly. "White is becoming to you, but so are other colors. We must write Madame Camilla and see what she suggests."

"Madame Camilla is my dressmaker, but I will choose my own clothes." Amanda left no doubt in Jennings' mind of her displeasure.

"Of course. Perhaps, though, you could ask her to send you copies of the latest plates."

Amanda considered her maid's suggestion and then nodded.

The next few days were filled with meetings with Drew, Major Besley, and her lawyer. Drew insisted that she write the man and request his presence. At first, she had protested, declaring that Drew's word was all she needed. But he insisted. Somehow putting their relationship on paper made it seem so shabby, so false, so temporary. More than once she had to remind herself that it was merely a convenience, that it would be over before the end of the year. Signing the legal documents made it all so real, so harsh.

The lawyer, who had worked for her grandfather for decades, drew up the documents, protesting the entire time. Finally realizing that they would simply find someone else, someone less discreet, he agreed. "You are certain this is what you want to do," he asked them very formally. They both nodded. He pursed his lips and pulled down his waistcoat over his rounded belly. "Your grandfather would not approve, Miss Desmond. You must know that." He stared at her, but she stared right back, refusing to allow him to see her doubts. "And you, sir. How can you do something so unethical?" A faint flush of red crept into Drew's cheeks.

Jeremy finally forced the lawyer to complete the task. He picked up the papers from the desk and handed copies to Amanda and Drew. "Sign these," Jeremy said, his voice harsh and cold. "The terms are the same you discussed: neither of you will have control of any property belonging to the other, and either may ask for an annulment anytime during the first six months of the marriage. Is there anything else?"

"But there must be settlements, a jointure," the lawyer said in horror.

Amanda shook her head. "Nonsense. Grandfather provided me a handsome income."

Her lawyer nodded in agreement.

"And I have more than I will ever need," Drew said quietly. Finally, they signed the papers.

That unpleasant task out of the way, Amanda had another task for the lawyer. "Major Besley and I wish to make a more formal agreement about Robert, my ward."

"Certainly."

"Do you need us, Amanda?" Jeremy asked, his hand already reaching for his hat.

"Not now. Drew must be included later. Remember you are to come to dinner on Thursday," Amanda said quietly, wondering why it was harder each time she said good-bye to Drew.

"I will see you tomorrow," her husband-to-be said quietly as he bent over her hand. She raised her eyebrows. "I think we should discuss the information I received from my mother." Amanda nodded reluctantly. His mother. She vaguely remembered a tall elegant woman, quietly reserved, whose eyes had seemed to follow her son wherever he went. Oh, well, it was best to get through unpleasant things quickly.

Her meeting with Major Besley helped keep her thoughts away from Drew's mother. Admitting that he did not truly care for children, the major had agreed to relinquish to her his rights as Robert's guardian. "Lady Mainwaring, the day you take on that title is the day our agreement will take effect," he promised. In fact, he insisted that the document read, "Full personal guardianship of Robert Shilling granted to Amanda Desmond Fairleigh, Lady Mainwaring, with his financial affairs under the advisement of Jeremy Desmond, Esq., and Andrew Fairleigh, Lord Mainwaring." He read the document again and signed it quickly.

The major said pompously, "Lord Mainwaring and your cousin will need to sign it too." He paused. "I suppose you will continue to spoil the child, but at least the problem will no longer be mine. I will see you again before the wedding to discuss the final arrangements with you when Lord Mainwaring is present."

As the door shut behind him, Amanda wondered why she was not feeling more relief.

10

When Amanda showed Drew the document the next day, he raised an eyebrow. "What is wrong?" she asked, worried by the look on his face.

"Did you realize that this document may no longer be valid if our marriage is annulled?" Amanda's face revealed her horror. "Only Lady Mainwaring is Robert's guardian."

Amanda gained control of herself quickly. "The major will be in India. How will he know what we do?"

Drew gave her a look that told her that she was not living in the real world. "Ships sail every day. And several people know how to write letters."

"He will still have to take action. And that will require some time. I'll think of something," she said, her chin set in a determined line.

Drew decided not to press the issue further. Instead, he asked, "Would you and Robert join me for a picnic?"

"A picnic?"

"A ride in the country and then a stop to eat food from a basket."

"I suppose you brought it with you," she said, noting his empty hands.

He grinned boyishly. "No. I hoped you could persuade Cook to supply one. I'll get Robert."

She laughed at the eager expression on his face and agreed.

A short time later they were on their way, Robert in the

lead on his pony. "Come on, Drew," he called. "I'll race you."

"Where are we going?"

"Manda and I have a favorite place. We go there lots. Last time I saw a squirrel and a rabbit. But Manda won't let me get close to the cliffs, though."

"No, I won't. In fact, young man, I believe it would be best if you ride with us the rest of the way."

Overjoyed to be outside and with them, Robert agreed.

"Tell me more about this picnic spot, Amanda," Drew said, moving his horse, a black stallion, alongside her gray mare.

"And I thought this picnic was your idea," she said teasingly.

"My idea, yes, but you are choosing the spot. Now, tell me about the place where you and Robert are taking me. Does Jeremy accompany you on these picnics?"

"Jeremy? Surely you jest, sir. Jeremy is usually so involved with sleeping or with business that he rarely sees the outdoors until the middle of the afternoon. Except when he is fishing or during hunting season, of course." She glanced up and noticed that Robert was some distance ahead. "Robert, wait for us," she called.

Obediently he pulled up.

A short time later Drew and Amanda sat down under a tree, watching Robert as he chased a rabbit across the open field. Drew leaned back, resting against the tree, and said quietly, "He is a fine boy, Amanda. You have done a good job with him."

She blushed. "Jeremy has helped."

For a few minutes there was silence, the comfortable kind between friends. Then Drew asked, "Have you ever regretted turning down those other offers of marriage?"

Amanda dropped her eyes, staring at the grass. Her hand clenched around the crop she had placed on the ground beside her. She shivered slightly. When she answered him some time later, her voice was carefully controlled. "Some times. But since I've had Robert, they have been fewer." She pulled a sprig of grass and slowly shredded it. "What about you?"

He shrugged and looked up to check on Robert, who was crouched over a hole watching something. Amanda began laying out in front of him the contents of the basket he had carried. Drew stretched out on his back, looking at the white fluffy clouds that dotted the blue sky. When he answered her, she was surprised because he had been silent so long. "I was busy, first with Wellington." He smiled sadly. "As hard as those times were, they were exciting." He breathed deeply and pushed the lock of hair that had fallen over his forehead back into place. "When I came home, there were so many details to see to."

"And too many women to choose from?" Amanda teased him gently, much as she would have done Jeremy.

He laughed. "That too." His face grew serious. "And they all seemed so young." He sat up and took a roll she offered him. "I felt as though they were mere babes—as young as Robert there. Their meaningless chatter depressed me. I want more from marriage than a compliant wife who will live her own life while I go my own way." He noticed Robert edging farther away. "Robert, come have something to eat."

The boy glanced up and then pelted toward them, throwing himself to the ground. "Did Cook send any cakes?" he asked, gazing over the array of food.

"You need to eat something else before that. You know the rule," Amanda said firmly.

"Healthy food before treats," he said, a resigned tone to his voice. He reached for a roll and piece of thinly sliced ham.

"Try a peach," Drew suggested, peeling one and handing it to Amanda piece by piece. "Here let me." He grabbed a napkin and dabbed at her chin where the sticky juice dotted her face.

"Manda made a mess," Robert said in singsong fashion.

"But we won't tell, will we?" Drew reminded him gently.

"No." Robert sat back, his meal finished. "Come see a bird nest I found. It is on the ground. What kind of bird

would it be?" He took their hands, pulling them toward
the spot. Deciding they were moving too slowly, he broke
free and ran ahead.

Amanda stumbled and Drew took her arm, holding it
even when there was no longer any need. Shyly, she tried
to pull away, but he entangled his fingers with hers. A
small thrill coursed through her. She looked at him from
beneath her eyelashes, surprised.

For the next hour or so they followed Robert from one
spot to another, stopping finally on the crest of the hill
above Bath. The spring sunlight glinted off the pale-gold
stone of the houses in the town, suffusing the spa with a
soft golden glow. Then they moved back under their tree.
Robert lay beside them on his stomach, his head on his
hands, struggling to stay awake. Drew, too, drifted off to
sleep. As Amanda sat there and watched them, she felt at
peace, enjoying happiness she thought lost to her forever.

As she had a few times when he was at the manor,
Amanda inspected Drew carefully. His skin was
beginning to regain its brown color. His hair, with the
one lock that refused to stay in place drifting to his
forehead, glinted with gold highlights. She leaned closer.
His eyelashes too were tipped with gold. A butterfly
landed on his hair. She reached up to brush it away but
then hesitated. He moved restlessly and flung an arm
across her lap. Its heavy warmth across her thighs stirred
something in her, something she was afraid to even
acknowledge. As she looked at them sleeping there,
Amanda admitted to herself that she had lied. She longed
for a husband and children. She was simply too afraid to
try. Lulled by the quiet sounds of the countryside, she too
drifted off to sleep.

When she woke a short time later, Drew was propped
up on one elbow beside her, a wistful expression on his
face. Startled by his nearness yet not afraid, she smiled
hesitantly. Slowly, as if to give her a chance to pull away,
he bent and kissed her tenderly, his kiss as light as the
butterfly. She held her breath, surprised, but she did not
pull away.

He stood up and pulled her up beside him, his arm

circling her waist and holding her close to him. "Amanda," he whispered in a tone so tender it made her ache. She wanted to move closer, but she was afraid. Realizing her hesitation, he dropped his arm. Quickly he stepped back and began putting the picnic goods back into the basket. Then he stopped. "Amanda, the doctor has given me permission to move to Bath."

She stopped folding the cloth and looked at him, a hint of unease in her eyes. "When?"

"In the next day or two." He paused and then hurried on. "But I want you to visit me in Bath. You and Robert. Jeremy too if he wants to come. I'll ride back out here also." He took the cloth she handed him and tucked it away in the basket. "You will, won't you?" Although Amanda found several excuses, Drew was finally able to persuade her that visiting him in Bath was well within the bounds of polite behavior.

When she arrived at Drew's home in Lansdowne Crescent some days later, she was agreeably surprised at the size of the house. Its gates, high arches made of ornate ironwork, framed the entranceways. Drew apparently had been watching for her. Before the butler could do more than usher Amanda and Jeremy into the foyer, he was there, limping even less than he had been only days earlier. He hurried toward Amanda almost as if he planned to take her in his arms. Then he stopped short, a few feet away.

Amanda told herself she was pleased that he had not tried to pretend that their relationship was more than it was. But she had to admit that seeing him smile at her made her feel better. A short time later she was trying to remind herself that she was pleased to see him.

"What do you mean?" she asked as he seated her beside the teatray. He sent a warning glance at the servants, and she glared at him. Slowly, as though counting to herself, she prepared three cups of tea and had the footman distribute the first two.

Finally the servants were gone. Amanda turned to Drew again and asked, "What do you mean about entertaining?"

Drew took a sip of tea, followed by a bite of one of his favorite chocolate hazelnut cakes. Amanda just stared at him, not really patient but refusing to let Drew know that. Jeremy sat back in his chair, enjoying the sizzling glances that shot between the two of them. He consciously tried to make them forget his presence. He succeeded quite well.

When the silence had grown thick with tension, Amanda asked again, this time in tones so sweet and soft that Jeremy caught his breath and prepared for the storm to follow, "What do you mean by entertainment?"

Apparently Drew had read the signs accurately too, for he said quickly, "Oh, my mother suggested that since so many of my family will be making the trip to Bath as soon as the royal wedding is over, we would need to plan some parties—a Venetian breakfast, a few dinners, and a ball." His voice dropped lower and lower until his last words were little more than a whisper.

The ruse did no good, however. Amanda heard every word. "A ball?"

"Not a large one. Just for my family and yours and a few of your friends. Mama asked that I send her your list as soon as possible. She has already ordered cards printed."

Amanda stood up, the deep-rose-pink flounces of her carriage dress flaring around her. She walked across the room as though she were leaving and then returned to her seat again. "Why?"

Both Jeremy and Drew looked at her curiously. "Why what?" Drew asked.

"Why must we have all these things?"

Jeremy provided the answer. "You want everyone to think that this is a real marriage, or have you changed your mind?"

"No." Amanda clasped her hands tightly together.

Drew said quietly, "According to my mother, the announcement in the paper has created quite a stir. Apparently our families had quite given up on us."

"On me, you mean," Amanda said, her voice harsh. "As soon as I set up my own household, my mother's family forgot about me." She adjusted her ruff more precisely and traced the pattern of braid on her skirt and sleeve.

Drew made a conscious effort to divert her thoughts. "Let me have the housekeeper show you over the place. Grandfather was quite farsighted when he bought a double house here, so there should be enough room for whatever we plan. Mama, of course, has already begun planning the ball. She also told me to tell you that you were welcome to stay with her in London if you needed to visit a dressmaker."

Once more Amanda felt trapped in a runaway carriage. She simply smiled and nodded where appropriate. Finally realizing that she had merely been sitting there without saying anything, Drew quieted. He noted with dismay her folded hands and tightly pressed lips. He glanced at Jeremy as if seeking advice. Then he crossed to the bellpull.

"Tell the housekeeper Miss Desmond is ready to inspect the house," he said firmly, raising an eyebrow in question at Amanda. She nodded. As soon as the door closed after the footman, he crossed to Amanda's chair. He held out his hand. She put hers in his and stood. "Remember, the only reason we are doing these things is to protect Robert."

"And you," she reminded him.

"And me." He crossed his fingers surreptitiously. "Everything must seem as normal as possible. But I will try to eliminate as many activities as I can. We can use your mother's absence as an excuse and the royal wedding as another."

To his relief, she nodded.

After she had left with the housekeeper, Drew turned to Jeremy. "Thank you," he said sarcastically.

"For what?" Jeremy asked, his voice amused.

"For not helping me get out of that."

"You created the situation. I decided you could solve it. Drew, I would like to remind you what could happen when you push too hard." Drew paled. "She may have become less impulsive, but Amanda usually gets her own

back," Jeremy said, his voice half-serious, half-amused.
"Now, tell me more about what you have found out about
that girth."

Drew sat down across from him. "The groom I had
with me that day admitted that he did not sleep alone
that night. He said anyone could have damaged it."

"Then you think it was deliberate?"

"You saw the girth. What do you think?"

Jeremy tapped his fingers on the arm of his chair.
"Hmm. That poses some interesting questions. Do you
have any ideas?"

"Not really. Almost anyone had access to it."

"But who would want to hurt you?" Jeremy asked.
Drew raised his eyebrows suggestively. "All right. Who
would want to see you dead?"

Drew rolled his cane between his hands. "If I knew
that, I could find out why," he said. "With the announcement of the wedding, I may have forestalled any more
attempts."

"Are you going to tell Amanda?"

Drew looked at his friend in horror. "No."

Just then the door opened and Amanda entered. "I
decided to see the house more thoroughly some day after
your mother arrives," she said. "Your housekeeper and I
decided on two menus for those dinners you mentioned.
And, if you agree, I thought everyone could drive out to
the manor for a Venetian breakfast."

"You're sure?" Drew was actually asking more than one
question.

"Yes." Amanda looked at him, noting the worried
frown on his face. "After lunch I must visit a library. I
promised to find Robert a present. He wanted to come,
but he is behind in his lessons."

"You must bring him along next time. His governess
could not be so cruel as to separate us too long."

"Here! Here!" Jeremy nodded. "I never liked the
woman. The least she could have done was helped with
the nursing instead of remaining at the squire's where she
was visiting."

"Jeremy, you know Doctor Weston refused her permission to return. Besides, she spent most of the time at her mother's," Amanda said, her face disapproving.

Drew stepped in quickly. "What else do you want to do this afternoon?"

The rest of the visit was accomplished successfully. Over the next few weeks Drew and Amanda took turns making the journey from Applecroft Manor to Bath. They visited the Pump Room, where Drew drank a glass of the steaming water in spite of his protests. Because of the excitement in London, fewer people than usual were there. Those long-time residents of Bath, however, found countless reasons to approach the couple, exclaiming over the engagement.

One afternoon after she returned to her home following a visit to Bath, Amanda curled up in her chair, letting Jeremy pour the tea, much to the footman's dismay. "You would think that no lady my age ever married before," she said bitterly.

"Come now, Amanda. You must admit that you and Drew are not your typical couple," Jeremy said patiently.

"No, but we should be."

"What do you mean?"

"Jeremy, have you ever thought how much of a wrong we do to those young ladies of the *ton*?" She looked at him. "No, it is not what happened in Brighton talking. I promise you."

"Then what is it?"

"Consider most of the latest crop of young ladies. They are carefully protected—even from using their minds—and then are put in charge of homes, most with servants, and expected to run them competently. Humph! They are little more than babies themselves. They know the rules but not how to apply them."

"What do you suggest?"

"Let them have some time. Too many families insist on settling their daughters that first Season. Is it any wonder there are so many unhappy marriages?"

"But what are they to do in the meantime?" Jeremy asked, intrigued in spite of himself. "Most households already have someone in charge—the mother. Do you want her to abandon her reins?"

"No. that is not it at all. It just seems to me that there must be a better way—something like Grandfather did for me."

"But even he had reservations. If you had finished that second Season . . ."

"I know." Amanda sat up straight and looked at her hands.

Jeremy looked at her curiously. "If you are regretting the promise you made Drew, I am certain he will release you," he said hesitantly, knowing that Drew would have his head on a pike if he heard the offer.

Amanda was silent for a moment, making Jeremy hold his breath. Then she shook her head. "No." She curled back up again, getting comfortable. "I got a letter from my mother today."

"And?"

"She is overjoyed. Lord Ainsworth is arranging transport immediately and will be coming with her."

"He will?"

"Apparently someone was needed to make a report to the Regent. He volunteered."

"Prinny should like that. Weren't they good friends for a time?"

"Yes, but some time ago. The Prince's memory is not always very long. I hope his mission is successful. He will stay in London for a while, but Mama plans to come here directly." Amanda laughed at his curse. "You can always remain at Hedgefield."

"And if I do, she will complain every time she sees me." Jeremy looked so disgusted that Amanda laughed long and hard.

"You do know my mother," she admitted. "However, between insisting that I redo the plans for my wardrobe and for the wedding itself, I expect her to be fully occupied."

"When do you expect her?" he asked, his voice resigned.

"She was not certain. They planned to leave as soon as there was a suitable ship."

"That means she could be here today." Jeremy pulled himself out of his chair and headed toward the door. "I think I will visit Drew for a time."

"Coward," Amanda called after him. But in spite of that, she too decided to make some decisions on her own before her mother took over. She hurried up to her rooms and called for Jennings. "Have those fashion plates arrived from Madame Camilla?"

The maid nodded and brought the designs to her. Noting the fullness at the ankles and the wealth of flounces many of them contained, Amanda frowned. "I just ordered several new dresses from Madame Camilla. They look nothing like these."

"Now, Miss Amanda," her maid reminded her firmly, "you ordered those dresses — and quite becoming they are too — before the start of the Season. With all those comings and goings to Paris that Thompson has been reading about to us, there are bound to be changes." She paused and then asked a question designed to promote action in her mistress. "Is Lady Ainsworth bringing your wedding dress with her from Vienna?"

Amanda glared at Jennings, remembering full well the dresses her mother had chosen when Amanda was first out — white with white, white with silver, white with turquoise, endless white accompanied by demure pastels, and each covered with laces and bows that made Amanda feel as though she were a confectioner's delight spun out of sugar for the gentlemen's delight. Oh, she had not minded the first Season; everyone else was wearing similar clothing. But the next Season, when all she wanted was to sink into the obscurity of Hedgefield, her clothing drew attention. Her mouth thinned as she thought of the unwanted attention she would be forced to receive this time. She had been so eager to sign those agreements. Now she was once again the center of conversation. A gleam entered her eyes. "Give me pen and paper. If Mama expects me to be the demure bride-to-be, she has a surprise in store."

11

Even while Amanda was ordering a wardrobe of clothes she did not want and writing letters to acquaintances whose letters of best wishes poured in, some to people whose names she had almost forgotten, she found herself stopping, listening for voices. Even though she visited with Robert every day, she was lonely. He was back into his routine, carefully controlled by Nurse and the governess he had already decided he was too old for. The activities with which she had filled her time only weeks earlier seemed boring now. It was not as enjoyable riding with Robert because Drew was not making her laugh or flirting with her. Jeremy, too, had deserted her, spending much of his free time in Bath with Drew.

Amanda found herself yielding to temptation. Finding countless errands to be run, she made at least two and often more trips each week to Bath. Each time she arrived, Drew would meet her, often giving her advice on which ribbons would complement some silk she had found or which suede gloves set off a soft aqua carriage dress to perfection.

He too found errands to run. Amanda had to help him choose a waistcoat for the wedding, a task that required four visits to his tailor before he found just the right material.

On the weekends Drew deserted Bath for Hedgefield, usually arriving early on Friday afternoon. Most weekends involved dinner parties or routs, for those families who had chosen to remain in the country for the

Season enjoyed the opportunity of dashing off letters to their friends in London with details of the engaged couple's behavior.

After one such evening when she had had to endure countless questions from ladies that three months earlier had had little to do with her, Amanda issued an ultimatum. "No more dinner parties. I will develop nervous exhaustion or, or the measles, but I will not attend another of these functions."

"Have you forgotten the ball?" Drew asked, his voice rather cool. "My mother has already issued the invitations."

Jeremy sat back in the corner, waiting to see what would happen.

"Oh, I did not mean that. It is just these, these . . ."

"Gossips?" Jeremy asked.

Amanda nodded, the diamond stars pinned in her curls twinkling in the moonlight.

"I suppose Jeremy and I could go alone," Drew said, smiling at her.

"Maybe it would be easier if you were the one who made the refusals," Jeremy said to Drew. "You could always say your leg was bothering you."

"And when I was seen galloping across the countryside? What would they think then?" Drew asked.

"You would have to give up your visits to Hedgefield for a week or so."

Drew and Amanda exchanged looks of dismay, neither wishing to lose those peaceful moments. Later, after they had left Jeremy at Hedgefield, as they usually did, they sat in uneasy silence, each wishing the other would speak. Finally, Drew cleared his throat and said, "If you really wish to cancel the rest of our engagements, I will stay in Bath."

"No!" Fearing to reveal her own emotions, Amanda said quickly, "Robert would miss you. I will go. It is simply so hard to know how differently I am treated now that I am engaged." She turned to him, her face serious. "Before, I was a threat to their way of life. Now, all these women see me as one of them."

"You are Amanda Desmond, soon to be Lady Mainwaring. What they think of you does not matter."

"But it does. For years I convinced myself that I did not care what they said about me. And all the time I was lying to myself. I hated being the center of gossip. I still do. And what will they say when our marriage is annulled?" Her eyes were bright with tears.

Drew turned her into the corner of the seat so that she was facing him, and cupped her face with his hand, one finger softly stroking her cheek. "One day at a time, Amanda. That is all we can live. One day at a time. We will go ahead with our plans and deal with each new situation as we find it." He put a finger under her chin, forcing her to look up at him. "Right now all we need to worry about is getting ready for our marriage." His blue eyes held hers, promising her his support and something else. She drew a shuddering breath and nodded. Reluctantly, he pulled away and sat back, his hand clenching at his side.

Amanda moved to face forward once again. Then she put a hand on his arm. "Drew." He turned to face her, his face serious. "Thank you."

"For what?"

"For understanding what I have been going through. For listening to me without laughing at me."

He smiled at her, the kind of smile that lit up his entire face. He tucked her hand under his arm, pulling her closer to him. "It is my pleasure."

For the rest of the journey, they sat silently, their fingers laced. When the carriage rolled to a stop, Drew climbed down and handed her out of the carriage himself, his hands lingering on her waist. She swayed slightly toward him. Unable to resist the temptation even though he knew the servants were watching, he kissed her lightly and said, "Until tomorrow." He let her go and watched as she entered the house.

The rest of the weekend did much to restore Amanda's sense of purpose. After church on Sunday they had dined with Jeremy and spent the afternoon arguing good-naturedly about the games they were playing, games simple enough to include Robert.

The next week their simple life changed. With the royal wedding an accomplished fact, Drew's mother arrived in Bath. Summoned to renew her acquaintance with Lady Mainwaring, Amanda gathered all her courage and her most formal manners, ready for the inspection. The reserved elegant woman she was ready to face did not appear. Instead, she was swept up by an excited, loving woman who welcomed her with open arms.

"I had quite given up on him," Lady Mainwaring said as she led Amanda to the yellow satin settee. Amanda, in spite of feeling more and more trapped by her false position, smiled back at her. "Now, sit next to me and tell me everything." The older woman settled her lavender skirt about her and straightened the lace cap she wore perched on top of her piled curls.

"I am certain Drew has explained."

"Men! My dear, men never tell one the details. And I want to know everything."

Gallantly, Amanda tried. She answered more questions than she had ever thought possible. Just when she was about to rebel, Drew entered. Amanda smiled at him, relieved to have his support. Looking from her son to his betrothed, Drew's mother sighed happily and smiled.

Drew said firmly, "Mother, you have had her closeted in here for long enough. It is my turn now."

"Why, we have not even discussed the ball. And I did not tell her about members of the family that will be arriving within the week." Amanda begged him silently for rescue. "Besides, in my day an engaged couple was not allowed to be alone."

His mother still protesting, Drew swept Amanda from the sitting room to the library. "I am always saying thank you for rescuing me," she whispered as she san into a deep, comfortable leather chair.

"She didn't upset you, did she?"

"No. She was so welcoming, so friendly." Amanda leaned forward. "Drew, she will be so hurt."

He cut her off. "Amanda, remember our promise."

"One day at a time." She sighed and nodded, leaning back in the chair and closing her eyes. "But I really wish there were some other way."

Had she been looking at him at that moment, Amanda would have been surprised at the look of determination on his face, the possessiveness in his eyes as he watched her.

"How is Robert?" he asked, willing her to open her eyes and smile at him.

She opened her eyes, but she did not smile. "Drew, that man has changed his mind."

"Who? Robert?"

"No, Major Besley. He has decided that he will be 'derelict in his duty' if he gives Robert over to my care completely. He has taken rooms here in Bath so that he can 'get to know the lad better.' " She mimicked the man perfectly.

"When did you discover this?" Drew frowned, not pleased with the situation.

"Yesterday afternoon. He sent me a letter stating that he will arrive at the end of the week and wants Robert to stay with him." Again she sat forward in her chair, her face serious. "What am I to do? Robert says he will not go."

"I'll have a talk with the lad. And perhaps we can persuade the major that Robert would be more comfortable here." He paused. Then he said hesitantly, "Perhaps with my mother here, you could stay as well."

"But Lady Mainwaring mentioned that she was expecting more of your family. Surely I would be in the way."

Drew laughed heartily. "In the way? My dear, you are the reason they are descending on me like a cloud of locusts."

After a morning of questions from his mother, Amanda had more than she could bear. She stood up, her face flushed and anger in every line of her straight body. "This elaborate affair was not my idea. If you do not like the results of our arrangement, I will be happy to release you."

The words seared Drew. He stopped laughing and stood up. Crossing to her side, he put his hands on her waist. She twisted away from him. "Amanda," he pleaded. "Did I say I wanted out?" He crossed to stand behind her. She continued to stare sightlessly at the row of morocco-bound books in front of her, her heart beating heavily. "Amanda?" he whispered, his mouth close to her ear. A thrill raced through her. "Please look at me. If you don't want to stay in Bath, you don't have to. I only thought it would help Robert."

She turned slightly and then leaned back against the books in surprise when she realized how close he was to her. Her eyes grew wide, but not in fear. Her heart raced as Drew reached out and brushed a curl away from her forehead. His hand dropped lightly to her shoulder, and she found it hard to breathe. She stared at him silently for a few minutes. Then, acknowledging that she had reacted hastily, she said softly, "I will write to the major. If he agrees, Robert and I will join you for several days."

The worry that had plagued Drew disappeared. He smiled slowly, first with his eyes and then with his mouth. Before he thought about it, he reached out and pulled her into his arms, hugging her and twirling her in a circle. Amanda reached out and put her arms around his neck.

Neither of them heard the door open. Lady Mainwaring stopped just inside the door, her lips curved into a smile. But there was no smile to be seen when she said, "So this is the way the younger generation behaves."

Amanda pushed Drew away, but he refused to release her. He looked over her shoulder, frowning at his mother. "Go away, Mama."

"No, you outrageous man."

Amanda's face turned red. Giving up her struggle to be free, she hid against Drew's shoulder.

"Mama, leave this room at once. And next time knock before you enter."

"Well, if I must," Lady Mainwaring said with a sigh. "But I do so enjoy seeing you young people so happy." She smiled at them, a mischievous, twinkling smile. "Don't let him muss you too much, Amanda. Luncheon wil be served shortly." She closed the door behind her.

"Let me down," Amanda said firmly, pushing against him.

"Why? She's gone." He smiled down at her and tightened his arms, lifting her higher so that her eyes were level with his.

"You might hurt your leg."

"Lifting you?" His voice was amused.

"Drew, please put me down." Recognizing the pleading look in her eyes, he nodded and let her slide down his body until her feet touched the floor.

She stepped back hastily, as if afraid of the fire tingling through her veins. He breathed deeply and turned away, struggling to control his reactions.

"Drew, no one will believe us when we ask for an annulment if you continue to treat me this way," Amanda said., her voice full of regret she only halfheartedly acknowledged.

"Amanda, I did not mean to frighten you."

"Oh, you didn't." She blushed as she realized what she had said and whirled around to stare at the door. Drew grinned, the worried expression he had worn only moments earlier completely gone. "I mean, I know you would never harm me." She glanced back at him, frowning when she saw his grin. "But we have to think of the future." He started to say something, but she cut him off. "Now, shall we join your mother?"

"In a minute." He crossed to her side and carefully smoothed her curls back into place and adjusted her skirt. "Now, shall we go?"

Her face becomingly flushed, she swished out of the room.

With the major's reluctant agreement, Amanda and Robert took up residence in the house on Lansdowne Crescent that Thursday afternoon. After careful consideration the major had realized that unless he was to care for the lad personally and curtail his own evening entertainments, he would need to enlist the services of several servants. Amanda's suggestion saved him time and money.

Lady Mainwaring was delighted with Robert. "Call me Nana," she urged him, noting with pleasure his careful bow and correct greeting.

"Why?" Robert asked.

"When my son marries Amanda, we will be related. I have a grandson close to your age, and that is what he calls me. What do you think?"

Amanda held her breath as she watched Robert consider Lady Mainwaring's words. She was just about to say something when Robert asked, "He won't mind if I call you that too?"

"No." Lady Mainwaring smiled at him.

"Then I will." The older woman patted the settee, and he sat beside her. "I never had a grandmother before. What does a grandmother do?"

When the major was shown in a short time later, Robert and Lady Mainwaring were deep in conversation. But Robert, with Amanda's urging, greeted him politely but coolly. Lady Mainwaring inspected him closely, making him wonder if there were something wrong with a piece of his clothing. She frowned her disapproval when she learned that Robert would be gone until teatime. "You will see that he eats properly and takes a rest," she said in a tone that reminded Major Besley of the wife of his first commanding officer.

"Nana, I am not a baby," Robert protested.

"Nonsense, sir. You will not speak until you are spoken to. Now apologize to Lady Mainwaring," the major said sternly, frowning at Amanda.

"No, Robert," the older woman said gently. "I forgot you are not as young as my other grandson. Now give me a kiss and enjoy your day with the major," she said, glaring at the major and daring him to correct Robert again.

Robert kissed her and then Amanda. With one last look over his shoulder, he straightened up and marched out the door at the major's side.

"Major Besley, ha! More like Major Beastly," Lady Mainwaring said contemptuously. Her look of disgust made Amanda feel better. Drew leaned down and kissed his mother's cheek. "And what was that for?" she asked.

"For reminding that man that Robert is not his to criticize."

"Humph! As if I would allow that man to take advantage of a little boy." She turned to Amanda, the light of battle in her eyes. "Amanda, do not receive that man alone. I do not care for the way he watches you."

"Watches her?" Drew asked sharply, his eyes narrowing dangerously.

"Thank goodness your marriage was arranged before he appeared. He strikes me as a man with a frustrated plan."

Amanda shivered slightly. Drew noticed and put his arm around her shoulders protectively.

"He will soon grow tired of this role he is playing," Drew told her. "And whenever he comes to get Robert, I will make a point to be here."

Drew's predictions were absolutely correct. When Robert returned from his day, he was bubbling, but the major looked exhausted. "Manda, we walked down by the river. There are lots of ducks there. I chased one. And we had Sally Lunn cakes for tea. I had four."

"But those cakes make him ill," Amanda said, her face disapproving.

"I wish you had told me sooner," Major Besley said, his face a granite mask. "Then I might have been spared the embarrassment he put me through. I had to return to my lodgings for fresh boots."

"And he did not hold my head properly, Manda. I wanted you or Nurse, but he told me I was being childish."

Three pairs of accusing eyes turned toward the major, who was backing toward the door.

"He is only a child. Surely you know how a child exaggerates. Tell them, Robert, about how much fun we had," the major said, his words tumbling out like apples spilling from a basket.

Lady Mainwaring stood up, as regal and commanding as Amanda had ever seen her. She held out her hand. "With all the excitement I am certain you will be happy to take your leave, Major. We will see you at the ball and the wedding, won't we?" She continued to smile until he had left the room. Then she crossed to Robert. "Come along, young man. Tell me about those ducks you found." She ushered him out of the room.

A moment later Robert ran back in. "Will I have to spend another day with him, Manda?"

"We shall see, halfling," Drew said, his laughter well-hidden. Robert made a face and dashed out. "So you did not tell Major Besley that Robert was always ill when he ate those buns? Amanda, you have not forgotten any of your tricks."

"Tricks? I simply forgot." Amanda sounded hurt.

"Don't worry. I do not plan to tell the man."

"Maybe now he will think twice about living with a small child," she said, her tone smug.

Delighted by the return of the mischievous girl he had known eight years earlier, Drew laughed heartily. His laughter continued so long that Amanda began to laugh too.

When Jeremy entered a few minutes later, he stopped in astonishment. His questions created a fresh storm of laughter. Finally, Drew and Amanda sat down, holding their sides, as exhausted as if they had fought a battle. But they were also relaxed. Even when they tried to explain, Jeremy just stared at them. Finally, they gave each other a smile. Drew shrugged. He looked at Jeremy who said, "No don't explain. I do not think I want to know."

That evening when Drew and Amanda saw the major in the Upper Assembly Rooms, they were polite but reserved. Forcing themselves to look around the room

instead of at each other, they escaped the encounter
without bursting into laughter again. As the next set
formed, Drew bowed to Amanda, his dark looks
enhanced by the black and white evening clothes he wore.
His fine white stock held the only piece of color in his
outfit, a large sapphire that matched his eyes.

She curtsied, her silver net dress over a slip of rose
sarcenet forming a pool of color around her. Drew noted
a trifle anxiously the small puffed sleeves of silver net that
seemed perched on her shoulders, leaving her arms free.
Her neckline, although not as low as others in the room,
made him want to smother her in a cloak for the rest of
the evening. Rose-colored gloves and pearls completed
her outfit. As he had done earlier in the evening, Drew
decided that she would dance only with Jeremy or him.
He swept her to the floor.

Had he thought to tell Amanda his decision, she would
have been much happier as the dance drew to a close. She
noticed Lady Mainwaring seated near one of the doors
with Major Besley at her side, his eyes fixed on them. She
stiffened and almost missed a step. As Drew turned her in
the figures of the dance, he inspected the spot she had
been watching carefully. As soon as she came close to
him, he said quietly, "Jeremy told me that he wanted the
next dance with you."

"He does?" she asked, and looked at her cousin, who
was whispering compliments in his latest flirt's ear.

Drew moved her carefully around a patch of wax that
had fallen from one of the chandeliers overhead, his face
flushed. "That is what he said," Drew lied, knowing that
Jeremy would agree to help protect his cousin. Catching
his friend's eye, Drew motioned him to the spot where
they would finish the dance.

Between the two men and a few of the married men
Amanda trusted, her card was filled for every dance.
Only in the intervals did the major have a chance to
approach her. Even then he was kept at a distance by
Lady Mainwaring on one side and either Drew or Jeremy
on the other. As the servants rushed to replenish the

candles during one interval, the major approached again, glasses of lemonade in his hands. He handed them to the ladies. "Perhaps we could sit this dance out, Miss Desmond. You look a trifle flushed," he said bitingly. "I wish to discuss our ward."

Before Amanda could frame her own answer, Drew had her by the hand and was drawing her to the floor. "Her dance is promised." He smiled down at her. "Mama has asked that we make this the last one for the evening as she wishes to return home."

"Then perhaps I should call tomorrow morning," the major said, his jaw locked.

Amanda nodded, happy to postpone the confrontation, and gave herself over to the dance, the music, and Drew's hand on her waist.

12

Amanda was still slightly bemused when they arrived at the house on Lansdowne Crescent a short time later. That state did not last long. A groom was waiting with a message from Thompson. "My mother will be here when?" Amanda asked weakly.

"Tomorrow afternoon. Shall I order a carriage for you now, miss?" the groom said, his face impassive.

"Nonsense. Drew, tell your butler to arrange quarters for this man. Amanda, you go to bed. First thing in the morning will be soon enough to deal with this." One by one Lady Mainwaring sent them on their ways until only she and Drew were left in the entrance hall.

"Thank you, Mama," he said just before he kissed her on the cheek.

"Don't thank me yet. You have quite a way to go before your bride-to-be is ready to be a wife." He pulled up, a frozen expression on his face. "No, that look will get you nowhere. Handle her gently, son, and your marriage will be a success." she laughed ruefully. "Remember to treat her gently. She is not very comfortable around gentlemen."

As she walked up the stairs away from him, Drew marveled once again at how much his mother saw. Not for the first time he wished that he could tell her everything, to enlist her help.

The next morning it was Lady Mainwaring who helped Amanda with all the details of her departure. "No, you do not have to wait on the major. I am certain Drew and I can handle him as well as you." She glanced at her son, who nodded, his face not revealing the satisfaction that the interview would give him. "Robert will be down in just a short while, and then you may leave. How long has it been since you have seen your mother?"

Amanda smoothed an imaginery wrinkle in the aqua carriage dress she was wearing and straightened her gloves. "Last year after they returned from Brazil. She spent several weeks with me while Lord Ainsworth arranged for a house in Vienna."

Lady Mainwaring glanced at her curiously but held back her questions. Amanda's flat tone told her more than she wanted to know. "You will have to bring her into Bath so that we can renew our acquaintance. It has been years since I have seen her." Remembering the fluttering social butterfly Amanda's mother had been the last time they had met, Lady Mainwaring wondered at the difference between mother and daughter.

Just then Robert dashed down the stairs. "I am ready," he called from the landing. Before the footman who was following with his portmanteau could reach him, Robert mounted the banister and slid around the curve to the waiting group below. Amanda, her heart beating so hard she could feel it in her throat, stood frozen. Drew, on the other hand, moved rapidly and snatched the child off just before he crashed headlong into the decorative marble dolphin that topped the bottom newel post.

Drew held Robert by the shoulders so that the boy was eye to eye with him. "You are never to do that again! If you had hit your head on that marble, you could have died."

The excited flush in Robert's cheeks faded. He paled. "I didn't know."

Drew put him on the floor. "I know that, brat." He gave him a swat and sent him over to Amanda.

She reached out and hugged him convulsively, her face still white with strain.

"I am sorry," the child said, his eyes filling with tears.

"Apologize for frightening Lady Mainwaring. Then we

must go. But you are never, never to do that again."
Amanda's voice still was not quite steady.

Robert was about to protest when he saw Drew's face.
He hung his head and made his apologies.

As Drew handed Amanda into the carriage a few
minutes later, he whispered, "The lad was just trying to
impress us. He did not mean any harm."

Amanda smiled at him. "Thank you for what you told
him."

He held her hand for a moment before turning it over
and placing a kiss on her palm. "Send me word when you
wish me to present myself for inspection," he said
jokingly.

There was no humor in Amanda's words. "Come
tomorrow afternoon. Please, Drew."

He looked at her eyes and nodded.

Drew's frustration at not being able to relieve all
Amanda's worries made him much firmer with the major
when he appeared later that morning. He stood up as the
man entered. "Major Besley."

The major made his bow to Lady Mainwaring and
then took the seat Drew indicated. "Will Miss Desmond
be joining us shortly?" he asked, his voice carefully
neutral, although there was a vein of impatience that he
could not completely hide.

"She had to return to the country. Her mother is
arriving today." Lady Mainwaring smiled, but there was
a faintly patronizing tone in her voice. "Her stepfather is
one of the members of the mission in Vienna, you know."

"Then I shall bid you farewell. I will be in touch with
her later." The major stood up, ready to leave.

"Perhaps I should be the one with whom you hold the
discussion," Drew suggested, standing up also. He smiled
pleasantly, but his smile did not reach his eyes. They were
cold.

The major cleared his throat and sat down again,
adjusting his cuffs nervously. "I simply wished to tell her
my reservations. After promising the lad's father that I
would care for him, I feel it would be wrong of me to
break my word."

Drew and his mother exchanged glances. "But have you thought of the difficulties having the child with you would cause?" Lady Mainwaring asked, her voice concerned.

"Rank is so difficult to achieve in peacetime," Drew said quietly. "And having Robert with you would limit the assignments you could accept. Or did you plan to leave him with your family here in England?"

Ready for angry rejection of his suit, the major was taken back by their sympathetic understanding. He hemmed and hawed for a moment and then said, "I had not thought to take the lad with me. But I really hesitate to release him completely into Miss Desmond's care."

"Had you forgotten, Major, that Miss Desmond will soon be my wife? Then I can share the responsibility with her."

Gritting his teeth, the major smiled faintly. "I did worry about the lad's future when you have your own children, your lordship."

Drew settled back in his chair and stared at him for a moment. "Robert may not be my son by birth, but he will have no doubt of my affection."

"I already consider him my grandson," Lady Mainwaring said bitingly. "And do you have any doubt about Amanda's attachment to him?"

"No, no. She obviously dotes on the boy."

"Then what is the problem?" Drew asked quietly but firmly.

Major Besley adjusted his cravat. The arguments with which he had hoped to intimidate Miss Desmond had little effect on the people in front of him. He began another approach. "Lord Mainwaring, I am certain you can understand my concern. If Miss Desmond's cousin wishes to do so, he could beggar the lad. And given her affection for her cousin, I am not certain Miss Desmond would stop him."

Drew and his mother exchanged glances. He has discovered just how much the boy is worth, Drew thought. A frown creased his forehead. "Are you accusing Mr. Desmond of being dishonest?" he said. His eyes narrowed.

Quickly, the major tried to retrieve his advantage. "I simply thought it would be best if someone outside the family had some control over the lad's finances." He smiled ingratiatingly. "Perhaps we should let the courts decide."

"And the document you signed earlier?"

"I changed my mind after careful consideration." He smiled again, this time with a hint of smugness.

"You know, of course, that the case might take months to get on the docket. I am not certain your superiors will appreciate your need to remain in England." Drew smiled too, his eyes promising trouble.

The major drew his breath in sharply, not pleased by Drew's response to his threats.

"Shall we arrange a meeting with our lawyers to discuss it, Major?" Drew asked, his eyes gleaming dangerously.

"Or we can wait until Sir Reginald arrives. Perhaps he could arrange for the case to be heard soon after the wedding," Lady Mainwaring suggested.

"Sir Reginald?"

"The chief magistrate in London," Drew explained. "When shall I have my lawyer expect yours?"

Major Besley shifted nervously, remembering that his lawyer had advised caution. "Perhaps I have been somewhat hasty," he said. He cleared his throat. "Maybe a simple gentleman's agreement would work."

Drew looked at him so closely that the major felt he was being inspected by a spyglass. "I think this has gone too far for that."

"You must realize that all I wanted was what was best for the lad."

"I understand completely." The major felt the same frisson down his spine he felt before a battle. Drew looked at his mother, who got up and left the room. As soon as the door closed behind her, Drew stood up and crossed to stand behind the major's chair, leaning over the man who slid forward. "I think that I must demand a statement from you, sir."

"Demand? Now see here, your lordship."

"No, Major. You should realize whom you are dealing with. I will no longer tolerate your threats to remove the boy from my fiancée's care or your changes of mind. My lawyer has the documents we agreed on. If you try to renege on them, the action will be brought to the attention of your superiors. Do you understand?"

Deciding that his career was far more important than the possible control of a fortune he would have to fight for in court, the major nodded. He stood up, wanting to escape from Drew's brooding presence.

"I shall be happy to explain the urgent business that recalled you to London to Miss Desmond," Drew said smoothly as though nothing had happened. He smiled pleasantly. "Will we see you at the wedding?"

Nodding, the major made his escape, cursing his luck.

As Drew went to tell his mother what had happened, he breathed a sigh of relief. Now the worst problem he had to face was Amanda's mother.

Amanda was already dealing with that problem. She arrived at the manor to find it in a state of readiness, the silver gleaming and the rich woods glistening with beeswax.

"I prepared the suite of rooms that Master Jeremy occupied," the housekeeper told her, jingling her keys nervously. Lady Ainsworth's visit last year had not been peaceful. "And several boxes arrived for you from London. I had them put in your room." She stood quietly as her mistress stripped off her gloves, spencer, and hat and handed them to a waiting footman.

"Is Aunt Elizabeth going to stay long?" Robert asked as he made his way up the stairs.

"Just until the wedding. Robert?" He turned to look at Amanda, the expression on his face full of dismay. "I will have Cook send you up something special for luncheon. Then you can join us for tea." He nodded and headed up the stairs again, muttering to himself.

"Come into my sitting room, Mrs. Thompson. I think we should consider several alternatives for this evening's meal." By the time they had the menus prepared for the next two days, Amanda's head had begun to ache. Requesting that a light luncheon be brought to her room, she too headed upstairs. There she found Jennings inspecting the contents of the boxes.

"The last of the dresses from Madame Camilla has arrived," the maid explained as she inspected a sky-blue muslin afternoon dress with a shirred bodice, a wide lace collar, and Marie sleeves banded with lace. She frowned as she noted the alternating flounces of lace and eyelet that completed the skirt. "Somehow this does not look long enough. Your ankles would be showing," the maid complained.

"If that is the case, we will simply add another flounce," Amanda told her. Remembering some of the gowns she had seen in Bath, she doubted that the dress was too short for the latest fashion. "Did my wedding . . . Oh."

Jennings unpacked the white muslin gown carefully. Made following the design they had seen on one of the fashion plates, the gown was a soft white muslin hand-embroidered with tiny white silk roses. It had sleeves puffed at the shoulder that tapered to the wrist. The bodice was cut low, with a tucker, its lace made of silk like the roses. The front of the skirt hung straight from the high waist but the back was fuller and had a demi-train.

"Just the thing, Miss Amanda. And here is your bonnet." Jennings pulled out a white satin village hat, its upturned brim decorated with white satin roses.

Amanda ran a hand lingeringly over the rich satin. "Leave it out. My mother will wish to see it." She laughed ruefully as she remembered how long it had taken her to decide on the material. She had been determined to wear blue. But it had turned out beautifully. And it was the only completely white outfit in her wardrobe.

By the time she had finished her luncheon and inspected the rest of her clothes, she was ready for the message that arrived a short time later. "Mr. Thompson said to tell you that a carriage has been sighted, miss."

The maid's eyes widened when Amanda paled.

"Tell him I will be right there." Amanda took one last look in the glass and hurried downstairs.

Her mother was the same as usual, a fact that always amazed Amanda, who was waiting for her mother to stop her fluttering yet determined ways.

"Darling," Lady Ainsworth gushed. "You must tell me everything. Your engagement is the talk of London and Vienna. And to think that I had quite given up on you. Tell me everything immediately." She turned toward the mirror and removed her large bonnet with its white lace veil designed to protect her complexion. She lifted it off carefully so that she did not disturb the high-piled curls underneath. "I do hope you are wearing a veil when you get out into the sun," she said, cutting off Amanda. "Sun is so dangerous to the complexion." She inspected herself closely in the mirror and smoothed one spot on her cheek. She turned around quickly, the mauve silk skirts of her traveling dress whirling around her. She took Amanda's hand. "Now tell me everything."

Once again, Amanda began the story she and Drew had decided on. To her surprise, her mother was much less critical than she had been in the past, simply raising an eyebrow when Amanda explained about Drew's fall and the measles.

"Well, I am pleased you made the most of your opportunities, darling. Now you simply must see the gowns I have brought you. I insisted that we return home by way of Paris instead of by ship. I knew my daughter had to have a dress by Leroy. It is not quite your usual style." She whisked Amanda up the stairs, hesitating only momentarily until Amanda pointed the way. "I told my dresser to unpack it immediately." As they entered the room, the dresser was just unfolding one dress on the bed. Of a light transparent silk over matching satin, the light lemon-yellow seemed to catch the light and glow. Its bodice, cut so low that the puffed sleeves rested on the very edge of the shoulder, was deeply décolleté and edged with grosgrain ribbon braided around puffs of silk. A small lace ruff edged with matching ribbons extended between the shoulders and slightly above them. The band under the bodice was crossed in front, and the skirt ended in deep flounces also trimmed in silk ribbon. Matching yellow kid gloves and slippers completed the outfit.

"Well, do you think you can find an occasion to wear it?" her mother asked a trifle anxiously.

"An occasion? Oh, Mother, it will be perfect for Lady Mainwaring's ball."

Her mother beamed proudly.

To Amanda's surprise, the days began flying past. Drew and her mother got along very well. Robert, especially when he learned the major had returned to London, was a model of polite behavior. In spite of a bit of coolness between them at first, Lady Mainwaring and Lady Ainsworth made their peace. Even Drew's relatives were less fearsome than Amanda had expected.

Although both Amanda and Jeremy had offered to open their homes to Drew's relatives, he had refused, electing instead to lease two houses in Laura Place for those who did not have a residence there. "With the hills between, they will find it more enjoyable to spend their time at the Pump Room or the shops than in Lansdowne Crescent. My younger cousins can take themselves to an inn."

Those younger cousins promptly followed Drew's example, forming a coterie of gallants around Amanda whenever she visited. Maybe because they were so young, she felt no fear in their company. But Drew took no chances. Before he allowed anyone to dance with her at the Assembly Rooms or to help her to her mount, he inspected him carefully, noting the slightest feeling of revulsion from Amanda and quietly warning the man away. Amanda was unaware of his actions. Jeremy, however, smiled and provided his assistance.

Although some members of Drew's family were as tiresome as her own family, when Amanda met Drew's sister, she realized that she had found another friend. Mary was only two years older than Amanda and had a son two years younger than Robert. Like Drew she had black hair and blue eyes. But while his eyes danced with mischief, hers were darker, sadder.

When Mary's husband arrived the day before the ball, Amanda discovered the reason for that sadness. "Mr. Van Courtland," the butler announced to the group assembled for tea. The cup that Mary had been handing to Amanda began to clatter against its saucer. Amanda took it quickly and looked toward the door. The man who stood there was not quite six feet tall. When Drew stood to welcome him, he seemed to shrink. His face, as white as any woman's, had deep lines from his nose to his mouth. His eyes, a pale gray, darted from one person to another as if taking their measure.

"A family party," he drawled. "How delightful." His thin lips never lost their slight sneer.

As Drew made the introductions, Amanda held out her hand politely. But she could not control her involuntary shiver as his mouth touched her hand. Drew's mouth tightened ominously.

"I thought you said you were not coming," Mary said quietly when he took his seat beside her.

"What? And miss this delightful addition to our family? Nonsense." He smiled and took a cup of tea.

Amanda had to fight the urge to make her excuses and leave. She blessed the stubbornness that had made her refuse to spend that night in Bath.

Later when they were driving back to the manor, her mother said suddenly, "I cannot imagine why the Fairleighs would choose a man like that for their daughter."

"Perhaps she did the choosing," Amanda suggested.

"If she did, it is as good an argument for arranged marriages as I have ever seen."

Although Amanda laughed lightly, she had to agree.

Her uneasiness was even more pronounced the next evening at the ball. As she stood beside Lady Mainwaring in the receiving line, Amanda was aware of Van Courtland's eyes on her almost continuously. She shivered.

Drew finished greeting the person in front of him and

looked around the room speculatively. His eyes hardened when they saw his brother-in-law. The man smiled mockingly and held up a glass of champagne as if in a toast.

"That man doesn't like you, Drew," Jeremy said quietly as he moved through the line.

Drew nodded. "Amanda's card is filled, but if you have any dances free, I would appreciate your keeping an eye on my sister," he said in a whisper.

Jeremy nodded and walked toward Mary.

As soon as the first crush had been welcomed, Drew bent down to Amanda. "Mama has arranged that several waltzes be played. Your mother told her the dance was all the rage in Vienna." He handed her a filled dancing card. "I have reserved them all for myself."

"And these others?" She looked in amazement at the names written there, but she had to admit that none of them was objectionable to her.

"You promised them dances. At least they told me you did," he said, a smile lighting his eyes.

Lady Mainwaring turned toward them. "The musicians are ready to begin the first set. Take your places."

Glad to be free, they quickly made their escape, forming a set with Jeremy and Mary. That set was the true beginning of the evening.

Amanda found that she enjoyed dancing again. If she was not entirely comfortable with anyone but Drew and Jeremy, at least she was not afraid. And waltzing with Drew, his hand on her back and her face close to his heart, was thrilling.

"Did I tell you how lovely you are?" Drew asked as he twirled her around the room.

She looked up, her eyes sparkling like the diamonds in her hair and around her neck. "Several times." She lowered her eyelashes coquettishly. "But it is something a lady never tires of hearing." Drew laughed heartily and pulled her closer. She pulled back and looked at him reprovingly. "What will all these people think?" she asked. Drew simply smiled.

Jeremy smiled too. He turned to his companion and said, "That is a very well-matched couple."

Mary smiled, but not with her eyes. "I certainly hope so." Her eyes searched the room until they found the person she was looking for, her husband. His eyes were fixed on the couple in the middle of the floor, and he was frowning.

Jeremy followed her gaze and noticed him too. He carefully hid his disquiet behind a mask of disinterest, turning back to his partner. "Why did you leave your son at home?" Jeremy asked. "He could have been the perfect companion for Robert."

"I can tell that you have forgotten how bigger boys hate to have younger ones tagging along behind," Mary said, her eyes happier than they usually were.

The rest of the evening slid by rapidly. Having seen the last of their guests to the door, the two families smiled at each other sleepily and headed for their rooms. Just before she left the room, Drew took Amanda's hand and pulled her back into the ballroom, where sleepy servants were extinguishing the guttering candles.

"Drew," she protested laughingly.

"One last dance." He swept her into his arms and around the floor, holding her closely against him. He hummed a waltz in her ear.

"Drew! What will the servants think?"

He reversed, bringing her back to the door again. He turned one last time and let her go. He took her hand and kissed her palm. "Good night, my lady," he whispered.

13

The days between the ball and the wedding seemed to fly by, bringing Amanda closer and closer to an event she was not certain she could go through with. As long as she was with Drew, Amanda was calm. Away from him, her fears built walls between them.

After a meeting with the bishop to discuss the service, Amanda tried to tell Drew how she felt. "I don't think I can make those promises when I know that I have no intention of keeping them. I feel as though I'm lying."

"But you do mean them. You do intend to marry me?" he asked, his face grim at the thought of losing her at this point.

"Yes." He smiled. "But not for 'till death do us part.' "

Drew pulled his curricle to a halt. He turned toward her. "Do you remember those papers we signed?"

"Yes." Amanda looked at her hands tightly clasped in her lap.

"Then perhaps you should remember the other alternative."

Her eyes grew wide. "What?"

"If after six months neither of us asks for annulment, the marriage will be permanent."

"Permanent? But you don't want to be married. That's why you are marrying me!" She gazed at him, amazement in every line of her face.

"People change. You and Robert have come to mean a great deal to me." He smiled down at her, letting her see his emotions clearly for the first time. "You aren't afraid of me, are you?"

Amanda shook her head, still startled by the idea. "Permanent?"

He nodded and signaled his horse to continue.

As Amanda made her final preparations for the wedding, more and more she thought of what Drew had suggested. When they were together, he noticed her watching him when she thought he was not looking. But she was more nervous too, jumping when he put his hand on her waist. Had he known that the minute he took it away she longed for it back, he would not have felt so much despair.

Finally the day arrived, all sunshine and blue skies. With her only attendants Mary and Robert, Amanda started up the long aisle, trembling so much that Lord Ainsworth looked at her in concern. The closer she got to the altar and Drew, the more she trembled. Her mother and Lady Mainwaring smiled at her as she passed them, but Amanda had her eyes fixed on the tall figure in blue standing beside the bishop.

Drew had watched her from the first moment she had begun to walk up the aisle. The bright morning sunlight flooded the church with a radiance that made the silk roses on Amanda's dress gleam. Though other people might bemoan the lack of stained-glass windows in the abbey, to Drew that clear sunlight was the perfect accompaniment for his bride. As she approached the altar, he stepped out to meet her, his eyes a deep blue like his coat.

Lord Ainsworth gave Amanda's hand to Drew and stepped back. Amanda swayed and turned even paler. Drew stepped closer, allowing her to lean against him slightly. She raised her eyes to his, noting his look of concern. Gradually, she gained control, managing a smile for Robert and Jeremy and, at last, for Drew.

As the bishop began the service, Amanda tried to forget how temporary the marriage might be. She focused on the flickering flame of a tall candle. But when

Drew made his first response, she looked up into his eyes. Slowly but clearly, he made his promises to her, his eyes holding hers. Her vows were little more than a shaky whisper. Resolutely, she tried to push her tears and guilt into the background, to feel secure in the warmth of his gaze.

That effort helped her endure the congratulations that followed at the wedding breakfast. The combined kitchens of three households provided a meal that became the mark by which all other wedding breakfasts in Bath were measured. There were soups—one a clear broth and one a cream—trout and lobster, barons of beef, ham and capons dressed with green peas and salsify, salad greens dressed in the French fashion, and all manner of vegetables and sauces. When the last remove was presented, the wedding cake created a stir. The rich fruit cake was covered with the usual marzipan frosting, but on top of that rested two exquisite white doves of spun sugar, their beaks holding a white sugar ribbon and their wings spread as if they had just fluttered to the top of the cake. Amanda hesitated for a moment as if unwilling to mar its perfection. Then Lady Mainwaring laughed happily, breaking the spell. "I think we may have started a fashion," she whispered to Lady Ainsworth.

The toasts made, Amanda and Drew made final preparations to leave for their week alone. They were going to a small estate on the coast, the visit a wedding present from one of his cousins. Amanda had tried to convince Drew that the trip was unnecessary, but he refused to concede.

While he kissed his mother, Amanda made her own farewells. She embraced her mother warmly and smiled her thanks at her stepfather.

"Now, darling, do promise me that you will insist that Drew bring you to Vienna. Unless, of course, you are increasing. I do hope you and Drew have a baby right away," her mother said, ignoring her blushes.

The words reminded Amanda of her mother's graphic description of a wife's duties and the pleasures of a marriage bed. She paled.

Hurriedly, Amanda turned away. Finally she stood before Jeremy and Robert. Her cousin reached down and pulled her into his arms. "Remember, brat, that you trust Drew," he whispered. "And if you need me I am here." Then he stepped back, his smile reassuring.

Robert, though pleased by the fact that Drew was now part of his family, was not certain he liked the idea of staying with Jeremy. His chin wobbled as he asked, "When will you be back?"

"In a week. I promise," Amanda said, hugging him. Drew nodded and held out his arms. Robert rushed into them. Amanda cleared her throat and blinked back her tears. "You obey Jeremy, pixie. Do you understand?" Then together she and Drew walked toward the carriage.

There in the entranceway were Mary and Van Courtland, his eyes as mocking as ever. "What's this? You are not traveling in your own coach?" Van Courtland asked. His eyes narrowed sinisterly.

"We decided to use Amanda's so that mine would be free for Mama and Mary," Drew explained, wondering why it made any difference. He handed Amanda into the carriage. Then he kissed his sister and shook Jeremy's hand.

As the coach pulled away, something in Van Courtland's manner caught Jeremy's attention. He watched, his lips in a straight line, as the man gripped Mary's arm, forcing her to return to the house. He followed slowly, determined to find out more about him.

While everyone in Lansdowne Crescent relaxed and made plans for their own departures or for an evening's entertainment, the atmosphere within the coach was tense. Amanda had realized finally that she was truly married to Drew. She sat stiffly upright, her back inches away from the gray satin upholstery, not certain what to expect but filled with fear. Drew made himself comfortable in the opposite corner, holding the straps as the coachman guided the team over the hilly streets. After one terrible jolt that had thrown Amanda against him, she jumped back as if she had been burned.

Drew said in his calmest voice, "I suggest you hold on."

Amanda started, but she did move into the other corner and took the other strap. She looked at Drew from under her lashes but turned away as he tried to get her to meet his eyes. She shivered as she remembered what her mother had suggested she do to make the journey more enjoyable.

In spite of wanting to reach out and pull Amanda to his side, Drew simply lay back and closed his eyes. Although he did not intend to go to sleep, he could watch Amanda from under his lashes. He noted with satisfaction the way she finally leaned back and snuggled into the corner. Her tension slipped from her as she dropped off to sleep.

When she woke up some time later, the tension returned immediately. She glanced around the carriage, her eyes wide with fear. What if he behaved like that other man had done? Or what if he expected her to act the way her mother had described? Her heart beat so hard she could hardly breathe.

Drew reached out a hand to soothe her. She jumped back in fear, cringing in the corner of the carriage. He tried to control his temper, but it was too much. "Damn it, Amanda. Don't do that!" She paled. He said more gently, "I promise that I will not hurt you." He sighed deeply. "Have I kept my promises in the past?" She nodded, still trembling. "Then, what caused this?"

Amanda blushed. She looked at her hands, clasped tightly in her lap. Shifting nervously, she whispered, "Nothing."

"Nothing? Amanda, it is obvious that something or someone has caused you to distrust me. Now, who or what was it?" Although he was concentrating diligently on making his voice as soothing as possible, a note of steel set in.

That note made Amanda stiffen. For the first time since leaving Bath, she glared at him, her eyes meeting his. "The problem is mine."

"Very well, your ladyship." Drew bowed his head

slightly, tilted his hat over his eyes, leaned back in the corner, and closed his eyes again.

Amanda stared at him angrily, willing him to sit up and talk to her. Instead, he began to snore. For a few minutes she simply glared at him, then a tiny smile tilted her lips, followed by a soft laugh.

When her laughter had faded to giggles, Drew sat up, abandoning his pretense of sleep. "That is better."

"Better than what?" Amanda asked, trying to frown at him but failing miserably.

"Better than seeing you sit there and shake as if I were going to pounce on you at any moment," he said. His voice was dry.

"Well, how was I to know. Mother said—"

"Oh! Now I understand." He smirked. "Your mother gave you the usual mother-to-daughter talk. I remember how confused Mary was after hers."

"She was not talking to my mother. Mother believes in complete candor." Amanda blushed and shut her eyes.

Drew leaned forward and whispered in her ear, "Tell me what she said so I can tell you if it is correct."

"No!" Amanda pulled back into her corner again, her heart racing partly in fear and partly in anticipation.

Drew leaned back and smiled wickedly. "Shall we make a small wager?" he asked.

"A wager?"

"You sound just like a parrot. I will bet you a pair of diamond earrings against . . ." He paused dramatically, a wicked light in his eyes. "Against one hundred kisses that you will tell me eventually."

"Never!"

"Then what harm is there in the wager? Would you rather have emeralds?"

Amanda closed her eyes for a moment and then glanced at him from under her lashes. "No tricks?"

"I promise." He sat up and took her hand, his face serious. "I do keep promises. Remember that, lady wife."

Amanda nodded and sat back. She did not, however, take her hand from his.

The rest of the journey, indeed the rest of the honeymoon, proved much different than what Amanda had
feared. Decreeing that she needed rest after the strains of
the last few months, Drew ordered Amanda to sleep late
each morning. He planned to spend those hours fishing
or riding about the countryside. Amanda, however, had
different ideas. The first morning she sneaked out to the
garden, almost running into Drew when she was
returning. The second morning, dressed in her burgundy
habit, she was tiptoeing down the hall to the stairs when
she felt a strange shiver run down her spine. She stopped
and turned around.

Drew was leaning against the door frame of his room,
his Hessians gleaming and his eyes sparkling. "Just where
did you think you were going?"

"For a ride." She stood up as tall as she could, but she
still felt tiny next to him.

"You are supposed to be resting."

"It's boring. I want to be outside."

Biting back the suggestive remark he was about to
make, Drew smiled. He held out his arm. "Then let us go
together."

For the rest of their stay they walked along the rocky
beach, fished in the streams, rode about the countryside.
The last afternoon as they sat on boulders along the
shore, Amanda watched Drew skipping stones across the
waves, the muscles in his shoulders rippling with each
throw. She said wistfully, "I have never been able to learn
to do that."

"It's all in the wrist."

"That is what Jeremy said. But I could never get it
right."

"Come here. I'll show you."

Standing in the circle of his arms a few minutes later,
Amanda felt none of the fear she had lived with so long.
Instead, every inch of her skin seemed alive and tingling.
Pulling a flat stone from his pocket, he handed it to her,
helping her arrange it so that her fingers held it precisely.
Then he leaned down so that his arm was behind hers,

holding her wrist lightly. He closed his eyes briefly, breathing the scent of roses that always seemed to cling to her. Amanda tried to ignore her racing heart and concentrate on following his directions.

"Pull your arm back like this. That's right. Now let it fly." They watched gleefully as the stone skipped once, twice, three times before it sank.

"I did it!" Amanda swung around, her face glowing. She stopped, still as a bird watching a worm.

Drew smiled down at her from only inches away. "I think your instructor deserves a reward."

"What kind of reward?" She knew she should back away but was reluctant to do so.

"A kiss?" His tone suggested that he was joking, but his eyes were serious.

Before she had a chance to grow frightened, she stood up on her toes and kissed him. She had meant for it to be light, much as she would give Robert, but their lips touched and then parted. Not really conscious of what she was doing, she put her hands on his shoulders. His hands lightly clasped her waist.

Breathless, she pulled away, her eyes wide, her breasts heaving.

Drew walked over to a boulder nearby and sat down. His emotions on a tight leash, he smiled at her and said, "With a little more practice, brat, you will be very good at that."

"What?" Amanda's turbulent emotions found a quick outlet. She ran toward him, "Why, you, you . . ."

She raised a hand to slap him when he grabbed her and put her on his lap. He kissed her quickly, lightly this time. "You are improving already. But I had better be the only one you practice on."

She pulled away again, her anger dissolving. "I will not make any promises," she said. She headed up the beach toward the house, swinging her hips saucily.

"Amanda?"

"Yes?" She half-turned toward him and stopped short, surprised by the serious look on his face.

"Nothing. Wait for me. I am ready to change for dinner, too."

"Food. That's all you think about." Expecting an answer, she glanced at him and then blushed at the look in his eyes. She picked up her skirts and ran ahead.

Later as she was bathing, she thought about the past week. All her fears had been for nothing. Of course, they had not been intimate, not the way her mother had described. But as she thought of their kisses that afternoon, she still tingled.

Dinner that evening was a time of shared glances, smiles, a blush or two, but little talking. It was almost as though both of them were afraid to say anything to spoil the mood, the sparkle between them. Neither Drew nor Amanda could ever tell anyone what they had eaten. For them the world danced in laughing hazel eyes and sparkling blue ones. Finally the butler asked, "Shall I serve your tea in here, your ladyship?"

Amanda blinked once or twice and shook her head. She rose and went into a small sitting room nearby.

The interruption gave Drew a jolt. Things were moving too fast. And Amanda was not ready to make any permanent commitments. Her skittishness that afternoon told him that. Even so, he wanted to be with her. "There is always the trout stream," he said aloud, remembering the cold waters.

Knowing that they would be leaving the next day added a poignancy to the evening. Neither of them wanted it to end. They played a game of chess but more often than not found their fingers tangled together. Finally, the candles guttering low, they walked up the stairs side by side but not touching. They stopped in front of her door.

"What time shall we leave tomorrow?" Drew asked, more to delay their parting than any real concern.

Amanda leaned back against the door, her head tilted so she could see his face. "I am not certain how long a journey it is. I slept part of the way," she said, a tiny smile playing around her mouth. "But we did tell Robert we would see him before supper."

Drew nodded. "Can you be ready by nine?"

"Jennings is almost finished with my packing already. After this is added, there will be little left to do tomorrow." She held out her bright-green skirt and made him a curtsy.

"I like that dress. It makes your eyes look like emeralds," Drew told her once again. A hint of mischief danced in his eyes. He bent his head and kissed her, deepening it until her lips parted to allow him to enter. He moved away slightly, "Did your mother tell you about that?" he asked in a whisper, his breath sending pleasant shivers down her neck.

"Yes." Then she pulled back abruptly. Her eyes took on a calculating look. "You do not want me to have those earrings, do you?"

He shrugged and laughed. "I would rather have your kisses." He was still laughing a few minutes later when he collected a towel and a robe and headed for the stream.

Refreshed by his cold swim, Drew finally managed to fall asleep. Amanda was not as lucky. The minute she dozed off, she was in his arms, feeling those kisses again. Waking up once again after reaching for Drew, Amanda finally lit a candle and opened the novel by her bed-side.

That restless night provided Amanda the perfect way to pass the journey. Almost before the carriage pulled away from the door, she was asleep, her head lolling back on the cushions. Less afraid of startling her this time, Drew untied her bonnet, throwing the straw decorated with cherry ribbons on the seat in front of him. He arranged Amanda's head on his shoulder, running his fingers through her short curls. Before long, he too drifted off to sleep.

When Amanda awoke, she was startled to find herself curled against Drew. He had propped himself in the corner and had moved the opposite footrest into place so that he was lying diagonally across the carriage and she was curled up on the seat beside him, her torso resting on his. Gently, she tried to pull away, but he had a hand tangled in her curls. His arm around her waist tightened.

Giving up the struggle, she closed her eyes again and nestled closer.

The next thing she heard was his voice. "Wake up, Amanda. We are almost there." She sat up and blinked her eyes sleepily, slightly confused. Had it been a dream and had she been asleep in this corner the whole way? She refused to believe that, noting Drew's crushed cravat and wrinkled waistcoat. "Amanda? Are you awake?"

She sat up straighter and reached for her bonnet, settling it on her curls in a rather haphazard fashion. "I am sorry I was such a boring traveling companion." She smiled at him.

He reached out to smooth the imprint of a flower from her face. His smile, like hers, promised things they were not yet ready to speak. "You were not boring at all."

Before she had time to ask him what he meant, they had pulled to the entrance of Hedgefield. There on the steps stood Jeremy and Robert.

Jumping up and down in his excitement, the boy dashed down the steps and into the carriage as soon as the footman opened the door. "Guess what? I had an adventure!"

14

"Let them get out, Robert. We will tell them about your adventure when they are more comfortable." Jeremy lifted the boy down. He stood back while Drew helped Amanda descend, inspecting his cousin closely. He noted the way their fingers touched while they were standing side by side and gave a sigh of thanksgiving. "I think you should plan to stay here for supper this evening," he suggested.

"Then this 'adventure' was serious?" Amanda asked, taking Robert by the hand.

Jeremy gave his head an almost imperceptible nod and looked at Robert. Amanda smiled, acknowledging his warning.

Once they were comfortably seated in the gold drawing room, Jeremy said, "Tell them your story, Robert."

His face lit up with excitement, Robert told them every detail. "It was on Thursday. Nana and Aunt Mary, she told me to call her that, Manda, took me with them to visit one of their friends. She has a little boy about my age, Aunt Mary said. But I never got to meet him."

"Why?" Drew and Amanda asked. They exchanged worried glances.

"That is the exciting part." He paused to see if they were really listening. "Cousin Jeremy and I had come into town to see if Nana wanted to visit Hedgefield, but she had to go to the country instead. So I got into the carriage with them. Cousin Jeremy missed all the excitement."

Patiently, trying not to let her anxiety show, Amanda asked, "What kind of excitement?"

Robert's eyes grew big. "We were going real slow. I wanted Nana to tell them to spring the horses, but she told me there were too many carriages. And there was a little hill, not like the one to the Assembly Rooms, much smaller."

Recognizing a master storyteller who could spend hours spinning a tale out, Drew looked at Robert. "Either you tell us what happened, halfling, or we will let Jeremy tell us."

"I was just about to," Robert said reproachfully. "We hit a bump, and something happened. The horses went one way, and we rolled down a little hill. I told Aunt Mary and Nana to be brave, and someone would rescue us. And they did!" He beamed proudly. "I even got a bump." He raised his hair and showed them a small blue mark on his forehead. "Nana said I was her little soldier."

"How exciting!" Amanda's voice was weak. "Let me see that bruise a little closer." Putting her arm around his shoulder, she led him away.

As soon as the door closed behind them, Drew turned to Jeremy. "What about the others? Was anyone else hurt?"

"Your mother and sister are bruised but fine. They left yesterday for London but plan to return after the Season is over. Your coachman, unfortunately, was more seriously injured. He held on to the reins, trying to control the team, and was dragged a way." Jeremy crossed to a table where a decanter and glasses sat. "Brandy?"

Drew shook his head. "What happened? From your tone I suspect it was no accident."

"It wasn't. Someone had filed away a part of the axle. The slightest strain and it was designed to snap. If you had taken it instead of Amanda's . . ."

"Amanda and I would have had the 'adventure.' "

"But on steeper hills it would have been more serious."

Drew stood up and crossed to the mantle feeling as

though he wanted to hit someone. "Who would want to harm my family?" he asked, his face bitter.

"Remember that girth, old man. It was *your* carriage. I think the time has come to find professional help."

"The Runners?"

His friend nodded. "Now that you and Amanda are safely home, I think I will make a quick trip to London myself."

Amanda stood in the door to the room, her face disapproving, "Missing your ladies already, Cousin?" she asked sweetly.

Jeremy looked at Drew. He shook his head. "That is as good an excuse as any," he drawled.

"How are your mother and sister, Drew?" Amanda asked anxiously, pointedly ignoring Jeremy.

Quickly Drew filled in the details, deliberately omitting their suspicions.

"Has anything else happened that I should know about?" Amanda asked, crossing to stand beside her husband.

"Your agent wishes to speak to you. And the major dropped by to say he would be seeing you before he sailed."

"Botheration."

"My thoughts exactly," Jeremy told her dryly.

After having a light supper, they collected Robert and his esssentials and headed toward the manor.

"Where are we going to spend the summer?" Amanda asked curiously, realizing that during the week alone they had never discussed their immediate future.

"I thought that until we make some kind of decision, you would be happier at the manor." He smiled at her, and hs eyes told her what he hoped her decision would be.

"And where will you be?" Her voice was sharper than she had intended. Quickly she looked at the floor of the carriage as if memorizing the way the boards fit together. She held her breath waiting for his answer.

"Why, with you and Robert. Mama and Mary have asked if they may use the house on Lansdowne Crescent this summer, but if you prefer to live in town, I will tell them no."

"Will Aunt Mary's little boy come too?" Robert asked.

"Yes."

"Good. I never had a cousin before, 'cept Cousin Jeremy and Manda, and they're too old."

"Too old for what, halfling?" Drew asked. Amanda had covered her face, trying to hide a laugh. How Jeremy would resent that statement.

"Too old to play with me. Do you think he likes puppies and kittens? Will he bring his pony?"

Amanda realized that the questions were but the first in a long line. "When he arrives, you may ask him," she said quietly. "Now, tell me what else happened while I was away."

Robert rattled on happily for a few minutes, detailing each minute of his days. Drew glanced at Amanda and she at him. Their eyes met and held. A current of energy sizzled between them.

In the weeks that followed that current grew stronger and stronger. At first Drew took every opportunity to touch and to kiss her. More than once Thompson had to exit and then reenter the breakfast room after clearing his throat loudly. Then he would find them seated primly at the table, their eyes laughing at each other.

Their behavior was a source of confusion to their servants as well. Despite their obvious enjoyment of each other's company, Drew and Amanda said their good nights and went off to their separate bedrooms.

"It ain't natural," a housemaid muttered as she deposited a load of sheets and other linen in the laundry.

"What isn't?" a tall footman asked, stopping to flirt with her.

"The way the two of them act." She pointed upstairs.

"Any more of this conversation, and you will find your-self looking for a new position," Thompson said coldly, running a disapproving eye over the footman as well. Straightening up, that man disappeared. "Have I made myself clear?"

"Yes, Mr. Thompson," the maid said, her voice shaking. But as soon as he was gone, she said under her breath, "But it still ain't right."

The confusion in the household over their behavior spread to other aspects of society. At first no one believed the gossip.

"Nonsense, my dear, you must have noticed the way his eyes follow her about the room," one grand dame said, sipping her glass of waters in the Pump Room.

"Or how close he holds her when they waltz," her niece, a young lady in her first Season, said, sighing.

"Scandalous. I will never understand why they decided to allow that dance at the Assembly Rooms." The older woman turned to her niece. "And if I ever see you dancing as improperly as Lord and Lady Mainwaring, I will remove you from the floor."

Before long, the gossip reached the ears of Drew's mother and sister. At first, like the others, they discounted it. But late one afternoon during a long weekend that she, Mary, and Daniel were spending at the manor, Lady Mainwaring pulled Drew aside. "What is the problem between you and Amanda?" she asked bluntly.

Drew stepped back. "Nothing, Mama."

"That is not what the gossips are saying."

"Since when did you start listening to gossip?"

"When it concerns my son and his wife." She looked at him closely, willing him to tell her the truth.

It took Drew only a few seconds to make his decision. He sat down heavily, his face serious. "I'm not certain I can pull this off, Mama."

"What?"

Stumbling, hesitatingly he told her the whole story. "You told me to go slowly, and I've tried, but I'm not certain how much longer I can hold out."

"Does Amanda know how you feel?"

"She knows I want the marriage to last. I have been afraid of frightening her if I try to push her too hard. After her mother's instructions on being a wife, it took some time before she did not shake with fear when I got too close."

"What was that muttonhead thinking of?" Lady Mainwaring asked, disgusted. Then she shook her head and sighed. "I am certain she was simply doing what she thought best. How does Amanda react now?" Drew's face glowed in embarrassment. "No, that is all right. Let me think about this for a while."

The rest of the weekend Lady Mainwaring was a much more observant person. She noted with satisfaction the way Amanda knew exactly where Drew was, her eyes lingering on him, the way she managed to stand close to him, almost but not quite touching.

When Jeremy joined them on Saturday afternoon, Drew's mother had another shock. Although he greeted Drew and Amanda cordially and made his bow to her, it was Mary who captured most of his attention. And Mary was not unaware of him. As little as she liked her daughter's husband, Lady Mainwaring believed in marriage. Although she had done everything in her power to convince Mary that Van Courtland would be an unsuitable match, as soon as they were married she had tried to be cordial to him even after it was evident that Mary was unhappy. She would have to do something. The problem occupied her for the next week.

During that week the major made a final visit to Applecroft Manor. Still as pompous as he ever was, he stayed only one night. "How soon do you plan to send the lad away to school?" he asked, a frown on his face.

"School? He just changed from a governess to a tutor. I do not believe it will be any time soon." Amanda, now that her claim to Robert was protected, felt no need to be more than civil.

"And when it is time for him to go away, Jeremy has put his name down for our old school," Drew said soothingly.

"Humph! Planning. That is what I like to do. I trust you will keep an eye on the lad yourself, Lord Mainwaring. Very taking little fellow, despite his lack of manners."

Before Amanda could say the angry words that Drew knew were about to burst from her, Drew said quietly, "Of course. But we had not expected to say our farewells to you until later this month. Have you been recalled early?"

"No. I still sail the last day of the month. But a friend and I decided to visit Brighton. Lord Ainsworth heard me discussing the trip and managed to get us an invite to the Pavilion for a look-see. Imagine I shall eat out on the description for some time after I return to India."

"When do you expect to return to England?" Drew asked, his eyes on Amanda. She had gone pale during the major's last speech.

"Not for some time. But I thought I would keep up a correspondence with the lad. Keep him informed about tigers and such," he said with a laugh. After the last interview with Drew and his mother, the major had reevaluated his position. He had decided to try to smooth things over with them. The connection had proved valuable when he mentioned the name in London. "Now, where is the boy? Looking through my things, I found something he might enjoy."

When Robert arrived, Drew and Amanda withdrew, taking refuge in the library. As soon as they were alone, he asked, "What is wrong? And don't tell me nothing."

For a few minutes Amanda said nothing at all. Drew watched her curl up in a big leather chair and waited impatiently. Her eyes shadowed, she finally said, "It's too soon."

"What is?"

"For this to be over. He will be sailing at the end of the month and we can get an annulment." Her voice was soft and full of despair.

"But we don't have to do that!"

"Will it be any easier later?" she asked, biting her lip.

"There is an alternative. No, don't look away. Amanda, you know I want this marriage to last, for you to be my wife in every sense of the word." He knelt in front of her and took her face in his hands. Although he wanted to reach out and crush her to him, never letting her go, he made his touch delicate. "Are you frightened of me?"

"No." The word was so low it seemed merely a sigh.

"Then, what is it?"

"What if when we're married—really married I mean," she asked, "if we are no longer happy?"

"Are you happy now?" She nodded. He got up and sat on the edge of the chair with her. She slid to one side and let him sit beside her. "In spite of our arguments?" he asked. Despite his efforts to keep his temper under control, they had had more than one shouting match, mostly over her necklines.

"Yes."

"Then, what is worrying you?"

"So many married people are unhappy. My mother seems happy with Lord Ainsworth, but she and my father fought constantly. And look at Mary and many of the others." Afraid one had said too much, she hushed.

"I know." Drew's voice was as sad as hers. He put his arm around her and then lifted her onto his lap. She put her head on his shoulder and listened to the beat of his heart, loving the feel of his hand as he stroked her side. "Are we going to let our fears cause us to give up before we make an attempt?" he finally asked, moving his hand so that it cupped her breast.

Instead of the comfort his stroking had given her, Amanda tingled. She wanted to press herself closer to him, to become part of him, but her years of fear made her push him away. She got up slowly and stood beside the chair, her hand still on his shoulder. She ran a finger down his cheek. He captured her hand and kissed it. Then he simply looked at her, his blue eyes shadowed. She turned away. "I don't know what to do," she whispered.

He crossed to stand behind her, encircling her with his arms. Then he waited a moment to see if she would pull away again before he drew her back against him. "The decision does not have to be made instantly," he said quietly. She moved against him and he almost gasped aloud, needing all his control to drop his arms and step back. "All I ask is that you do not start annulment procedures until you have given us every chance."

She turned around, her eyes bright with unshed tears, and nodded.

Then he smiled at her so sweetly that she caught her breath. Wanting to make her smile, he whispered, "Remember I plan to win my bet!"

Amanda responded as he had hoped. First she glared at him and then smiled.

As Lady Mainwaring prepared for her return to Fairleigh, both her children's marriages weighed heavily on her mind. Although Van Courtland had joined them for a few days and then left, Mary showed no signs of following him. Finally, Lady Mainwaring sent for Drew. "I want to oversee the conversion of the Dower House, but I want things settled here first."

"If you mean Amanda and me, you may have to wait for a while," Drew said, his face impassive.

"I have a suggestion. You take Jeremy and the two of you head north. I am certain that one or both of you have friends who will welcome you and provide you with some hunting or fishing."

"Yes, but . . ."

"Mary wishes to remain in Bath for a time. She can move in with Amanda. It is fortunate that the boys enjoy each other's company so much."

"Mama, I cannot speak for Jeremy, but I am not sure I can be away for long. My agent has written asking me to come up to London." In reality, he wanted to follow up on Jeremy's visit to the Runners.

"Is Jeremy going with you?"

"I don't know."

"Take him." Drew looked at her, puzzled. "For your sister's safety, take him with you." For a moment joy flooded his face. Then he frowned. He nodded. "And,

Drew, it might do your own situation some good if you stayed away for a while."

More and more, Drew decided his mother was right. Watching Jeremy react to Mary over the next few days worried him, for he could see no happy solution to their situation. And it was harder to control himself around Amanda.

To his surprise, she made no complaints about the trip. Nor did she ask why they were not going together. She merely asked, "When?"

It was Robert who was the problem. "Are you coming back?" he demanded, a worried look on his face.

"Of course."

"Then, why aren't we going with you?"

Instead of laughing as he might have done months earlier, Drew sat down and pulled Robert on his knee. His face was serious. "Did you go with Amanda and me on our wedding trip?" Robert shook his head. "Did we come back?"

"Yes."

"Then, what makes you doubt that I will return this time?"

"Faith was talking to a footman, and they said—"

"Robert, they do not know the facts. I will come back." At least this time, he added silently, hoping that Amanda would allow him to keep his promise.

Robert inspected him carefully. "And Daniel gets to stay with me while you are gone?" This time Drew nodded. "Well, I suppose it will be all right. You don't stay away long, though!" The little boy threw his arms around Drew and hugged him. Then he slipped down from his leg. "Manda is staying here too?" he asked, wanting one more reassurance. Drew nodded.

Jeremy was much harder to persuade than Robert had been. "I need to be here to oversee the harvest."

"You have an estate manager for that."

"But I like to keep an eye on it myself."

Drew looked at him sympathetically. Jeremy shifted nervously. "Jeremy, come to London with me at least. I am certain that the redheaded opera dancer that gossip linked you with last winter would be happy to see you."

Jeremy sat up straight in his chair. "You know!"

"Yes." His friend smiled sadly.

"Who else knows?" Jeremy's face was impassive.

"My mother." Jeremy sucked in his breath. "And Amanda maybe. Jeremy, I wish—"

"Don't. I knew from the start what it would be like. Like you and Amanda."

"At least we have a chance," Drew said, and then regretted it.

"And I have none." Jeremy's voice was sad. He stood up and took a turn around the room, looking anywhere but at Drew. "I suppose Amanda could check on Hedgefield and on the manor," he finally said, his voice carefully flat.

"Ask her. And then come north with me. Litchfield has invited us up to hunt. My mother has ordered me away too." The two friends looked at each other for a moment and then shook hands.

"Agreed!"

15

For Amanda the first days after Drew's departure were both full and empty. They were full of details Jeremy insisted only she could oversee. They were empty because she missed Drew, missed him so much that she ached with longing at times. It was those times that made her realize that their marriage meant more to her than she had ever thought it could.

When she was missing Drew, Mary helped. His sister told her one story after another about his childhood, the episode with the pony, one Christmas when they had gone skating on a pond without their parents' knowledge. Each one made Amanda realize how he had become the kind of man he was.

About the only complaint Amanda had about Mary's visit was Daniel's governess, a handsome woman with dark hair and eyes. One afternoon while she was in her room resting, Robert ran in, obviously disturbed.

"What has happened?" Amanda asked.

Robert looked at her for a moment. Then he asked, "I am not supposed to tell tales, am I?"

"What do you mean?"

"If I see someone else do something." He sat beside her, his eyes intent on her face.

"It depends." Amanda sat up straighter and pulled him up beside her. "If what you saw caused someone or something to be hurt, you should tell someone you trust. Also if what the person was doing was wrong."

"It was!" Robert clamped his lips together as if he were afraid of saying more.

"Then you need to tell me."

He thought for a moment. Then he looked at her again, as if considering his options. "But she will know who told."

"Who?"

"Daniel's governess, Miss Lampley."

Amanda turned so that she could look at him. "Robert, I think you should explain. Did she do something to you?" He shook his head. "To Daniel?"

"Yes." Robert's answer was only a whisper. "She told Nurse he fell down, but I saw her. She pinched him hard and he cried. She is not a nice lady." Hugging him close to her, Amanda held him while he cried too. Finally he sat up. "Will you make her stop?" he asked, his face serious.

"I will try. Now, you ask Nurse to see me right away and take Daniel to the stables for a riding lesson." She smiled at him and smoothed his curls.

A short time later, her face serious, Amanda talked to Nurse. "I was wondering how you were managing since Daniel has joined Robert in the schoolroom."

Her face impassive, Nurse said, "Very well, Lady Mainwaring."

"And Master Daniel's governess, Miss Lampley? How is she fitting in?"

Nurse sniffed. "Well, I would not wish to be a gossip, but I would not leave Master Robert in her care." She sniffed again.

"Why?"

"Her charge has far too many accidents. If I were Mrs. Van Courtland, I would dismiss her at once."

"Hmm. Robert does not like her either. I will talk to Mrs. Van Courtland, but until then, choose another maid, someone who has brothers or sisters of her own and who likes children, and assign her to help care for Master Daniel."

Nurse nodded, a militant look in her eyes. "She won't

be alone with either of them again. I'll see to that. And
Miss will think it a compliment to her," she said as though
making a solemn vow.

Amanda's interview with Mary was less successful. Beginning carefully, Amanda mentioned her own
governess, whom she had admired. Then casually she
asked about Miss Lampley. "How long has she been with
you?"

"Only since this spring. She's a connection of my
husband's. Apparently the family fortune is all to pieces."
Mary's voice was almost a monotone. "Since Daniel
outgrew his nurse, Van Courtland hired her as a
governess. I offered to send her home to her family while
I visited you, but she refused."

"I have asked Nurse to arrange for another nursery
maid while you are here to make her job easier. Perhaps
we should also include her in our excursions." Amanda
made her tone cheerful.

Mary's face contained as little emotion as her voice.
"Perhaps."

While Amanda was dealing with the governess and
completing the list of things that Jeremy had left for her
to do, Drew and Jeremy found London flat. Their clubs
were almost empty, the latest opera dancers had no
appeal, and the Runners had no news.

"I told you we should have gotten in touch with them
earlier," Jeremy said, staring deep into his glass.

"And be told earlier that there was nothing to find?"
Drew asked, wishing he were with Amanda.

His friend sighed. "When does Litchfield expect us?"

"I told him we would send him an express before we
left."

"Then send it. This place is depressing."

After he dashed off a note to his friend, Drew sat there
for a moment and then pulled another sheet of paper in
front of him. "Someone needs to know where we are," he
muttered. Then he smiled. If he could not be with
Amanda, at least he wanted her to know he was thinking
about her.

* * *

Before the letter arrived, Drew was in Amanda's thoughts. As she and Robert rode out in the mornings, she wanted him beside her, laughing at her. Each morning she completed some project until slowly, surely everything was ready for the harvest, the extra people hired, the wagons ready. Satisfied with the progress, they headed back to the house.

"Do I really have to do lessons today?" Robert asked, his voice plaintive.

"Yes."

"But Daniel . . ."

"Daniel may join you."

"He does not even know how to read."

"Neither did you at his age. Help your tutor teach him," Amanda said quietly.

He thought for a moment and then nodded. "I'll race you back," he shouted as he urged his pony forward.

Amanda let him get a good lead and then followed. Even so she had to concentrate to let him beat her. They turned their horses over to the grooms and then headed to the house.

In the front entranceway, Thompson handed her the mail. She recognized Drew's frank, and her heart beat faster. Hurriedly she sent Robert up the stairs. Just then, the clock struck the hour. Remembering her promise to help Mrs. Thompson mix the spices for the potpourri that kept both the linens and the rooms fresh all year, she sighed and hurried toward the backstairs to the kitchen and still room. She frowned as she noticed how dark they were. Perhaps Mrs. Thompson could arrange a lamp or two above them. But the letter in her hand was more interesting. She brought it up to her nose, trying to catch a whiff of the sandalwood that Drew preferred. She closed her eyes for just a moment. The next thing she knew she had a death grip on the railing and was on one knee near the bottom of the stairs.

"What happened? If that girl has spilled another pot of tea . . ." Cook said threateningly as she came to investigate the noise. "Lady Mainwaring? Here someone bring a light! What happened?"

A footman helped Amanda to a chair, Drew's letter still clutched tightly in her hand. "I was not watching where I was going, and I fell. I think my foot slipped on something. Those stairs need better lighting."

Cook pointed to the footman who had helped Amanda to a seat. "You, check each and every one of those stairs. Take an extra lamp. It is black as a winter sky in there."

"Where are the oil lamps? Why aren't they lit?" Mrs. Thompson asked as she bustled in. "What happened?"

"Her ladyship slipped."

"Are you hurt? Shall we send for Doctor Weston?"

"Nonsense. I wll go to my room for a short rest, and I'll be fine," Amanda said firmly, wincing as she stood up. "The potpourri will have to wait for another day, Mrs. Thompson."

The footman came back in, a curious expression on his face. "There is something slick all over one of the steps. But it isn't grease or candlewax. Smells funny too." Both Thompson and Cook hurried to take a look.

"How fortunate you were not seriously injured, Lady Mainwaring," a cultured voice said.

Amanda started. "Miss Lampley! Thank you for your concern."

"If you are increasing, I would suggest quite strongly that you call your doctor." The governess smiled and returned to her pot of tea.

Amanda shook her head, suddenly thrilled at the thought of bearing Drew's child. She looked down at the letter in her hand and smiled.

Suddenly Jennings was at her side. Noting the gaping observers, she sent them on their way. "You two see that there is hot water for Lady Mainwaring's bath, and you see that she has tea. Now, my lady, you come along with me."

They headed up the stairs, now lighted with oil lamps, moving cautiously past the step where the youngest maid was scrubbing diligently. Cook and Mrs. Thompson supervised.

"A pomade of some sort. Though what it would be doing here is anyone's guess," Mrs. Thompson said. "Had a very definite scent." Cook nodded, her face serious.

In her room in a tub full of hot water, Amanda soaked her aches out and read and reread Drew's letter. He missed her. She looked once more at the closing. He loved her. Why did he have to go to Scotland? Or why didn't he suggest she accompany him?

Laughing at herself, she emerged from the tub and dressed quickly, paying little attention to her toilette. Without Drew to impress, clothes were merely covering to protect her body. She hurried downstairs to find Mary waiting for her.

"Are you all right? My dresser said you fell." Mary's face, normally pale, was even whiter than usual.

"It was just a mishap. I had a letter from Drew and was not looking where I was going."

Mary looked at her for a moment, her face worried. Then, very casually, she asked, "Did Drew say when they are returning?"

"Not for a while. They are heading to Scotland to visit a friend, Lord Litchfield. As usual, Jeremy sent me another list of things to see about. Oh, well, when we move to Fairleigh, he will have the joy of overseeing both places himself."

Mary blinked rapidly to hide her tears of disappointment. "When do you and Drew plan to make the move?" she asked.

Amanda blushed. "We have made no definite plans." But we will, she promised herself. Her smile seemed to light up the entire room.

"I suppose I should be making plans to return home myself," Mary sounded wistful.

"Nonsense. Unless you are bored. I know that waiting for me while I supervise the estates is not exciting."

"No. I am enjoying myself. You know how lazy I am. Having someone else take charge of the household and let me sleep as late as I like is delightful."

Amanda looked at her, trying to decide if she were just being polite. Mary did look more rested, the lines of strain fading from her face. The deep-blue muslin dress she wore matched her eyes. "If you don't mind waiting until day after tomorrow, we can leave the boys with Nurse and spend the day in Bath," Amanda suggested. With the nursery maids and Nurse on duty, both boys were thriving, and she had no fears about their safety. Robert had told her that the governess no longer was pinching Daniel.

The next day Amanda worked on completing Jeremy's list. She arranged for the thatchers to repair the roofs of cottages at Hedgefield and then on her own property. The stonemasons agreed to restore the balconies at Hedgefield and erect a wall between the bottom of the garden and the stream. Amanda had raised her eyebrows when she read that, for Jeremy had always declared that part of his delight in fishing was being able to watch people riding up to the house and then to lie down hidden if he did not wish to see them. The wall would make that impossible, but at least she would no longer have to worry about Robert or Daniel falling in when she allowed them to play alone in the garden when she met with Jeremy's agent.

Having given him Jeremy's instruction, Amanda continued. "Then I will need you at the manor. I want you to check every stone. Master Robert has begun to climb on everything. Maybe we will find a way to make it safer."

"He'd not use it if we did, your ladyship. Boys like the danger," the master stonemason said, his own face mischievous. Amanda raised her eyes to heaven. "But we can try, we can try."

The next day Amanda, Mary, and Miss Lampley headed for Bath. After her refusals to accompany them in the past, Amanda had been surprised when the governess accepted the invitation.

"If Mrs. Van Courtland will agree, I should like to visit a friend of mine who has a school in Bath."

"Of course. Had you told me sooner, we could have arranged for you to see her regularly," Mary said.

"We will set a time and a place for a meeting. Will your visit be a short one, or do you need several hours?" Amanda asked.

"As much time as you can spare," the governess said quietly, her eyes mocking.

Achieving an agreement, the group split up. As she and Mary entered one of the shops along New Bond Street, Amanda noticed a man leaving a shop farther down the way. "Isn't that your husband?" she asked Mary.

"Where?"

"Just down the street."

Mary glanced that way and then turned back. "I don't see anyone. You must have been mistaken. He is visiting friends in Sussex."

Wondering about it but not wishing to make an issue of it, Amanda nodded. "Jennings gave me instructions to buy ribbons for one of my bonnets. I hope I can find ones that match the dress."

When it was time to leave, she had found not only her ribbons but a host of other things. Stopping by the circulating library on Milsom Street, she had selected an armload of books before they hired sedan chairs for the trip to Lansdowne Crescent. After a late luncheon, they were just pulling on their gloves when Miss Lampley arrived.

Although Mary promptly closed her eyes and leaned back to sleep for the drive home, Amanda could not help noticing the difference in the governess. There was a sparkle in her eyes that had not been there when they have arrived. Her lips were red and slightly swollen. And when she bent down to place a package on the floor, Amanda had to hide her gasp behind a cough. The tucker the woman had been wearing was missing, and under her spencer, Amanda saw the definite outline of teeth marks on her neck.

Amanda quickly closed her eyes. She would have a word with Thompson when she arrived home. Someone was certain to have seen Miss Lampley that day. And no matter if she were Van Courtland's connection, if she were the loose woman she seemed to be, Miss Lampley had better hope her lover could support her. Amazed that she was not more shocked, Amanda marshaled her forces mentally.

Unfortunately for all Amanda's plans, Miss Lampley had been careful, very careful. When Mary decided to leave a few days later, Miss Lampley was once more in charge of Daniel. But because of Amanda's insistence, the new nursery maid, Ellen, was going too. Amanda had taken the girl aside and given her two things—specific instructions about how she was to behave, and enough money to buy her passage home if she needed to. "You keep this with you at all times," Amanda told her, handing her the small packet of coins and a note of explanation wrapped up in a small pouch full of potpourri. "Tell them you promised your old granny to wear it always if anyone asks about it." The girl nodded, her eyes wide.

Although the carriage would be crowded, Mary had decided to use only one, putting Ellen on top with the coachman. They were almost ready to drive away when Daniel missed a picturebook Robert had given him. "I think I know where it is," Miss Lampley said. "I will get it." She left the coach. Amanda noticed Robert getting too close to the horses and called him to her, moving closer to the front door. Then Ellen screamed. Everyone ran forward to find out what was wrong only to turn in horror as a stone window ledge crashed where they had been standing, sending shards of stone and dust over everyone.

Totally stunned by their close brush with death, Amanda wrapped her arms around Robert and stood there trembling. Mary, her mouth a straight line, looked remarkably like her brother as she climbed down from the coach. "Take everything back inside," she said briskly, motioning the footmen and maids into action. "And have everyone who was standing out here checked for injuries." Her eyes narrowed as she watched her governess pick her way through the rubble. "You see that this coach is unloaded." Then she turned to the girl who sat trembling on the top of the coach. "Ellen, you take Daniel and Robert up to the schoolroom, where you should all have some tea." She watched as the coachman lifted the girl down to a footman. "We will discuss your reward later."

"Reward. Oh, no."

"Nonsense." She helped Daniel down and then crossed to her friend, lifting her skirts as she tried to avoid the largest pieces. "Amanda, let him go and come with me," she said, her voice firm. Like someone under the power of Dr. Mesmer, Amanda obeyed. The boys, beginning to chatter wildly, ran up the stairs to Nurse. "Here is what we are going to do."

By the time Amanda had stopped trembling and gotten angry, Mary had written to Jeremy and Drew, rifling Amanda's desk to get the address. When she had sent the groom on his way, she had supplied him with ample funds. "Do not worry about expense. Get there as quickly as possible," she said, her mouth hard. But although her first impulse had been to send for her mother, she reconsidered that idea.

All there was left for Amanda to do was to talk to the master mason. And even before he arrived, she knew his answer. "That stone was as solid as mortar can make it, Lady Mainwaring. I had my own son walk on all the ledges to test them for Master Robert."

"I know. Please check everything once again. And if you find anything unusual, I would appreciate your telling no one but me." He nodded and set to work.

As she had expected, Amanda was deluged with visitors for the next few days. Some, like the county magistrate, came to offer his help. Most, however, were merely curious. For the latter Amanda and Mary developed a routine: tea with plain cake, a quick thank-you for their concern, a discussion of the visitors' families, and farewell. Thompson entered into the spirit of the occasion by providing a variety of situations that required their instant attention.

"If I had known it could be this easy to handle

unwanted visitors, I would have stopped dreading them. Who taught you how to do this?" Amanda asked as she curled up in her chair, completely crushing her soft-blue afternoon dress.

"Mama. But unless it is necessary, as it is now, you should not do this very often. People learn to evade your attempts to dislodge them."

"Like the vicar's wife?"

"Yes, but she may be a complete natural. How did she find out that the stone was loosened deliberately?"

"I wish I knew." Amanda stretched. "I'm for an early night. A farmer on the other side of Hedgefield sent a message that he needs a new roof. I've promised to inspect it first thing tomorrow morning."

"Take a groom with you, Amanda. Humor me," Mary begged.

Amanda just laughed.

When Mary awoke, she glanced at the clock. She stretched and then called her dresser. When she made her way downstairs a short time later, she fully expected Amanda to be there, laughing at her and teasing her about her tardy appearance. "Did you see Lady Mainwaring this morning, Thompson?" she asked when he appeared to open the door to the sitting room.

"No, Mrs. Van Courtland. But the footman told me she sent word that Masters Robert and Daniel were to join you for luncheon." He bowed and closed the door behind him.

Mary looked at the clock on the mantel and then picked up her embroidery. Half-listening for hoofbeats, she was startled when the door opened and the boys rushed in.

After making their bows, each boy kissed her on the cheek. Then Daniel leaned over and whispered in her ear, "Guess what?"

"What?"

"I learned to write my name, Daniel Andrew Van Courtland. See!" He pulled a crumpled paper from his pocket and handed it to her.

"Very good, my darling. Did Robert help you?" He nodded, and Mary smiled at the other boy over Daniel's head.

"Where's Manda?"

"She had to see a farmer about a roof this morning."

"I know. She let me ride part of the way with her. Then Hilton brought me home."

Mary's eyes widened. She had gone alone. Then she heard hoofbeats and gave a sigh of relief. "I am certain she will be here shortly," she told him, giving both of them a hug.

A few minutes later she wished she could recall those words.

"May I see you out here, Mrs. Van Courtland?" Thompson asked, his face impassive but very pale.

After telling the boys to wait, Mary went out into the hallway, pulling the door closed in front of them. "Lady Mainwaring's horse has just returned to the stables."

"Her horse?" Mary lost what little color she possessed. She put her hand to her throat as though she were choking.

Thompson glanced at her and then explained. "Hilton believes the mare was frightened by a gunshot. She is scored on her right flank."

"Gunshot?" The word slipped out in a whisper as Mary sank to the floor. Both Thompson and the footman tried to catch her. Before they could reach her, the sitting-room door flew open.

"Mama!" Daniel screamed, and threw himself at her.

"What has happened to Manda, Thompson?" Robert asked, his whole body trembling. He was trying valiantly to keep his voice steady. "Where is Manda?"

A bronzed hand reached out and took his shoulder. "I think we both need an answer to that question, Thompson."

16

His blue eyes glittering with exhaustion, Drew picked up Robert and held him close. Then he noticed his sister and Daniel. "What is going on?"

Jeremy, who had entered on Drew's heels, rushed to Mary's side, pushing the footman away. He lifted Daniel and gave him to the footman and then carried Mary into the sitting room, putting her on the settee. "Get some water," he demanded.

As soon as his sister was taken care of, Drew turned to Thompson once more. "Where is my wife?"

"We do not know, your lordship. Her horse came home alone, its side scored by a bullet." This time Thompson's voice shook.

Drew turned as pale as he could with his tan. Carefully, he hugged Robert and put him on the floor. "You look after Daniel, Robert. I'll find Amanda." He stood up, stretching. "Where was she going?" Robert quickly supplied him with directions. "Jeremy, let's go."

Torn, Jeremy stood for a moment and watched Mary. Then he too stretched and headed for the door. Within minutes they were mounted on fresh horses and away. Pushing their horses at breakneck speed, they took each fence they came to, leaving the grooms following them certain that there would be yet another accident to worry about. Just as they crested a small hill, they saw her in the valley below, her green habit torn and her hat gone, trudging steadily homeward.

Drew shouted. She looked up and broke into a run. He

galloped toward her, pulling up only inches in front of her. His heart pounding as fast as it had when he first got Mary's letter, Drew reached out and gathered Amanda into his arms, crushing her against him.

Amanda, her only thoughts of him, reached up and pulled his head down. She kissed him, wrapping her arms around his neck when he picked her up. "You are home, my darling," she whispered.

Startled, he raised his head, but their moment together was over.

Jeremy swung off his horse and walked over to where they were standing. "Amanda, are you all right? What happened?"

She pulled away from Drew but only slightly. "I am bruised and angry. And my feet hurt."

Drew pulled her close again. "Nothing else?" She shook her head. "Then there are some very worried people at the manor we need to reassure." He lifted her on his horse and swung up behind her.

Jeremy mounted up and led the way back. For Drew, with Amanda in his arms, the ride was too short. Only the thought of Robert and Mary made him spur the tired horse on.

For Jeremy the ride was endless. Already exhausted over his own struggle with his feelings about Mary, he felt this last strain was almost too much. He slumped in the saddle and more than once swayed alarmingly. By the time they reached the manor, it was all he could do to swing down from his horse. But the grooms had arrived before them. Mary stood on the steps. And the sight of her put new vigor in his movements.

"Are you all right?" Mary called, trying to keep Robert and Daniel firmly by the hand.

Robert broke free and headed toward Amanda at a hard run. He wrapped his arms around her and held on as if he were afraid she would vanish.

"She is all right, Robert," Drew assured him. "Let her go change clothes, and then we will talk." Hesitantly, the boy stepped back. "You can stay with me while I change."

With the first uneasiness over, the servants set to work providing three baths and fresh clothing. Thompson also provided teatrays and sent word to Cook that luncheon would be delayed. Their valets still somewhere on the road behind them, both Drew and Jeremy relaxed for a few minutes in the warm water and then made quick work getting dressed, choosing comfort rather than elegance. Robert, although he would rather have been with Amanda, relayed some of Drew's clothing to Jeremy and waited impatiently while the two men put the finishing touches on their attire.

"Where is Manda?" Robert demanded as the three of them entered the red-and-ivory sitting room.

Mary, who had been feeling rather left out, said quietly, "Still changing." She smiled up at Jeremy and then turned away in confusion at the warm light in his eyes.

"Tell us about that ledge that fell," her brother demanded as he sat beside her. "Your letter was incomplete."

"It was exciting. Ellen screamed. We ran to see what was the mtter, and a big piece of rock hit behind us," Robert said, his eyes wide. "Then Daniel had nightmares."

Drew glanced at his sister for confirmation. She nodded. "If that girl hadn't been looking up or if they had not moved so fast . . ." She shuddered.

Jeremy stood behind her, his hand on her shoulder. "What were the damages?"

"Thompson was sprayed with rock and received a few cuts. So was a footman. The rest of us were merely shaken." She closed her eyes and sighed. "It was frightening."

"Did Amanda call in the mason?" Jeremy crossed to a chair directly in front of Mary.

"She did not have to. He was here that very afternoon, checking everything." She took a deep breath. "He said the ledge had been tampered with."

"What?" Both men sat up straighter.

"Someone dissolved the mortar. All it took was a slight push to move it."

All of their heads whipped around. Amanda stood in the doorway, looking as fresh as if she had just awakened. Robert dashed to her, once more wrapping his arms around her, crushing her dress, her newest muslin in her favorite red.

Drew was not far behind. He slipped his arm around her and then tilted her face up. "Are you certain you are all right?"

She smiled and nodded. Disengaging Robert, she said, "Thompson said luncheon will be spoiled if we do not eat soon." Although Jeremy and Drew started to protest, Amanda nodded to the boys, and the two men bit off their remarks abruptly.

Luncheon was finally over, although only the children had done justice to the succulent chicken or the light omelets. Then Mary took the boys back to the schoolroom, over Robert's protests. Only Mary's promise that she would stay with them made the two boys agree to go. "You still owe me an explanation, Amanda," Mary said as she walked out into the hall.

"Now would be a good time to tell us everything," Drew suggested, his arm once more around her waist.

"I wish I knew what was going on myself." Amanda glanced at her cousin and then back at Drew. "This morning someone shot at me."

"Are you sure?"

"Was anyone hunting in the area?"

"All I know is what I told you. The gunshot startled my mare, and she headed for a fence, where she lost me."

"It did more than startle her. She was hit."

"Is she all right?" Amanda's eyes were wide. She could deal with possible injuries to herself but not to a helpless creature.

Drew patted her hand. "Thompson said she was scored. She'll be fine shortly. Thank heavens the shot wasn't higher. You could have been hit."

"But that's just it. I could have been hit. Maybe it was just a poacher."

Jeremy stood up. "And maybe it wasn't. I am going to Hedgefield to make some inquiries. I'll send you word if I discover anything." Amanda and Drew stood up to walk him to the door. Before they reached it, he turned and hugged Amanda. "You be careful, brat. You are the closest family I have, and I would be lost without you." His eyes filled with tears. Amanda nodded, her throat too full to speak. The two men walked out together to view the front steps.

When Drew returned a few minutes later, his face was grim. "Hilton said he asked to go with you this morning, and you refused."

"He had to bring Robert home." Amanda smiled at him.

Drew glared at her. "You are never to go riding again unless Jeremy or I go with you."

"And what am I to do if you are not here?" Her tone was pleasant, but her eyes were not.

"Ask Hilton! How dare you put yourself in danger. Do you know what it would have done to Robert or Jeremy or to me if you had been injured this morning? Amanda, you must start thinking about us." He glanced at her. A large tear trickled down her face. She sobbed, and the one tear became a torrent. He reached out and pulled her into his arms, soothing her, whispering his love in her ear.

"I was so frightened," she sobbed. "And you weren't here. Mary tried, but she was afraid too." Amanda cried so hard that Drew grew worried. He gave her a little shake, picked her up and then crossed to the settee. Holding her tightly, he sat down with Amanda on his lap. Gradually her sobs decreased. He took his handkerchief and wiped her eyes and cheeks. Then he handed her the square of linen. "Blow." Amanda did. Then she nestled her head between his neck and his shoulder, her breaths still shuddering. When she was finally calm once more, Drew suggested, "You go wash your face and then go see Robert. He is as worried about you as I am." He stretched tiredly. "I want to talk to Hilton." Then he yawned.

For the first time Amanda noticed the exhaustion in his face. "When was the last time you slept?"

"Sometime yesterday morning. Jeremy and I stopped to

change horses, and we slept for a couple of hours." He yawned again.

"Take a nap, then talk to Hilton." Drew shook his head. "Then go see the man so you can go to sleep. I'll visit Robert."

Stifling yet another yawn, Drew nodded. "You are not to leave the house alone. Promise me!"

For a moment Amanda considered arguing with him. Then she remembered how tired he must be. "I promise." She smiled up at him.

Drew could not resist it. He leaned down and kissed her the way he had been longing to do for so long, deeply and passionately. His tongue made forays between her lips.

Instead of pulling away, Amanda wrapped one arm behind his head and the other around his neck as if she were trying to imprint his pattern on herself. Their kisses deepened.

The minute Drew felt his last bit of control slipping away, he stepped back. Amanda moaned softly in protest, her breaths coming in pants. He ran his hands over her shoulders, holding her at arm's length. "You have to talk to Robert," he said in a husky voice.

Amanda blinked and nodded. She headed toward the door. As soon as she was gone, Drew slumped in a chair, his face radiant. Then he stretched again. "First Hilton and then a nap," he told himself. A picture of Amanda lying beside him, her eyes heavy-lidded with passion, sent him to the stables at almost a run.

After stopping by her room to smooth her hair and let her cheeks cool, Amanda headed for the schoolroom. While the boys finished their naps in their bedrooms, she told Mary what she knew. Mary sat quietly in the rocker while her friend paced around the room. Neither noticed that the door behind them was open just a crack.

"I simply do not understand why this is happening," Amanda said, angry once more.

"Have you had problems with any of your tenants?" Mary asked, her face serious.

"No. And except for that stone, the other accidents seemed designed to scare me or injure me slightly, not kill me."

"If you had been pregnant, all of them would have been enough to injure the child."

"But, Mary . . ." Amanda blushed. She turned and walked to the window, her face heated. "Would you mind if we do not join you for supper this evening?" Mary lifted her eyebrows. Amanda blushed again. "Jeremy has gone to Hedgefield, and Drew has gone to bed. I thought we could have supper in my sitting room when he wakes up."

Mary smiled, her face carefully schooled to hide her disappointment in Jeremy's absence. "I will join the boys." She walked across to look out the window too. "Now that Jeremy and Drew have come back, I should return home. I will need some rest before the Little Season. Do you and Drew plan to come to London?"

Longing to ask Mary to stay, Amanda bit her tongue. "I suppose you had better ask Drew. He has been away from Fairleigh so long he may need to go there."

"Not if my mother has anything to say about it. She is deep in the restoration of the Dower House and has warned everyone to stay away until it is complete."

Just then a noise caught their attention, and they hurried to their children.

By the time Amanda returned to her rooms, she was emotionally drained. Robert had held on to her as though he expected her to disappear in a puff of smoke. She looked longingly at the bed. Jennings untied her ribbons and unhooked the back of her dress. "His lordship had me open the door into his bedroom."

"Is he there?"

"Fast asleep, poor man. Hilton told Thompson they had ridden all night." She untied the last of Amanda's laces and slipped her corset off. Wrapping her mistress in a thin robe, she put her to bed. "Go to sleep. We have had all the excitement we can endure today." Amanda smiled at her maid's proprietary tone and obediently closed her eyes. After making sure all the draperies were securely fastened, Jennings left.

Some time later Amanda awoke. She rolled over and began to stretch, a lazy smile on her face. Suddenly her smile grew broader. Seated on the foot of her bed, his blue eyes fixed on her face, was Drew. "Hello," she said in a voice made husky by sleep. "Have you been awake long?"

"No." Drew cleared his throat. Amanda blinked sleepily and sat up, pulling her robe about her primly. They looked at each other for a long time. Then Drew slid off the bed and held out his hand to Amanda. But before she could put her foot on the steps and take his hand, he picked her up, holding her so that they could look at each other face to face. "I have missed you," he said quietly.

Amanda leaned forward, her lips just barely brushing his. Then she smiled. "Put me down." As soon as her feet hit the floor, she took his hand and led him to his door. "Supper will be served in my sitting room in"—she glanced at the clock above the fireplace—"half an hour. Don't keep me waiting." She kissed him again and shoved him through the door, startled by her own daring.

On the other side of the door Drew stood for a moment, his heart racing. Then he ran a hand over his cheek and headed for the washbowl, wishing that his valet had arrived.

He was already in the sitting room when the footmen entered with supper. Quickly he had them set it out, light the candles, and leave, promising to ring if they needed anything.

Then the door to Amanda's bedroom opened and she came in. Her gown was a sheer pale-pink muslin so fine that Drew imagined he could see through it. He knew that had she worn that neckline, cut wide across her shoulders and plunging to a V between her breasts, anywhere but there, he would have bundled her up immediately. As it was, he was having difficulty breathing. Eating supper was almost as difficult. Amanda flirted with him shamelessly. But when he started to grow more serious, to ask her the question he longed for her to answer, she shied away.

Finally he refused to cooperate any longer. He crossed to the bellpull. Then he said, "You wait in your room until they clear this away."

Amanda opened her mouth to protest. She glanced at him and thought better of it. She whisked through the door and closed it behind her with a snap.

When he opened the door later, he saw her seated on her chaise, her legs curled beneath her. "They are gone," he said, and held out his hand. For a minute he was not sure she would respond. Then she got up slowly and walked toward him. "I think it is time that we have our talk." His eyes were as dark blue as the evening sky.

Amanda merely nodded. Drew seated her in a chair and pulled one for himself right in front of her.

"Drew," she whispered, and reached out to touch his cheek.

He drew back and captured her hand, his fingers tangling with hers. "Amanda, don't play with me anymore." She tried to pull away, but he held her fast. "I have to know. Are you ready to be my wife?"

Amanda looked down. Then she took a deep breath, and her dress slid farther down, revealing the creamy-white tops of her breasts. She leaned forward. Drew gasped. "Yes."

"What did you say?"

"I want you to be my husband." Her eyes promised him more.

He reached out and grabbed her, burying his face in her breasts. Suddenly she realized that he was crying. "Drew?" She raised his head and brushed the teardrops from his cheeks.

"I was so afraid that you would say no. Amanda, I love you. From one of those afternoons when you swished into my rooms bringing a scent of roses with you, I have loved you." He pulled her from her chair and onto his lap.

"But you agreed to my proposition." Amanda stroked the black line of his eyebrow, fascinated.

"I took a chance. That's why our agreement made a permanent marriage a possibility." He hugged her and nibbled her ear.

"What if I had said no?"

"You didn't." He stood up, holding her in his arms. "Amanda, if we had not been friends, if I had not thought that you cared for me, I would have called everything off when you suggested it."

Amanda wrapped her arms around his neck. "Thank you."

"For what?"

"For teaching me to love you. For being patient with me. Drew!" she cried as he lifted her up higher and buried his face in her breasts again, this time covering them with kisses. "Drew . . ." This time his name was more of a purr than a word.

He pulled her even closer, letting her slide down his body until just the tips of her toes touched the floor. Then he kissed her. Her lips parted and this time her tongue was as active as his. One of his hands stroked her side. The other cupped her bottom, fitting her into his hips. She gasped, but she did not pull away.

Finally he stepped back. "Let Jennings get you ready for bed."

She stood for a moment as if she did not want to leave him. Then she moved backward toward the door.

Just before she reached it, he said clearly, "I love you."

Her answer trembled on her lips, but she could not make herself say it. Once inside the bedroom, Amanda sat down, shaking with emotion. She wanted Drew, but now that she was alone, she was afraid. Jennings unhooked her gown, complaining the whole time about the way Amanda had forced her to ruin it by ripping out the lace tucker it had originally had. But the nightrobe she chose for her mistress was her sheerest, a silk so fine that wearing it was like wearing a moonbeam. She tied the last bow and helped Amanda into bed.

By now Amanda had started to shiver. "He is my husband. I love him," she whispered. But still she shook.

Drew stepped in, his powerful form covered with a robe that matched his eyes. He smiled at her and then stopped short. He took a deep breath and hurried to the bed. Amanda sat there trembling.

"I don't know what is the matter with me," she quavered. "I like you to hold me." She hiccupped.

"Then I will." He slid into bed beside her, keeping his robe pulled tightly around him. He put his arms around her, waiting for her to pull away. She moved closer.

"What's wrong with me?" she asked, trying to force herself to be still.

"Reaction. I've seen it in battle. When a person has had more than he can bear, he does strange things. After everything that has happened to you lately, I should have expected it." He wrapped his arm around her shoulders and began listing everything that had happened on his fingers. "The only time that has been uneventful lately was our honeymoon." He laughed gently.

She pulled his head down and whispered in his ear, "Even then I was afraid of you sometimes." Then she added honestly, "And of me."

Drew slid down in the bed and pulled her with him. She tried to pull away, but he held her and gave her a little shake. "Go to sleep."

"But I thought that you would . . ."

"Later."

"Oh." He closed his eyes, trying to count backward from one hundred. He had reached seventy-two when Amanda asked, "You know about Brighton, don't you?" He nodded and opened his eyes. A look of shame covered her face.

"I don't know the details. Jeremy only told me because he was afraid I might frighten you. My darling, there is nothing to be ashamed of. He was the one who did something wrong. You were merely his victim."

"My mother did not think so."

Drew bit back his angry words. "Well, I am your husband, and my opinion is the one that counts." He put her head on his shoulder. "If you ever want to tell me about it, I will listen."

"Now?"

"Whenever."

Suddenly the story came pouring out. The girls had

been trying on bonnets when the door to her cousin's room had been opened stealthily. Then, before they could prevent it, they had been locked in with a madman. They had tried to hide behind the furniture, but he had grabbed their long hair, taking pleasure in using it to dash them against the bedframe or into walls. "We screamed. Oh, how we screamed," Amanda whispered. Drew forced his hands to unclench and stroked her back. "A maid heard us and ran for help. They used the housekeeper's keys to open the door. When the footmen came in, the man let us go and wandered out into the hall." She shuddered, burrowing closer to him. "The next morning I cut my hair. Mama didn't understand, but Grandfather did."

"And so do I. Now, go to sleep, my darling. I'm here to protect you now." Drew listened as Amanda's breathing slowed, saying a silent prayer of thanksgiving for the fact that she had not been more seriously hurt. He wrapped one of her soft curls around his finger and tried to sleep himself.

Some time later Amanda opened her eyes, surprised by the flickering candlelight. She tried burrowing her head deeper into her pillow. Then she raised her head. Drew was in the middle of her bed, and she was lying half on top of him, her face pressed against his bare chest. She wiggled slightly, trying to move away.

"If you do that much more, I may attack you," Drew said, running his hand up her leg under her gown. He waited to see if she would pull away. She didn't. Instead, her hand wandered across what she thought was his chest. He stopped moving. Her eyes grew big, and she removed her hand immediately.

"Don't be afraid. I'm almost like Robert," he told her. "Just bigger and with a little more hair." He took her hand and put it on his chest this time. Slowly so that he did not frighten her, he turned them on their sides. Then he kissed her, using the moment to pull her nightrobe to her waist and to press her against him. His kisses covered her face and her neck at first. Then he laid her down and he untied the drawstring at her neckline, exposing her breasts. Once again he started to kiss her, letting his kisses roam lower and lower.

Realizing that she would not push him away, he lowered his head to her breasts, kissing first one and then the other, teasing one with his tongue or with his fingers. His other hand crept lower, smoothing her stomach, drifting down a leg before working its way to her inner thighs.

She grew still at first. Then her hands and mouth caressed his chest, soothed his shoulder. She rubbed her breasts against his furry body, enjoying the sensations but wanting more. She moaned softly and parted her legs as his hand went higher. His knee followed his hand, forcing her legs farther apart. She writhed as his hand found the spot he had been looking for, beginning a rhythm both old and new.

When his control was almost gone, he dropped his hand and moved over her, trying to make his entry slowly, carefully. But she surged up against him, her arms and legs locking him close. His control gone, he moved rapidly to his climax and then collapsed. When he could think again, he was still buried deep within her, his body held tenderly by hers.

He raised his head and kissed her. Then he tried to pull away, but she tightened her hold. Suddenly he flipped over and pulled her over on top of him, fondling her breasts, stroking her back. She wiggled slightly, and he gasped, pulling her over him and entering her slowly. He pulled her down to him. "And did your mother tell you about this?" he said, giving his hips a twist and smiling up at her, watching her eyes widen with desire.

"Yes." She leaned forward as far as she could and whispered something.

"Your mother?" Amanda nodded. "I think you just lost our wager. I'll take my first kiss now."

17

By the next morning Amanda had almost finished paying off their wager. Drew, of course, disagreed. She still owed him, according to his reckoning.

They woke and breakfasted in their rooms, only emerging when Jeremy sent for them. Amanda blushed as Jeremy inspected her carefully. "Wish you happy, brat," he said, winking at her. "And you had better keep her that way."

Drew laughed. "I plan to." The two men exchanged knowing looks and pounded each other on the shoulders. "But I'm sure this is not why you asked to see us."

Jeremy shook his head. "I asked my tenants if they had seen anyone new in the area. But with the harvesters about . . . ?" He shrugged. "They have noticed someone who rides out toward Bath in the early afternoons. Has Mary been riding?"

"Not alone. At least I don't think so. Shall I call her? She should be ready to come down anytime now."

"She always was a slug-a-bed. She made our governesses so angry." Drew smiled at Amanda, reminding her how they had spent the morning.

Jeremy turned away. He crossed to the mirror to straighten his cravat, his back to the door but using the mirror to watch for Mary. Drew too looked at the mirror, seeing not just his friend, elegantly dressed in a chocolate-brown coat and buff inexpressibles but a man who was suffering. Amanda, too, watched her cousin, her own joy dimmed by his pain.

The door opened. Mary entered, dressed in a muslin dress of her favorite blue. Jeremy squared his shoulders and turned around, his face as expressionless as he could make it.

"What is wrong? Has something else happened?" Mary asked.

"Nothing. Jeremy just needs to ask you a question," her brother said quickly.

As if as reluctant as he, Mary turned toward Jeremy.

"Have you been riding to Bath several afternoons a week?" he asked.

"Me?" Mary shook her head. "You might ask Miss Lampley, though. She asked permission to ride in the afternoons while the boys napped."

"Your governess?" She nodded. Drew looked from one to the other. "A governess? Really, Jeremy, I think you are looking in the wrong place."

Amanda led Mary to the settee and sat down beside her. "Personally I would believe anything about that woman."

"Why?" Mary asked, truly puzzled.

"Did you notice how she looked that afternoon when we all came back from Bath? If those were not teeth marks on her neck . . ."

"What? I cannot remember that. Are you certain?"

"As certain as I am that she was mistreating Daniel. Both Robert and Nurse noticed that."

"And you did not tell me? You let that woman go on caring for my son," Mary exploded. She paced around the room for a moment, so angry she could not speak. "And you say you are my friend."

"I tried to talk to you about her, but you kept saying she was some connection of Van Courtland's." Jeremy muttered something under his breath. Amanda glared at him. "Then I made certain she would never have another chance to hurt him again."

"The new nursery maid!"

"That is right. Now, tell me what else I should have done." Amanda glared at Mary.

"I still wish you had told me. I will discharge that woman immediately."

"No!" Jeremy was emphatic. Drew looked at his friend and indicated he should explain. "At least keep her until we find out if she is indeed the one." Jeremy crossed the room and took a seat.

"But I must leave for home soon. What am I to do then?" Mary asked, glancing at the tall man who sat slumped over, his eyes on the floor.

"Take Ellen, the nursery maid. And since Daniel has been learning so well, take Robert's tutor also. We can send Robert to school with the vicar until the man comes back," Amanda said, checking Drew to see if he agreed. He nodded.

"But I still do not understand why she would be involved," Mary said.

"I think I had better return to London, Drew. Now that we have more evidence maybe the Runners can find something to go on."

No one had noticed that Thompson had entered with a teatray. He cleared his throat. They all jumped. "If you are sending for the Runners, Mr. Desmond, you should ask Cook for the sample of grease she took from the stairs."

"Stairs? What is he talking about, Amanda?"

"Did something else happen?" Jeremy asked.

"Lady Mainwaring fell down the kitchen stairs because there was grease all over one step," Thompson said, his voice ringing with anger.

"And Cook has a sample?" Drew asked, watching Amanda as if something else were going to happen to her in the next instant.

"Four accidents in one family in less than eight months cannot be a coincidence," Jeremy said, his face worried.

"More than that. In Scotland someone shot at me," Drew explained. "I thought it was an accident. Now?"

After the horror had died down and Drew had reminded Amanda that he had been in less danger than she had, they began to make their plans. Mary would return home, keeping Miss Lampley busy with anything she could find. "Perhaps Mama could use her help with the Dower House," Drew suggested, winning a smile from Amanda.

After all the evidence had been collected, Jeremy would head for London and stay there for a time to make sure the Runners remained on the job.

"Remember. Maintain your image," Amanda told him.

"And what will you two be doing while I am in London?" Jeremy asked. Drew looked at Amanda. She blushed. "Hmm. Why not remove to Fairleigh?"

"I have promised my mother a free rein until Christmas. She has said the Dower House will be finished then. She says I make her nervous," Drew said.

"I think she just wants to say her good-byes privately," Mary said, her own eyes sad.

"She does not have to leave. Drew, she could share the house with us."

"Amanda, I offered. She refused."

"A wise woman. No household should have two mistresses," Jeremy said.

"And where did that bit of wisdom come from?" Amanda asked. The look on her face told him she knew it could not be original.

"Some book I found in the library." He smiled at her, looking more like Robert than an adult. "Where are the boys this morning?"

"Studying." Mary sighed. "I looked in on them before I came down. Do you want to explain to the tutor or shall I?" She sighed again. Between them, they gave the task to Drew, who frowned but agreed. "When you talk to him, tell him I must leave the day after tomorrow."

"And bring the boys down to luncheon," Amanda called. "I wonder what Cook is having. Somehow I have missed my meeting with Mrs. Thompson the last two days."

"And the house is still running?" her cousin teased.

Despite Amanda's worries, luncheon was a delight. The lighthearted sparring she had always enjoyed with

Jeremy carried over to Drew and Mary. In spite of all their problems, no one wanted to leave the table. Finally, Daniel's head bobbed. He caught himself and rubbed his eyes sleepily.

"Naptime for you two," Amanda said firmly. She exchanged a quick glance with Drew and hurried the boys up the stairs.

As exciting as Drew's and Amanda's afternoon was, they would have worried if they had heard Jeremy ask, "And what about us, Mary?" He held the door to the garden open and waited for her to pass through it. Their walk ended a short time later when Mary ran in, her face covered with tears. She turned to look back for a moment. Then she walked slowly up the stairs to her room. Until the morning of her departure, Jeremy stayed away. Then his eyes seemed haunted.

After seeing them off, Drew grabbed Jeremy by the shoulder and pulled him into the library. He poured him a brandy.

Jeremy took a sip and then put it down. "My information is almost complete. I plan to leave for London within the week. Is there anything else I should know?" He glanced from one to the other.

Amanda cleared her throat. Drew looked at her proudly. She wore a dusty-rose riding habit with white braid trim. "No, I was probably dreaming."

"What?"

"Amanda, at least give us a chance to make up our minds," Drew said, his voice crisp with command.

Amanda stared at him but dropped her eyes before he did. "That day when the three of us went to Bath, I thought I saw Van Courtland there."

"Mary's husband?" Amanda nodded. "Did Mary see him?"

"She said she did not. Maybe I was mistaken."

"I will add it to my list," Jeremy said, almost as if to himself.

"Manda?" Robert was standing in the hallway, shouting.

"In here, halfling," Drew called.

"Do I still get to go to school today?"

"Yes, the vicar has been told to excuse you until ten. But you must be on your way."

Robert smiled at her and ran out the door. "Hilton, I have to go to school," he shouted, ready to join his new friends, who were teaching him games.

"At least that is a success," Jeremy muttered. Then he said aloud, "I will stay in town for a while. Expect me only when I arrive."

"But you must come to Fairleigh for Christmas. I will not have you alone here." Amanda was very adamant. "If you stay here, I will be here too."

"No. Your place is with your husband."

"And yours is with your family. Promise." Knowing that she was as good as her word, Jeremy finally gave in. Then she smiled at him sweetly. "Would you mind running a few errands for me while you are there?"

"A few?"

"Just some of my Christmas presents. I will purchase the rest in Bath."

"Are you certain you shouldn't order a few more? The shopkeepers will be weeping over the size of this order."

"All the way home," Drew added, trying to peer over Jeremy's shoulder.

"Yours is not there," Amanda said smugly.

"I don't get one?"

"If you knew how much time Amanda puts into her list, you would not ask that, Drew." They all laughed.

Over the next few weeks Drew and Amanda laughed a lot. They also argued. But the result was always the same: they ended up in each other's arms saying, "I love you." Their days were not adventurous, for the accidents had ceased, but they were as rich and full as the autumn. They saw Robert off to school each morning. Since Amanda's last accident, Robert needed reassurance. Then they would go for long rides, coming back covered with hay. Thompson had all he could do to keep the gossip at a reasonable level.

At other times they were all business. While Amanda met with estate agents, Drew wrote letters to his. But they were together. They entertained, inviting people to dinners. The only things that marred their happiness were their worries about Jeremy and their impatience with the Runners.

Finally after yet another depressing note from her cousin, Amanda told Drew, "You go to London. He needs you."

"Then you come too." She shook her head. "Why?" Drew wore a hurt expression.

"I do not want to take Robert out of school, and I cannot leave him. You go. But make your visit a short one."

By the time he left, Drew had decided she was right. Besides, it would let him do a little Christmas shopping himself. He knew just what he wanted.

Amanda kept all her time filled, hoping to keep her loneliness at bay. She did not succeed any better than Drew did, but they both accomplished a great deal.

The Runners, although they had no firm evidence, had a few real suspicions. With Drew's permission they posted down to Fairleigh with letters to his mother. When the family started gathering, they would be in positions where they could keep their eyes open.

Also at Drew's suggestion, Lady Mainwaring was to invite Mary to come early. When Van Courtland had refused to allow Miss Lampley to leave, Mary had promoted her to her companion, keeping her busy with Christmas projects. The Runners wished an opportunity to observe her more closely without too many people around.

There was little Drew could do for Jeremy. He did secure his promise to join them at Fairleigh shortly before Christmas.

After Drew arrived at the manor, Amanda had little time for anything but for him and for Robert. But there was a radiance about her that was new, a special happiness. When she was sure, she told Drew. She was lying close to him, her head resting on his shoulder. "Drew."

"Hmm," he said sleepily, and pulled her closer.

"I have a surprise for you." He turned his head and blinked in astonishment. According to Jeremy, Amanda never gave her Christmas secrets away early. He just looked at her. She smiled so beautifully that he caught his breath. "We are going to have a baby."

"A baby? Are you sure? Are you all right? Why did you let me . . ."

Her smile became a laugh. "Come here." He lay back down beside her as if afraid to touch her, but Amanda would have none of that. She wrapped her arms around him and explained. "It is perfectly natural. Jennings said I will be just fine, and so did Doctor Weston."

"A baby." Drew's face was as happy as Amanda's. He wrapped his arms around her protectively. "When?"

"In the summer."

"You are sure you are all right?"

"Yes." She let her fingers begin to explore him.

"Should we do this?"

"Except at the last—for six weeks or so."

He put his hand on her stomach, stroking it lightly. "A baby."

To their surprise, when they told Robert about the baby the day before they were to leave for Fairleigh, he was not happy at all. His chin wobbled. "You'll be the baby's mama and papa?"

"Yes." Amanda hugged him, but he pulled away.

Drew watched him anxiously. "Will I still live with you?" Robert asked, his eyes big.

"Of course. You will be baby's big brother," Drew told him.

"I can't be."

"Why not?" Amanda tried to brush back his curls, but he pulled away.

"You are not my mama and papa. They are dead." His voice shook, but he stood straight and tall.

Amanda and Drew exchanged worried looks. Then

Drew sat on the settee, Amanda beside him. "Come here," he said firmly. Robert reluctantly obeyed. Drew lifted him up between them. "Do you remember when we told you we were going to marry?" Robert nodded. Amanda tried to say something but her throat was so tight no words would come out. "We promised then to be a family. What do you think a family is?"

"A mama, a papa, the children." He looked from one to the other confused.

Amanda cleared her throat. "Robert, darling, you are my little boy. I have loved you since the first moment I held you."

"Like a mama?"

"Exactly like a mother." She reached out and hugged him.

Drew then put his arms around them both. For a few minutes they just sat there, holding one another. Then Robert wiggled free, a thoughtful look on his face. "Is baby going to call you mama and papa?" They nodded. "And I'll be baby's big brother?" Again they nodded. "Then I should call you mama and papa too."

Tears streaming down her face, Amanda nodded. "If that is what you want, darling."

Robert looked at Drew, who was beaming. "Why is she crying?"

"You made her very happy, halfling. Me too!" He reached out and grabbed Robert, tickling him until the boy was helpless with laughter. Then they both hugged him again and sent him up to finish collecting his toys for the move.

As soon as he saw Thompson in the hallway below, Robert shouted, "Guess what, Thompson! I'm going to be a brother."

Drew pulled Amanda over to him and wrapped her in his arms, patting her stomach as he often did now.

When they reached Fairleigh, Robert, as usual, was the first one out of the coach. He dashed up the stairs to where Lady Mainwaring and Mary waited with Daniel.

"Nana, Aunt Mary, guess what? I'm going to be a brother."

Drew smiled ruefully at his wife. "I told you what he would do."

'I don't mind. I got to tell you." She smiled at him as he lifted her from the carriage as carefully as though she were a piece of fine porcelain.

"Welcome home, my darling." He started to kiss her, but his mother and sister were beside them instantly.

The next few days were quiet ones. With everyone insisting that she must rest, Amanda found herself with little to do. She had toured the house, making notes of a few things she wished to change. Drew had promised her that she could redo their suite in her favorite ivory and red. She visited the Dower House, on which the last of the work was almost done, although Lady Mainwaring had decided to remain at Fairleigh until after Christmas. With Drew conferring with his agent and Robert once more with Daniel and the tutor, she found herself with more time on her hands than she liked.

She had written to Jeremy about the baby. His reply, a delightfully risqué comment on their behavior, had made her laugh so hard she knew Drew heard downstairs. After talking to Mary for a few minutes, she headed downstairs to the library. She was so happy she almost skipped. Just then one of the new footmen, a Runner, started up the stairs. His eyes widened, and he took the stairs two at a time, reaching her just before she reached the middle step.

"Stop, your ladyship!" Amanda glanced at him curiously, but she knew who he was. She stayed where she was. "Look."

There on the step in front of her were several hanks of yarn, almost the color of the steps. "You could have fallen," the Runner explained.

Amanda clutched her stomach as if protecting the baby. Then she grew pale and swayed.

"Let me help you, Lady Mainwaring," the Runner said, worried. He put the yarn in his pocket and helped her to a chair at the foot of the stairs. "I will find his lordship. You stay here."

By the time Drew arrived a few minutes later, Amanda was crying. Gently, he picked her up and headed upstairs. Calling Jennings, he had the maid undress her and put her to bed, sitting beside her until she drifted off to sleep. "Stay with her, Jennings," he said, his face grim. He headed back to the library.

"Well, do you know who did it?" he asked the Runner, who was waiting for him.

"We are almost sure, your lordship. As soon as one of my men returns, we should have all the information we need to prosecute."

"Well, make sure nothing happens to my wife in the meantime." Drew headed back upstairs, sick with worry.

For both Drew and Amanda the accident had dampened their enjoyment of the holidays. Amanda retreated to her former behavior around most men, jumping when anyone came close to her. And when Jeremy finally arrived on December 23, she cried all over him.

"What's wrong, brat? Has Drew been beating you?" he asked, his voice humorous. He shot a questioning look at his friend.

"There was another accident," Drew told him, his face grim.

"You are all right? And the baby?"

"Fine." Amanda sniffed inelegantly and held out her hand for the handkerchief Drew had ready. "I seem to be a watering pot these days." She wiped her eyes. "I'm so glad you are here."

"So am I. You can help keep an eye on her." Drew smiled.

"Did you bring me everything I asked for?" Amanda asked, her eyes glistening.

"And some you didn't. But those will have to wait."

"Do we get to open presents on Christmas Eve?"

"She is always like this, Drew. She wants to open her present but doesn't want us to open any of ours." Jeremy smiled at Amanda.

"I do not. Drew, if I can open one of mine, you can open one of yours."

"Lady wife, at Fairleigh we do not open our presents until Christmas morning," Drew told her, teasing. Her face fell, "But we do decorate our tree together."

The next afternoon everyone in the family helped set up the tree. The children dressed the lower branches, the ladies the middle, and the men the top. In spite of Robert's pleas, however, Drew refused to put candles on the tree. "It is too dangerous," he explained. Jeremy nodded his agreement. After a friend of theirs had returned to school after Christmas with burns on his hands and arms, they had made him a promise that they had kept.

With hot cider for everyone, the tree was quickly ready. Even Van Courtland had helped with a few decorations. Finally all that was left was the star at the top.

"Amanda is the newest member of the family. Let her put it on," Van Courtland suggested.

Jeremy glared at him.

"No. It's too dangerous. I'll do it," Drew said.

"I'll help hold the ladder," Jeremy promised.

18

While they all stood around laughing and joking, Drew sent a footman for the tallest ladder. Jeremy stood off to one side, his eyes fixed on Van Courtland. He tried to convince himself that his dislike for the man was merely jealousy, but he knew that was only part of it.

Mary had surrounded herself with children, Robert and Daniel to the forefront, and stood close to the tree. She glanced up to see Jeremy watching her and quickly lowered her eyes. Van Courtland narrowed his speculatively. Then he crossed to his wife's side and whispered something in her ear, laughing softly when she jerked away.

Jeremy controlled himself with effort. He crossed to where his cousin stood, close to Drew.

"I think I should have a chance to put the star on top," Amanda demanded.

"If any one but Van Courtland had suggested it, I would have said he did it to put you in a revealing position." Jeremy leered at her comically. Her face turned red. "But I do not trust the man."

Drew nodded his agreement. "Keep an eye on him for me. The Runners have discovered some disquieting facts about his finances," he said. He glanced at Mary. "Fortunately, my father tied up Mary's portion very well." Drew looked at his brother-in-law again, wondering what Van Courtland was saying to Miss Lampley. The woman stood in front of him with a tray of cider, effectively shielding him from the rest of the room.

She shook her head and then turned around. He grabbed her and pulled her into the corner, whispering something into her ear. She nodded and walked away, this time with a smile on her face.

Just as Drew started that way, Amanda put out a hand to stop him. "The ladder is here," she said quietly. Smiling, they headed for the tree.

Deciding how to brace the ladder took careful consideration. Finally it was placed just right, and several sturdy men moved to brace it. "You be careful," Amanda told Drew as she handed him the star.

Van Courtland smiled as he watched his brother-in-law take the first rung.

Drew had just climbed the first few rungs when the door flew open. "Get off that ladder, your lordship," a gruff voice said. Drew stopped and turned slowly.

Van Courtland paled. His eyes darted around the room.

The rest of the group broke into horrified whispers. "A servant! Well, what are we coming to?"

"He should discharge him immediately."

"How dare he!"

Lady Mainwaring, Amanda, and Mary drew closer together. Jeremy, braced against the ladder, said quietly, "See what he wants, Drew. We can finish later."

Carefully, Drew descended. He drew the man, one of the Runners he had hired, to one side. As soon as he could, Jeremy joined them. Amanda and the other two women made their way to that side of the room. Van Courtland edged his way closer to the door and the small group of men, his eyes trying to pull the information he needed from their faces. He rubbed his hands nervously.

Noticing the stares, especially Van Courtland's, Drew took them all to the library. "Tell me! What is the matter?"

Van Courtland followed slowly, pausing outside the open door as if using the mirror in the hall to straighten his stock.

"The ladder, your lordship. One of my lads saw

someone tampering with it but paid it no mind, you and your ladyship not usually around the things." The Runner paused and wiped his brow. "When he heard belowstairs what was going on up here, he told me at once." He mopped his forehead again. "Closer call than I like."

"You could have been killed!" Amanda grabbed Drew as if she were afraid he might vanish.

Jeremy's face was serious. "You said one of your men saw who it was. Tell us."

The Runner glanced around the room nervously. He cleared his throat and glanced at the ladies, dressed in their Christmas reds and greens. "It wouldn't be proper, sir."

Lady Mainwaring walked over in front of him. She drew herself up, as elegant and commanding as any lady who helped rule the *ton* quickly learned to be. "Whether we hear it from you or from them, we will hear. I suggest you stop wasting our time and tell us. We have guests waiting." She glared at him, and he wilted. Amanda stifled a giggle and Mary twittered.

Neither was laughing a few minutes later. "Are you sure?" Drew asked, glancing at his sister anxiously. Van Courtland glanced down the hallway, his eyes narrowed dangerously. Then a crafty smile crossed his face. He ran up the stairs.

All thoughts of propriety forgotten, Jeremy crossed to Mary and pulled her against him. She hid her face against his chest.

"Your brother-in-law fixed those rungs himself. If you had stretched to put that star up there, you would have had no way to protect yourself."

"You would have been killed!" Amanda grabbed Drew again and held him close.

"But he was not their first choice." Jeremy looked at Drew, his eyes hard.

Drew's arm closed around his wife. "Amanda?"

Mary burst into tears. His arms around her, Jeremy looked over her head at her mother. She walked slowly to his side as if the strain were almost too much to bear. "Here, let me have her. You need to find him." Jeremy nodded.

When Drew stepped back, Amanda ran to her friend's side. "Oh, Mary, I am so sorry." She patted her shoulder.

Mary brushed her tears from her face. "I should be saying that to you."

"Nonsense. Neither of you is to blame. The man is a bad 'un, through and through." Lady Mainwaring stepped back and inspected them both. "Mary, you go to your room and freshen up. Amanda, come with me. I am certain that our relatives are agog at what has happened already. If we are to brush through this successfully, we will need all our wits about us."

Their faces serious, Amanda and Mary agreed.

"Now, put on a pleasant smile and follow my lead." Lady Mainwaring threw open the door to the drawing room, where the tree had been set up, and laughed merrily. Everyone turned around.

Drew said quietly, "Van Courtland is not here."

Robert, with Daniel at his heels, ran over to Amanda. "Where is Papa going?"

"He will be back shortly. There is a problem with the ladder."

"Let me climb it," Robert demanded.

"No, not that one." Quickly, quietly, Amanda told the footmen to remove it.

As she did, Lady Mainwaring visited one group after another, explaining. "Fortunately, the man is loyal. I have known some households where the servants would have enjoyed seeing the master fall to his death," she said. Their relatives nodded wisely.

By the time Lady Mainwaring had finished her circuit of the room and the room was once more buzzing with the latest gossip of the day and happy anticipation, Mary and the men had returned.

Amanda glanced at her husband, and he shook his head slightly. Jeremy's face was somber. Quickly she asked, "What carols shall we sing?"

For the rest of the afternoon they had no time to discuss anything. But finally everyone drifted away to nap before a very late supper and the midnight service. Amanda personally delivered Robert and Daniel to Nurse, who had already begun to eye her proprietarily. Then she hurried back to the library.

Drew handed her a cider. She sat down in a chair next to his. "Well?"

"The Runner who was supposed to be watching the stables was the one who saw the ladder being tampered with. No one saw them leave, but Van Courtland, Miss Lampley, and a curricle are missing."

"Then they must plan to return soon. A curricle in this weather?" Lady Mainwaring shivered.

"And what will you do if he does come back?" Mary asked. She looked exhausted and her voice shook.

Drew and Jeremy exchanged glances. "A trial is out of the question," Drew said firmly.

"But I know him. He will stop at nothing to get what he wants," Mary said. She sat on the edge of her chair, staring in front of her.

"According to the Runners, he needs money. Maybe we can strike a bargain," her brother suggested. His mother nodded. "Now, if we are not to sleep through services tonight, we had better get some rest ourselves." He sent his mother and Amanda off with a kiss, but he stopped Mary at the door. "This has nothing to do with you. Stop worrying."

"Of course it does. If I had not married him, he would never have had the opportunity."

"That is not what I mean, and you know it. There is nothing that you can do at this point. You did not cause it to happen. He did. Remember that." He took her in his arms and held her close. "Also remember I love you," he said as he let her go. She brushed tears from her eyes and nodded.

When the door had closed behind her, Drew turned to Jeremy. "Well?"

"I do not know how I am going to do it, but that man

will never have a chance to hurt her again," Jeremy said, his voice icy cold. Drew nodded solemnly.

Although Mary was still subdued the next morning, Amanda was not. Drew was safe, Robert was happy, Jeremy was there, and it was Christmas. She and Drew had exchanged their special gifts very early that morning. For them those early-morning hours were the best. She had opened her eyes to find him propped up on one elbow watching her, a definite gleam in his eye. He slid his hand over her slightly rounded stomach caressingly before moving lower. Amanda freed her hands from the covers and did some exploring of her own before she pulled him down to her, moaning softly.

Later he watched with obvious enjoyment as she slipped from bed and crossed to a small cabinet. "I am ready for another Christmas present," he said suggestively, winking at her. She found what she had been looking for and ran back to bed, picking up her robe where he had thrown it the night before. "You don't need that," he said, and tried to take it away from her.

She laughed and put it on. "I told Robert he could join us for chocolate later." Drew nodded. "Well?" she asked.

"What?"

"Where is my present?"

He laughed and leaned over to a pitcher beside the bed. He turned it over and shook a package out. "Here you are, sweet!" He laughed at her indignant expression. "Now, where is mine?"

They both held rich leather boxes. Amanda's eyes widened as she opened hers. "Drew, oh, Drew." He lifted out a pair of diamond earrings, really a series of diamond teardrops, and fastened them on her ears. He pulled her close and whispered, "I want you to wear these when . . ."

"Drew!" Amanda laughed happily, her eyes making him a promise. "Now, look at yours."

He opened the box carefully. There was a signet ring with a large sapphire, the color of his eyes. Carved into it was an initial "A." "For Andrew and Amanda," she whispered. "Look inside."

He read the date and looked at her, beaming proudly. "The day you really become my wife!" He bent his head and kissed her. Then they heard voices.

"But they said I could, Jennings," Robert protested.

"Knock first."

Drew slid out of bed and into his robe before Amanda had time to do more than sit up against the pillows. Then they both called, "Come in."

"Happy Christmas!" Then Robert frowned at them. "You are not dressed. It is almost time to open our presents, and you are not dressed." Had Christmas been put off for weeks he could not have been more indignant.

"We will be shortly. We promise. Now come here." Robert crossed to the bed and climbed up.

"Do ladies wear earrings to bed?' he asked curiously, kneeling close to Amanda to see them more clearly. She blushed.

"They were a Christmas present. Like this one." Drew sat down on the edge of the bed and handed him a package.

Robert ripped it open and then stopped. Then he reached for the small pocket watch complete with chain and fob. "For me? It's really for me?" He opened it slowly and then read the inscription inside. " 'To Robert, from Mama and Papa with love. Christmas 1816.' Oh! It is beautiful." He hugged both of them and then began jumping up and down like the child he was. "Get up. Hurry!"

Laughing, they obeyed. Soon they were all downstairs with the rest of the family. Only a few incidents marred the day. Mary picked up one of her presents and then put it down again, shoving it deep under the tree. Amanda later learned it was from Van Courtland. Jeremy was more somber than Amanda liked, but he could not resist teasing her. "A trifle formal for breakfast, brat." He touched one of her earrings and laughed when she blushed. But when he received his gift from Amanda and Drew, he was speechless.

"Do you like him?" Amanda asked anxiously when he simply stood there and stared at the beautiful Arabian stallion the groom was holding. "Is he what you wanted?"

"Wanted? He's beautiful. Where did you find him?" Jeremy did not bother to find a coat but rushed outside, Robert at his heels. He ran his hands down the horse's legs, lifted a hoof, and stroked his nose.

Drew and Amanda stood inside the house, smiling. When she noticed Robert beginning to shiver, Amanda called, "Come inside. It is time for breakfast." Reluctantly they obeyed. And for the rest of the day when the women missed any of the men they knew they were in the stables.

Although they kept expecting Van Courtland to return at any moment, he had not done so several days later when everyone began to leave for their own homes. Lady Mainwaring moved into the Dower House, taking Mary and Daniel with her in spite of Robert's objections. Jeremy stayed at Fairleigh with Drew and Amanda, determined to be at hand if Mary should need him.

Early one afternoon as the three of them played cards, the butler appeared. "There is a gentleman to see you, your lordship."

"Well, show him in."

The butler bent close to his ear. "He says that it would be best if you met him alone."

Drew raised his eyebrows but nodded. "Put him in the library. I will be in shortly." He looked at the cards in his hand. "And I could have won with these." He threw them down.

A few minutes later the butler was back. "His lordship requests that you join him in the library."

Wondering, Jeremy and Amanda made their way there. As soon as they came in, Drew demanded. "Tell them what you told me." The man, a hearty-looking gentleman, glanced at Amanda. Then he repeated his story.

According to someone who had seen it only a short

time before the accident must have happened, the curricle had been traveling very fast. The driver was whipping the horse and took a corner, almost turning over. Then they had reached the bridge. There had been some ice, and a wheel had come off. Jeremy looked up suddenly. Drew, too, had the same look in his eyes. The driver and his companion had been thrown onto a low stone railing and then to the water below. "Bodies were found on Boxing Day. We found the man's card and sent a messenger to his home. When the man returned with word, I came right here. Was the lady his wife?"

"No." Jeremy stood up, his shoulders straighter than they had been in a long time. "Shall I tell her?"

Drew shook his head. "I am her brother. I will tell her. But you can come with me."

"I am coming too. She will need me," Amanda said firmly.

"What are we to do with them?" the magistrate asked.

"We'll send someone for the man. And we will pay for the woman's burial." Drew looked at the other two for their approval. They nodded. "If you will see my agent?" Drew scribbled a note and handed it to him. "I need to go to my sister."

When Drew told Mary, her reaction was not what he expected. She turned pale, but she did not lose her composure. She asked, "Will Daniel have to know when it happened?"

"No. And now there is no need to publish our suspicions abroad," Drew said quietly. "A private burial in the family plot and a notice in the papers. That will take care of it."

"Better put your lawyer's name in the notice. We don't want his creditors disturbing Mary," Jeremy said. He had taken a seat beside Mary and held her hand tightly in his.

"I do not want to return to that house again," Mary said, steel in her voice.

"But . . ."

"Then you will not. Drew, you and I can represent the family at the funeral. Amanda does not need to make another journey and Mary can be prostrated by grief. Will that do?" He turned to Lady Mainwaring.

She looked from Jeremy to her daughter and back. She nodded. "Tell the lawyer to find a good agent."

"Or a tenant," Amanda suggested.

Mary nodded. She asked, "May I use the house in Bath for a while?"

"Nonsense, you will stay right here with me," her mother said.

"Would't you be happier in the country?" Amanda asked when Mary refused her mother's offer.

"Yes, but I won't . . ."

"Then why not stay at Applecroft Manor. The servants already know you."

Mary's face lit up. "You wouldn't mind?" Amanda shook her head. "Then I will stay here until after the funeral. After that I accept your offer."

As they drove back to Fairleigh, Jeremy was happier than Amanda had seen him in months. "Thank you, brat."

"Now it is up to you," she reminded him.

"Not if my sister has anything to say about it," Drew said. "You know I will welcome you to the family."

"Wait until it happens. Early congratulations make me nervous," his friend said, but his smile was as bright as fresh winter snow.

"Why do you suppose he did it? Van Courtland, I mean?" Amanda asked.

"He was probably afraid he was going to be caught. He panicked."

"Not that. Why did he try to hurt us? What did he hope to gain?"

"Money," Jeremy said.

"How? Until recently my money would have come to you or Robert," Amanda reminded him.

"But Drew's would go to Daniel. And Van Courtland would be his son's guardian and capable of drawing on his inheritance."

"But he wouldn't have been."

"What?" They stared at Drew.

"My father trusted few people. His will creates an unbreakable trust for any male heirs who are under age. The trust is governed by a lawyer, a banker, and one male relative outside the immediate family unit. It is so complicated that we have kept quiet about it." He sighed deeply. "Now I wish we hadn't."

The next few weeks were busy ones for everyone. Drew and Jeremy, accompanied by Lady Mainwaring, attended Van Courtland's funeral. Mary's mother had stated firmly, "Someone must see to the house and Mary's interests there." Leaving her behind to supervise the closing of the house, the men headed to London.

A few meetings with the lawyers did much to relieve their minds. "Do you think your father knew about Van Courtland?" Jeremy asked as he reviewed once more the arrangements Drew's father had made for Daniel only a short time before he himself had died.

"He couldn't have known everything, or he wouldn't have let her marry him. But he must have found out something. If Van Courtland had had any idea . . ."

"Thank God he didn't. At least Daniel will have an unencumbered estate now." Jeremy sat back in his chair, his face somber.

"And with a good tenant for the next few years, the expenditures can be regained. But when Daniel gets a little older, you need to persuade Mary to return to his estate occasionally. He needs to grow up knowing his tenants and they him." Jeremy nodded, his own right to control Daniel's life unquestioned. Drew glanced down at the letter he held in his hand. "Amanda says my mother has returned to Fairleigh."

His friend knew exactly what he meant. "Then it is time to send that notice to the papers." They had withheld it to allow time for the legal affairs to be put in order. "Put it in the papers," Jeremy said once again, his voice hard.

* * *

Instead of occupying the Dower House on her return, Lady Mainwaring had joined Amanda and Mary at Fairleigh. As unpopular as Van Courtland had been, when the notice of his death appeared in the papers, they were deluged with condolence visits.

Amanda and her mother-in-law refused to let Mary appear, describing her to those people who were determined to see her as devastated. "And I am too, but not with grief," Amanda said after a particularly obnoxious guest had left. "Only the knowledge that it would hurt Mary and Daniel keeps me from laughing in some of these people's faces. I do not know how you manage."

"Discipline, my dear, and years of experience. Now, let us see what those grandsons of mine have been doing."

By the time Drew and Jeremy returned from London, the worst was over. Mary smiled once in a while. And when she saw Jeremy, she glowed, although she quickly dropped her eyes. Lady Mainwaring took one look at them and announced that she would accompany Mary to Applecroft Manor, at least for a few weeks. Jeremy simply smiled at Mary and nodded.

When their coaches rolled away, at first Fairleigh seemed quiet without them, especially to Robert. But to Amanda and Drew it was a quietness they treasured, a time to be a family, alone.

One afternoon while Drew was out on the estate, Amanda was finally unpacking a box of papers from her desk at Applecroft Manor. She picked up one packet and opened it. Her eyes widened. Her smile was as brilliant as the brightest candles. She tucked it into her pocket and hurried to her bedroom.

That evening as she lay in bed beside Drew, the candles still lit, her breath beginning to return to normal, Amanda reached up to stroke his cheek, marveling once again at the softness of his skin after he had just shaved. Then, evading his arms, she rolled away. Leaning out of bed, she reached for something on the table. She handed the packet to Drew.

"What is this?" he asked, remembering his last surprise.

"Read it."

Opening the packet carefully, Drew read the first few words and laughed. "And what lawyer did you find to draw up these terms, lady wife?" He pretended to frown as he continued to read.

"I served as my own counsel, sir," she said, spoiling her pompous speech with a giggle. "Are the terms agreeable?"

Drew looked once more at the paper in his hand and then smiled at her, his blue eyes sparkling. "Excitement?" She nodded. He pulled her closer and lowered his head until his lips were barely touching hers. "Then excitement is what you will get," he promised.

As Amanda frequently told her curious and slightly scandalized granddaughters years later, their grandfather never made a promise he did not work very hard to keep.

About the Author

Barbara Allister is a native Texan who enjoys reading and traveling. An English teacher, Ms. Allister began writing as a hobby after experimenting with techniques to use in her creative writing class.